The Downstairs Room

By Kate Wilhelm

The Downstairs Room

AND OTHER
SPECULATIVE FICTION

by Kate Wilhelm

DOUBLEDAY & COMPANY, INC.
GARDEN CITY, NEW YORK
1968

SF

c.5

ACKNOWLEDGMENTS

Baby, You Were Great, copyright © 1967 by Damon Knight;
originally published in *Orbit* 2.

When the Moon Was Red, published in *Amazing Stories.*
Copyright © 1960 by Ziff-Davis Publishing Co.

The Feel of Desperation, published in *Alfred Hitchcock's
Mystery Magazine.* Copyright © 1964 by H.S.D. Publications, Inc. (Published as *A Case of Desperation*)

A Time to Keep, published in *Fantasy and Science Fiction.*
Copyright © 1962 by Mercury Publications.

The Planners, copyright © 1968 by Damon Knight; originally published in *Orbit* 3.

Windsong, copyright © 1968 by Damon Knight; originally
published in *Orbit* 4.

The following stories are copyright © 1968 by Kate Wilhelm:
*Unbirthday Party, Sirloin and White Wine, Perchance to
Dream, How Many Miles to Babylon?, The Downstairs
Room, Countdown, The Plausible Improbable, The Most
Beautiful Woman in the World.*

BL

NOV 12 71
Library of Congress Catalog Card Number 68–22513
Copyright © 1968 by Kate Wilhelm
All Rights Reserved
Printed in the United States of America
First Edition

To Ann Meredith, my mother, with love

Contents

Introduction

IT IS THE NATURE OF FICTION, and particularly of shorter fiction, to move from linear representation toward a quality we can only call vision.

This is especially true, it seems, of American fiction. We have taken naturally to the short story, and our major contributions have been within this medium. Emerging from the romance rather than the novel proper—and with its heritage in Irving, Hawthorne, Poe—American literary development has been from and toward a fiction of extremes. Representation, however accurate, has never seemed in itself an end; our aim has been toward a form which, rather than ascending from journalism, descends from poetry. The 1920's were our most fertile period, and the most characteristic stories of that time adapt themselves to the traditions of realism which were then dominant —but it has become an intensely *selective* realism. Situation is condensed to a point where the stories appear virtually plotless; theme and intention remain implicit, often realized in stream-of-consciousness or symbolism; the story has become a regenerating form of words, a total suspension of force, motive, and process. These stories achieve a large measure of ambiguity and resonance, and exhibit the elliptical, visionary qualities of the best non-realism. There must be a periodic return to natural, casual forms—a kind of re-tooling—but always the urge is simultaneously toward something more complex and subtle, toward a form closer in quality and texture to life itself. (In some part, this inclination accounts for the uncertain nature of our fiction; we have no single representative voice.) Of course the short story is almost by definition metaphorical, in that it offers a reconstructed image of life. And in embracing the form so fully, we accept as well the processes *of* the form.

I suppose it is with Chekhov and Joyce (particularly the Joyce of "The Dead") that many of us find our clearest antecedents; and perhaps Thomas Pynchon's "Entropy" and Tillie Olsen's "Tell Me a Riddle" are two of our more characteristic contemporary stories. Surrounded by new and often more popular or comprehensive forms, in a deluge of media and genre art, the contemporary writer looks to stake out a specific ground for fiction: to realize a quality and form with which nothing else can compete. He rejects the circumspect, circuitous "literary" style as false. He eschews breadth for depth, penetrating, whether by Olsen's leaps in chronology and viewpoint or Pynchon's intensely symbolic structures, as deep as he can on a limited field. The process is from the outside—from the skin—in, thus recalling Chekhov's economy and the "symbolic naturalism" of Joyce. He wants to pierce directly to the essential qualities of experience, and to accomplish this will use any apparatus at hand; hence, the highly eclectic nature of our current fiction. At any rate, the story grows ever more complex and resonant yet, at the same time, ever more intangible. It is bare, unembellished . . . with the delicacy and inevitability of a colloidal suspension.

Now, this movement toward vision is threefold.

First, it is the process of any developing literature and has brought us, in America today, to a period of outstanding development within the short story form—while even our novel begins to borrow more and more from the mood and vocabulary of the shorter form.

Secondly, it is the record of fiction's summary impingement upon the reader. He begins by accepting a story's surface, its texture, and moves toward comprehension of its forms as the story occurs within him; a*d*sorption becomes a*b*sorption. The ideal story perhaps follows Thurston's advice to an assistant: it points one way and happens another. It is, like Durrell's grass, "an assassin of polish."

But this movement also manifests itself in the individual

writer's work. Here, it is the writer coming awake, discovering new possibilities in the fictional form and new direction in his own previous work, able to take on more tricks of balance within a single story—to distill image and concern into a new, more comprehensive form. A more mature and relevant fiction gathers out of old intimations, old intentions, old peripheral effects. This may occur consciously by way of retrospective analysis, or unconsciously, but inevitably in the serious writer it *will* occur. And often the writer will himself be surprised at what is coming onto the paper. He is working by instinct, and suddenly the work seems so much more aware, so much truer and more knowledgeable than its source; he marvels that he is able to control all this new material. Of course, it is simply that perception (sensation) is reconstructing itself toward conception (information) and that the ground between is always the artist's chief concern. But this is after all the great satisfaction of creative work: the sudden self-generated insight, the epiphany, the intellectual-sensual pleasure of coming onto structures that hold a vision in suspension.

Kate Wilhelm says in one of the introductions included here: "I am so much smarter, know so much more about everything when I am writing than when I am not." Elsewhere she gives evidence of her own development as a writer: "It happens occasionally that I don't know what one of my stories means until it is done. I will know everything that takes place in it, how the people feel and react with each other, what parts of it need emphasis, what parts need understatement, and still if I were to try to sum up the statement being made, I would be unable to, or wrong. . . . It felt right." And: "I was telling stories, directly, from my personal vision to the finished manuscript."

So it is that the writer becomes increasingly aware of the complex, basically indefinable material with which he works, and of the ambiguous processes by which a story exists in the world. Consequently the work takes on further substance, develops a more informing image and becomes, in short, something considerable, something larger and more conclusive than its parts. This is the attainment of vision.

The stories collected here cover seven years of work in the short story form and dramatically illustrate Kate Wilhelm's continuing development as a writer.

The earliest of them are unembellished, spare. Incident is clustered close about the structure; they demonstrate a remarkable clarity of sight, of observation. And from the first, in stories like "Sirloin and White Wine" and "A Time to Keep," a singular voice evidences itself. It is tough and feminine; light and mordant. A voice concerned with the everyday necessities of life and with external patterns which intrude upon that life. A voice filled by, pervaded with, urgency. There is something she must tell you: the desperation of understanding, the impossibility of decision, the inevitability of desertion. And they exhibit more than mere technical excellence though that, in such stories as "The Most Beautiful Woman in the World" with its double streams of language and image, and "How Many Miles to Babylon?" with its complex shifts in chronology and tone, is obvious enough.

They are, first of all, easily accessible; they open themselves easily to the reader, and have about them the quality of direct, lived experience. They are stories which have for the most part (as has, even if but peripherally, much of our best contemporary work) embraced the genre. This is the "limited field" within which Kate Wilhelm aims for depth, for ever deeper penetration—in the vehicle of thriller, mystery, science fiction. But this is not, for her, a prescriptive genre affording more strictures than freedom, not a form which necessarily carries its own content. She has accepted the genre form as comfortable, as one in which she feels most at ease and most able to realize her specific interests, and has discarded the trappings, the preconceptions, the implied structures. Her work is, in final analysis, one that generates its own idiom, a fiction in which it is virtually impossible to separate story-as-object from story-as-experience.

In the seven years over which these stories were written, Miss Wilhelm has published (aside from collaborations) three novels, and is currently at work on another. Each has been progressively more comprehensive and satisfying.

By symbolizing a purely destructive force in a robot, a second force (bound, for personal *and* social reasons, to the *robot's* destruction) in a man, *The Killer Thing* deals with a theme of social and personal responsibility in the vocabulary of science fiction. This dualism is carefully extended into the book's whole, and technical effects are often stunning, so that at times the style seems almost to sparkle. By implication Miss Wilhelm is examining the forces of war in this novel and is, like much of the best current science fiction, reconstructing the moral problems brought home to us now in Vietnam.

Her latest novel, *Let the Fire Fall*, is even more in control of its substance and in tone approaches the experimental—some indication of the freedom and depth she is yet finding. The most recent of her stories, "A Cold Dark Night with Snow" (not included here), is non-sequential, containing remarkably effective shifts in point of view, modulations of tone, and reconstructions of chronology and incident. This depth of vision is to be carried over into her next novel as well. Its first-person narrator may be observer or participant—stepping outside herself to record things dispassionately, visualizing entire scenes in which she takes no part and which may or may not be actual. There are ambiguous interrelations on several levels, real and/or imaginary, objective and/or subjective, external and/or internal.

Similarly, the stories collected here. The earliest are highly readable, enjoyable, accomplished. There is a gradual, easily evident evolution toward more regenerative forms and concepts; a new subtlety, a gathering intensity of expression. And in the most recent of them—most especially in "The Planners" and "Windsong"—it seems to me that the writer achieves, with deceptive simplicity, true vision.

Yet, abstraction has no place in Kate Wilhelm's work. Her theme is responsibility—but a *tangible* responsibility, one that shows itself (and is of account) only in day-to-day, person-to-person affairs. Just as the "statement" of *The Killer Thing* is carried in action and reaction, in pure narration, the awesome vision of "The Planners" is planted squarely in the actual workaday world of the scientist and that, in turn, in the mundane movements and preoccupations of its characters. This is, I feel, the essential quality of her voice, and it is by exploring this contrast that she in fact most often generates her story. Indeed, a story like "The Most Beautiful Woman in the World" is carefully built to this contrast, and it is difficult to account for the power of "The Downstairs Room" or "Countdown" or "Baby, You Were Great" in any more suitable terms.

Kate Wilhelm's central image, then, is this: some huge, indifferent pattern imposes itself (often gratuitously) upon small, personal concerns, forcing characters toward decisions which they are incapable of making.

This imposition may be objective, as with "The Planners," or psychological, as in "The Downstairs Room," or ambiguously either/both. It may occur to the individual ("A Time to Keep") or in the context of a social group ("The Planners" and "Windsong"). Wherever it does occur, the character's choice is threefold: he may attempt to flee ("The Most Beautiful Woman in the World"), accept the imposition and try to keep it shut off from his personal life ("The Planners" and "The Downstairs Room"), or accept it fully and disintegrate ("A Time to Keep"). Either way, desperation and desertion are inevitable: he surrenders contact with others and becomes, finally, sundered from life.

The strongest of these stories embody, in their imagery and language, the process of such disintegration. They are like verbal charts, registering the conflict of external and internal forces— at the same time objective and subjective, experience and object. They lay open for us the descent of the person into his personal hell, letting us experience the way in which he adapts, or gradually surrenders himself, to that hell. And the stories are themselves a progressive descent toward the final visions of "The Planners" and "Windsong," which carry in turn the seed of Kate Wilhelm's future work.

That work is to be much anticipated. I believe that her success in fitting her themes to genre forms has been a significant one and that now, gathering energy from her previous visions, she will move outward to a still deeper, more comprehensive fiction.

For what these stories finally demonstrate—in their themes and central image, their structures, even in their exploitation of the genre—is that experience occurs when order and chance intersect. That life is, in the words of Simone de Beauvoir, the reworking of a destiny by a freedom.

JAMES SALLIS
London 1968

The Downstairs Room

When human beings discovered language, stories came into being. A child at play tells himself stories throughout the day. Watch his lips move; watch him listen to his imaginary playmates, and you know he is telling stories. I told myself stories, then my younger brothers, then my own children, and one day I discovered that I could put my stories on paper and other adults would read them. I wrote my first commercial story in longhand, and with the check I received for it I bought a typewriter. Learning to write at the typewriter was difficult—the keys kept getting in the way, and my fingers were clumsy and demanded attention, but slowly the machine faded into the background, and again I was telling stories, directly, from my personal vision to the finished manuscript. You won't read the same story that I saw; my words can't push the same buttons for another that they push for me; our responses will be different. So a story has to do two things, at least: It has to bring to life that inner scene experienced by the writer, and it has to say something as nearly equivalent to that scene as is possible to the reader. Most of my stories are about a small part of life, but now and again there is one—like the first one in this collection—that seems to be about all of life, encapsulated. And again, perhaps it isn't that at all.

Unbirthday Party

WELLMAN blinked rapidly, then shook his head. He was on the wrong floor. He could feel the difference, although visually there was very little that was not familiar. The elevator must have come up too swiftly, left him dizzy and on the wrong floor. He gazed about wonderingly. So like his floor. The corridor was not as well lighted as was his own. He felt certain he should have ridden higher than this. The many doors lining the corridor were closed. At the far end there was one that was partially opened, and from it was issuing laughter and music that seemed to be inviting him to join. He shook his head slightly and moved backward toward the elevator. The distant door opened fully and a woman stepped out.

"Oh, come on. This is the place."

She was wearing a red dress that swirled gently about her long legs—chiffon, or something equally soft. She motioned from the doorway again and went back inside. He was drawn toward the noisy apartment, forgetting as he walked that he had meant to return to the elevator and his own floor.

The door resisted momentarily his push against it, then gave; there was a short shriek of pain, followed immediately by a louder peal of laughter. He had hit someone with the door. He looked about to apologize, but no one was paying any attention to him. Someone filled the space between him and the door and he was forced into the room, pressed by the bodies of the party-goers.

There was excitement in the room, much laughter, music, and the heady atmosphere created by champagne, good food and convivial people. Wellman decided he was glad he had come. He passed a table beautifully laid with silver and crystal, and decorated with tiny white rosebuds and shiny leaves of waxed philodendron. Some of the *hors d'oeuvres* were steaming, some icy cold, and the champagne was in silver buckets of ice. He helped himself. As yet no one had noticed him; no one had come up to demand his name or an explanation for his presence, or even to be introduced. He grinned to himself and refilled his glass, this time moving from the table, not wishing to be conspicuous and accosted too soon.

The apartment was very large with high ceilings and many rooms. He moved slowly for the next few minutes, getting nowhere near the door he had come in by. There were so many people he probably never would be noticed; even his clothes would draw no comment. Some of the guests were in formal wear, others in street clothes as plain, or even plainer, than his own. He caught a glimpse of the woman in red who had called to him and he started to make his way in her general direction, not caring if he got to her side or not. She must be the hostess, and it might prove embarrassing when she realized that he was not the man she obviously had thought he was in the dimly lighted hallway.

"Yar selgemid dex," a tall, handsome man said, smiling pleasantly. The man made no effort to detain Wellman, who sidestepped him and continued to cross the room toward the woman in red. Wellman glanced over his shoulder and found that the man was regarding him with an amused expression. The man raised his glass in a salute. Wellman stepped into the middle of a group of people and lost sight of the sardonic face.

He was shoved a step or two sideways before he noticed this group's preoccupation with a painting on a creamy wall. The painting was framed in what looked like a border woven of straws, red-striped paper straws. He turned his attention to the painting. It was a Rubens, he thought, but as he considered it the old master rotated out of the frame and was replaced by another work of art. This was a landscape, Gauguin, perhaps. It was replaced by a reproduction of a cereal box, complete with a price stamped on it. Someone clutched his arm and he turned to look into an alabaster-like face of an ascetic-looking woman with severe black hair pulled so tightly back that it seemed to be lifting her scalp. There were tears in her eyes.

"The beauty," she said huskily. "The beauty of it!" There were ropelike cords in her neck.

The cereal box vanished and a spiral of black and white was there. He felt that he was slipping into it, around and down, around and down. The hand clutched harder, nails cutting through his coat, through his shirt, biting into his arm.

"I can't stand it," the woman moaned.

Wellman couldn't either. He tried to disengage her hand, but she clung to him, and now her other hand was at his chest, scrabbling at his shirt. The next painting was a sprayed, gray, flat surface, unmarred by a line. The woman stiffened convulsively, her eyes rolling up until only whites showed. Wellman pried her hands loose and laid her on the floor; he stepped over her carefully and left the group. From nearby he could hear a voice:

"Five puz quak ler . . ."

He didn't turn to look at the laughing face.

Someone touched his arm and he was facing a girl with an intent look. Her hair was long, swishing back and forth as she gyrated to music that seemed suddenly to be beating into his soul. It was a throbbing, primordial sound, no melody, no cohesion, just a beat that was almost a pain stabbing him deeply. He swayed opposite the girl. Her hair was the color of pale straw; her eyes were closed, with incredibly long lashes that weren't quite straight. She wore a low-cut, beige dress that clung to her and was stretched tautly across her thighs. She was barefoot. Her movements became more animalistic. Her mouth parted slightly, showing white teeth clenched together. The intent look on her strained face became a grimace and she moved faster and faster with the beat, swaying toward him, away, toward him, away. He felt a film of perspiration cover him, and his hands began to tingle and clench. She was moving very fast now, not touching him, seemingly not even aware of him, but dancing at him without restraint. With a sudden gasping cry she fell to the floor, on her knees, her face buried in her hands, and still her body moved and worked, only slowly losing the intensity of the movements that had jerked her spasmodically. He began to back away from her, feeling horror and disgust. He drank his champagne, gulping it without tasting it, then he turned to fill the glass again.

"I say bomb them to hell and gone!"

Wellman spun around. A potbellied, red-haired man with a mottled face and quivering dewlaps was wagging his finger under the nose of a clergyman.

"Negotiate! You can't bomb everyone who has a different opinion or a different way of governing." Under a heavy wave of silver hair the clergyman's face was benign, unlined, his eyes mild. His features were arranged in an almost-smile.

"God damn all pacifists! Give the world away because you're running scared! Want a nigger in the White House? In your daughter's bed? Want a Castro in every South American country? A Mao Tse-tung in every Asian country?"

"And the universities? I suppose you would bomb them too?"

"Put the sons of bitches in the army and let them learn to love the country and fear God!"

"You bastard!" The clergyman went pale, as if surprised and frightened by his own words. The almost-smile remained.

"Atheist!"

The clergyman flung his glass of champagne into the face of the red-haired man. Sputtering and coughing, the red-haired man raised his hand to ward off a blow, or perhaps simply to wipe his face. The clergyman hit him in the solar plexus with a hard, white-knuckled fist. The red-haired man fell to the floor and lay there retching. Wellman ran, pushing his way through the clusters of people. Someone caught his arm.

"Do you know who our host is?" It was the woman in red. Wellman breathed a sign of relief. He would make his apologies for crashing the party and then go. "Is this your party?" the woman asked.

She was nearing middle age, he realized with a start. She had appeared so young, with a slender, graceful figure. But there were lines about her eyes that on closer inspection appeared cynical and tired. Her mouth had a sarcastic twist although her lips were full and soft-looking. She seemed aware that he was noting her lips. She moistened them.

"I thought it was your party," he said. She put her hand on his arm. Her laugh was like chimes in a gentle wind.

"And I was certain that you were our host. You look so grim and purposeful."

"Do I?" He was pleased by the description. "I was afraid that you were coming to toss me out."

"Really! The most charming man in the room . . ."

The hand on his arm was leading him gently, without pressure, and they were leaving the roomful of people, passing through a doorway with dark velvet hangings. This room was empty and cool, with dim pink lights above a low, large bed covered with a white spread. She led him to the bed, her hand caressing his arm, her other hand slipping under his coat.

Her dress was in two parts. The diaphanous red outer part hung in the air like a brilliant cloud before settling to the floor;

the inner, more intensely colored part fell to the center of it. The two parts looked like a large bloodstain, dried about the edges where the floor showed through the gauzy fabric, still dark and shiny in the middle.

She was frenzied when they met on the smooth sheets of the bed, and it came as a shock for Wellman to find that she was frigid. After it was over she bit him maliciously on his shoulder. Wellman closed his eyes in pain and opened them to find her gone. Far away he could hear someone screaming softly. He dressed and hurried from the pink room.

The party was still in full bloom, if anything more crowded than when he had left. He looked for the source of the screams. On the far wall there was a Dali painting, just rotating out of view when he turned his searching gaze to it. Replacing it was an ethereal, pastel-blue, Japanese scene. Someone in the group before the wall sobbed noisily. Everyone there appeared oblivious to the rest of the party attendees. Now and again within the group one embraced, or clutched, another, but seldom did an outsider enter their midst, or a member stray away.

Beyond that group he saw watching him the man who had been speaking gibberish. The man started to cross to him. Wellman turned his back. Didn't anyone else care about who had screamed, or why? He almost bumped into a pale man whose eyes were glazed. He was wearing glasses with oversized lenses emphasized by heavy black frames.

"Is this your party?" the man asked, grabbing Wellman's lapel, holding him firmly on the spot.

"No. I just wandered in," Wellman said. He kept tension on the pull, so that when the man let him go, he staggered backward a step or two. The man had gone paler with his words; his pallor was alarming. He was thirty, Wellman thought, and not, as he had assumed at first, drunk. He looked like a graduate student, the effect of the large glasses, and of his hands that were ink-stained with fingernails bitten off to the quick.

"We all just wandered in," the man said, his eyes out of focus disconcertingly. "It's nobody's party. No one was invited, yet here we all are. No celebration, yet there is champagne. Who planned it? Don't you even care?" He bit at the nail of his left forefinger.

"Nap hoil selsten baax quiful . . ."

"You! Leave me alone! I'll find out!" The ghastly young man spun about and elbowed his way through a throng of laughing people, leaving Wellman and the grinning man side by side.

"Why did you do that?" Wellman asked. "You understand us perfectly. Why are you making those noises?"

The man laughed harder, tears forming in his large brown eyes. He wiped at them with the back of his hand. He was holding a nearly full champagne glass, and very slowly he turned it upside down, laughing harder as he did so. Wellman backed several steps from him, turned and left as quickly as the pale man had done. Mad, he was as crazy as a loon. When he looked back, the man was gazing after him with a thoughtful, melancholy expression on his face.

Someone bumped into Wellman from behind and he swung around. It was the clergyman, and he was carrying a bucket of sudsy water and a mop. He thrust the mop at Wellman, who let him place it in his hand.

"You start over there, near the door. Someone spilled something over there. I'll get the paint."

"What are you talking about?" Wellman asked. "Are you the host, then?"

"Me! Gracious no. But think of his anger when he returns and finds his apartment in such a turmoil. He'll have us all thrown in jail."

Wellman stood the mop against the wall. "Anyone with an apartment like this has to have a maid," he said. "Let her clean it up. Or the person who spilled the stuff."

"What is your name?" the clergyman cried furiously. "I'll report you myself. I'll come down and visit you in your cell and laugh at you. People like you, selfish, lazy, taking, never giving, never helping, never fearing the consequences of your acts. We are responsible. You are, I am . . ."

Wellman left him sputtering, searching his pockets for a notebook on which to write Wellman's name.

He heard laughter like chimes in a gentle wind and turned to see the woman in the soft red cloud of a dress passing through the curtained doorway, leading a portly bald man. The man was half-turned toward the party; there was a look of pleading on his face. Wellman's gaze followed his, and he saw a tall, angular woman, hands on her hips, an angry sneer twisting her mouth. She was dressed in gray; her hair was gray and sparse; her skin was gray. There was fierce hatred in her sunken eyes. Wellman shuddered and turned from her. He wanted to leave the party and the assorted freaks who had wandered in. A loud clattering sound erupted, and everyone turned to look toward the buffet table. The pale young man was standing on a chair, hitting a silver tray with a heavy serving spoon.

"Will our host please reveal himself?" he shouted. There was an answering hoot of derisive laughter, and an excited giggle, and much shuffling about of feet. No one claimed the honor.

"I'll find out," the pallid man cried. "Anyone else curious? Let's find out. There must be something about here to tell us. Look in the drawers, in the closets, everywhere . . ."

He leaped from the chair, and several others swayed and pressed toward him. Within minutes they had pulled open drawers and closets and cabinets, strewing contents about. The rest of the party resumed as if there had been no interruption.

"I say everything has to be free of government control: labor, enterprise, prices, wages, education, everything. Soon as you control one aspect, you have to control them all."

"Let big business fix wages and prices again, like a hundred years ago? Is that your idea of free?"

"They weren't sucked dry by government tax collectors . . ."

"They starved."

"They starved free!"

"Bullshit!"

"Why don't you go to Russia if you like control and collectivism so much?"

"Why don't you go to hell!"

Wellman didn't see them, but he heard the sound of blows. He tried to find the source and failed. He was hemmed in so closely that all he could see was the third button of a dress shirt straight ahead of him at eye level. Turning his head slightly to the left he saw the soft swell of a pale breast with a faint blue tracery of veins. Behind him people were pushing, and he was forced to step upward. He was pressed against a deep-chested man with an open, sunburned face. The man was beaming at him. At his side was a woman with a lovely oval face the color of ivory; she had magnificent black eyes and softly curled black hair. Her beautiful lips were sharply drawn with pale pink. Her gown, from the abbreviated bodice to the soft folds about her golden-clad feet matched her lips exactly.

"There is no body," she said softly. "Only spirit. All else is illusory." She moved closer to him and was solid enough, scented with a heady fragrance that made him want to melt. The man took his hand and clasped it in a grasp that threatened to mangle.

"You have chosen wisely, my boy," the man said. "There is no body! Remember that. Always. There is only spirit. Adjunct of God. With God's power. You are an adjunct of God."

With that, Wellman was pushed from him, and he was beaming at the next person to be shoved up the single step. Wellman tried to turn to catch another glimpse of the most beautiful spirit he had seen, but already she was pressing against the next being. The new spirit was perspiring profusely, trying to get his arms around her.

"It is *your* body! *You* have made it. *You* have control over it. You have survived ten million years of incarnations to the highest point in the evolutionary scale attainable. Seize this control today. Demand it! It is yours for the taking."

Wellman gaped at the man speaking. He was holding one hand over a candle, and with the other hand was running a six-inch hatpin into his body. He pulled it out and stuck it in again. His emaciated body was covered only by a loincloth; his hair was light brown and curly, down to his shoulders. His skin was dry-looking and white. He had a pointed beard and narrow light-green eyes that seemed to be staring into a place where other eyes couldn't see.

The distraught young man searching for the host darted up

the step, past the beautiful spirit, his hands pushing aside all who got in his way, his face intent.

"He has to be here! Who is doing the cooking? Who bought the food and the drinks? Who pays the light bills?" He snatched his glasses off, wiped them furiously, and jammed them back on.

"It is illusory," the sunburned man said soothingly. "A wave of the hand. A flickering of light. A whim of God's."

"I drank the champagne and ate the food. I was hungry and now I am not. That is not illusion. Where do we go from here? Where do you go after the party?"

"Nowhere. Everywhere. Moments are eternal. Or nonexistent. A whim of God's."

The man in the loincloth stuck the pin through his throat. "It makes no difference," he said, "who opens the door through which we pass. You are here now. You can be your own master. That you are here demonstrates your correct decisions in the past. Make the next decision now. Seize control of that machine that is running you now. Be your own man!"

The pale man cursed him fluently and rushed past the group. Wellman followed him. "What do you mean, where do you go after you leave here? Back to where you came from, don't you?"

The young man let out a despairing cry that was nearly a scream of anguish and darted away from him.

"Apol grexel gwa noqit . . ."

"Who are you?" Wellman said. "Why do you do that?" The man laughed, but this time Wellman was closer, staring at him directly. There were tears in the man's eyes. They were haunted, tortured eyes. "You are as afraid as he is," Wellman said. "You pretend it is all nonsense because you can't find the answers yourself. You are as afraid as he is!"

A violent tremor shook the man. He steadied himself against the wall, staring intently for a second or two at the room full of people; he examined Wellman's face. He opened his mouth, but closed it again without speaking. His face was twisted with pain, or pity, or both. He handed Wellman his glass, a diamond stickpin shooting fire as he moved. Without a word the man passed Wellman and went to the window. He didn't pause, but lifted one leg over the sill, and without looking back, followed it with the other leg and slid over. Beyond the window the night was utterly black and silent. Wellman dropped the glass from a hand that had gone numb.

"See! You are helping to mess it up! You shall help to clean it up before he gets home!" It was the clergyman, again thrusting the mop at Wellman. He accepted it, not caring if he cleaned or not.

"Didn't you see him?" he asked. "Jumped from the window. Didn't you even see him?"

"That isn't my job," the clergyman said. "I have to keep this place clean, so that when he gets home he won't put us all in jail. Do you know what jail is like, young man?" But Wellman had dropped the mop and had gone.

From the corner of his eye Wellman caught a blur of red and white, and when he turned to look at it, the red chiffon was coming to a stop beside a girl in a long white dress. She looked very young, wearing white gloves, and a small white flower in her hair. Her hair was soft brown, almost childish in its simplicity. Wellman found himself going to them. The woman in red smiled at him mockingly. She had her hand on the arm of the girl, who turned large blue eyes toward him. Wellman put his hand on her other arm.

"May I get you something?" he asked.

"But we were going to talk . . ."

"She'll still be here later," he said, drawing her away from the woman in red. They danced, with his arm about her, and then they shared a single glass of champagne and a small turkey sandwich from a plate that she held. They laughed often. Her soft laugh held promises for him; there was a gladness in his breast that hadn't been there before. When she had to leave, even though he knew he would see her again, he felt empty and tired. The woman in the red-cloud dress caught his arm and hissed something at him, but he didn't catch her words. Her face was venomous. He shrugged away from her.

"But you'll come back," she said. "You'll come back, and in

your brain a memory will stir and you'll wonder when or where we met before."

He almost fell over the pale man, who evidently had given up his search and was sitting on the floor, huddled into a ball, his knees under his chin, his arms wrapped about his legs. He raised his head to look at Wellman, and his face was without hope. Mutely he put his forehead again on his knees.

Wellman saw the clergyman, his coat off, his sleeves rolled up, filth up his arms to his elbows, his attention fixed on the dirt on the floor that he was trying futilely to scrub away. He didn't look up as Wellman skirted him.

A new painting slid into the straw frame: a pencil sketch of a nude. It was followed by a geometric pattern like an Indian blanket. The group was more intent than before, more gaunt, less aware of the rest of the party.

Wellman stopped before a bookshelf and began scanning titles. He sat on the floor before the shelf and read a little in several of the books. He never had heard of any of the authors, but the books were beautifully written and illustrated, and handsomely bound. They treated many subjects from poetry to mathematical theories, from short stories to philosophical essays. Suddenly the book he was reading was snatched from his hands. A bespectacled young woman riffled through the pages and tossed it back to him; she pulled other books from the shelves.

"Not a single best seller," she said scornfully. "Illiterates." She turned and marched stiffly away, leaving several books on the floor behind her. Wellman picked them up and replaced them on the shelf.

He heard weeping close by and turned to see the chiffon-dressed woman. When she saw him looking at her, she drew up and said haughtily, "That Goddamned mattress has made my back ache."

The crowds thickened again and Wellman was being pushed by them. The surge was irresistible, and soon he ceased trying to struggle against it.

He caught a glimpse of two young men, arms entwined, rapt expressions on their faces. Behind them the curtains to the room with the pink lights stirred. There was a sinuous girl stripping in time to frenzied music, heavy with drums. Wellman saw her jaw moving and almost laughed as he realized she was chewing gum. A circle of men and women watched avidly as she stripped. There was a man with a green eye-shade hiding most of his face, his hands shuffling cards expertly, stacks of money in front of him. Across the table from him sat a white-haired man, and Wellman could see one of his hands under the table. It held a pistol.

He was swept on. His head ached then, and he felt sore from the jostling and pushing. Someone was moaning, a young woman clinging to the arm of a man who was reaching out with his free hand to pinch the breast of another girl who was not even looking at him.

Wellman tried to grab a pickpocket, but missed. He called to the man who had been robbed; the man grinned vacuously and vanished from his sight in a throng of merrymakers. Wellman felt his own pocket and knew the pickpocket had been there. He couldn't free himself from the mass that he was caught up in to do anything about it. His head was aching abominably by then, and he felt that he couldn't breathe in the haze-filled room. With an effort he forced his way to the side of the flowing tide of people, and stood leaning against the wall panting, his clothes disheveled. He pulled another man from the people streaming past. The man stared at him blankly.

"How do you get out of here?" Wellman asked, his breath still coming fast from his struggle to get free.

"Out?" the man said stupidly.

"Where is the door to the hallway?" Wellman asked.

The man indicated the direction with his thumb. "I thought you meant out," he said laughing. Someone in the crowd behind him picked that up and repeated it to someone else, and they both laughed. Wellman started to push his way through in the direction the man had indicated. The laughter was spreading through the party by then and he could hear "Out" being said again and again. At the door he turned to look at them, but no one was paying any attention to him. He turned the doorknob as someone said laughingly, "I say fifteen minutes, five dollars says fifteen minutes. It never takes longer than that."

Wellman pulled the door open then and started to step into the hallway. Someone slammed the door hard against his back, sending him sprawling to the wall on the other side. For a moment he was dazed; for a moment it seemed that everything was spinning away from him, memories of laughter, of champagne, a party . . .

Wellman blinked rapidly, then shook his head. He was on the wrong floor. He could feel the difference, although visually there was very little that was not familiar. The elevator must have come up too swiftly, left him dizzy and on the wrong floor. He gazed about wonderingly. So like his floor. The corridor was not as well lighted as was his own. He felt certain he should have ridden higher than this. The many doors lining the corridor were closed. At the far end there was one that was partially opened, and from it was issuing laughter and music that seemed to be inviting him to join. . . .

During brain surgery it was learned that electric currents could revive long-forgotten memories in patients. Snatches of conversations, music, scenes from the past could be replayed. More recently there has been a discovery that will permit sightless persons to "see" through the direction of an electric current into the brain. Electrodes in the brain can stimulate all of the emotions on cue—anger, love, timidity. . . . Through the ages writers have examined their own society and its discoveries, and sometimes they have found themselves leaving the familiar space-time dimensions in search of a frame that would fit the story more closely. Such stories might appear to be about someplace else, or some other time, or some other people, but actually they are about us in our time. Stories are twined about pegs so that ideally neither the story nor the pegs could exist without each other. The pegs might be historical, contemporary, futuristic; they might be mundane or fantastic. Whenever a story cannot be told without its own particular pegs, and when those pegs are based on the scientific possibilities that either exist, or could exist, then the story is science fiction. I never label a story until I have finished with it, and sometimes not even then. I think this one is a story about us, here and now. You may disagree.

Baby, You Were Great

JOHN LEWISOHN thought that if one more door slammed, or one more bell rang, or one more voice asked if he was all right, his head would explode. Leaving his laboratories he walked through the carpeted hall to the elevator that slid wide to admit him noiselessly, was lowered, gently, two floors, where there were more carpeted halls. The door he shoved open bore a neat sign, AUDITIONING STUDIO. Inside he was waved on through the reception room by three girls who knew better than to speak to him unless he spoke first. They were surprised to see him; it was his first visit there in seven or eight months. The inner room where he stopped was darkened, at first glance appearing empty, revealing another occupant only after his eyes had time to adjust to the dim lighting.

John sat in the chair next to Herb Javits, still without speaking. Herb was wearing the helmet and gazing at a wide screen that was actually a one-way glass panel permitting him to view the audition going on in the adjacent room. John lowered a second helmet to his head. It fit snugly and immediately made contact with the eight prepared spots on his skull. As soon as he turned it on, the helmet itself was forgotten.

A girl had entered the other room. She was breathtakingly lovely, a long-legged honey blonde with slanting green eyes and apricot skin. The room was furnished as a sitting room with two couches, some chairs, end tables and a coffee table, all tasteful and lifeless, like an ad in a furniture-trade publication. The girl stopped at the doorway and John felt her indecision heavily tempered with nervousness and fear. Outwardly she appeared poised and expectant, her smooth face betraying none of the emotions. She took a hesitant step toward the couch, and a wire showed trailing behind her. It was attached to her head. At the same time a second door opened. A young man ran inside, slamming the door behind him; he looked wild and frantic. The girl registered surprise, mounting nervousness; she felt behind her for the door handle, found it and tried to open the door again. It was locked. John could hear nothing that was being said in the room; he only felt the girl's reaction to the unexpected interruption. The wild-eyed man was approaching her, his hands slashing through the air, his eyes darting glances all about them constantly. Suddenly he pounced on her and pulled her to him, kissing her face and neck roughly. She seemed paralyzed with fear for several seconds, then there was something else, a bland nothing kind of feeling that accompanied boredom sometimes, or too complete self-assurance. As the man's hands fastened on her blouse in the back and ripped it, she threw her arms about him, her face showing passion that was not felt anywhere in her mind or in her blood.

"Cut!" Herb Javits said quietly.

The man stepped back from the girl and left her without a

word. She looked about blankly, her blouse torn, hanging about her hips, one shoulder strap gone. She was very beautiful. The audition manager entered, followed by a dresser with a gown that he threw about her shoulders. She looked startled; waves of anger mounted to fury as she was drawn from the room, leaving it empty. The two watching men removed their helmets.

"Fourth one so far," Herb grunted. "Sixteen yesterday; twenty the day before . . . all nothing." He gave John a curious look. "What's got you stirred out of your lab?"

"Anne's had it this time," John said. "She's been on the phone all night and all morning."

"What now?"

"Those damn sharks! I told you that was too much on top of the airplane crash last week. She can't take much more of it."

"Hold it a minute, Johnny," Herb said. "Let's finish off the next three girls and then talk." He pressed a button on the arm of his chair and the room beyond the screen took their attention again.

This time the girl was slightly less beautiful, shorter, a dimply sort of brunette with laughing blue eyes and an upturned nose. John liked her. He adjusted his helmet and felt with her.

She was excited; the audition always excited them. There was some fear and nervousness, not too much. Curious about how the audition would go, probably. The wild young man ran into the room, and her face paled. Nothing else changed. Her nervousness increased, not uncomfortably. When he grabbed her, the only emotion she registered was the nervousness.

"Cut," Herb said.

The next girl was brunette, with gorgeously elongated legs. She was very cool, a real professional. Her mobile face reflected the range of emotions to be expected as the scene played through again, but nothing inside her was touched. She was a million miles away from it all.

The next one caught John with a slam. She entered the room slowly, looking about with curiosity, nervous, as they all were. She was younger than the other girls had been, less poised. She had pale-gold hair piled in an elaborate mound of waves on top of her head. Her eyes were brown, her skin nicely tanned. When the man entered, her emotion changed quickly to fear, and then to terror. John didn't know when he closed his eyes. He was the girl, filled with unspeakable terror; his heart pounded, adrenalin pumped into his system; he wanted to scream but could not. From the dim unreachable depths of his psyche there came something else, in waves, so mixed with terror that the two merged and became one emotion that pulsed and throbbed and demanded. With a jerk he opened his eyes and stared at the window. The girl had been thrown down to one of the couches, and the man was kneeling on the floor beside her, his hands playing over her bare body, his face pressed against her skin.

"Cut!" Herb said. His voice was shaken. "Hire her," he said. The man rose, glanced at the girl, sobbing now, and then quickly bent over and kissed her cheek. Her sobs increased. Her golden hair was down, framing her face; she looked like a child. John tore off the helmet. He was perspiring.

Herb got up, turned on the lights in the room, and the window blanked out, blending with the wall, making it invisible. He didn't look at John. When he wiped his face, his hand was shaking. He rammed it in his pocket.

"When did you start auditions like that?" John asked, after a few moments of silence.

"Couple of months ago. I told you about it. Hell, we had to, Johnny. That's the six hundred-nineteenth girl we've tried out! Six hundred nineteen! All phonies but one! Dead from the neck up. Do you have any idea how long it was taking us to find that out? Hours for each one. Now it's a matter of minutes."

John Lewisohn sighed. He knew. He had suggested it, actually, when he had said, "Find a basic anxiety situation for the test." He hadn't wanted to know what Herb had come up with.

He said, "Okay, but she's only a kid. What about her parents, legal rights, all that?"

"We'll fix it. Don't worry. What about Anne?"

"She's called me five times since yesterday. The sharks were too much. She wants to see us, both of us, this afternoon."

"You're kidding! I can't leave here now!"

"Nope. Kidding I'm not. She says no plug up if we don't show. She'll take pills and sleep until we get there."

"Good Lord! She wouldn't dare!"

"I've booked seats. We take off at 12:35." They stared at one another silently for another moment, then Herb shrugged. He was a short man, not heavy but solid. John was over six feet, muscular, with a temper that he knew he had to control. Others suspected that when he did let it go, there would be bodies lying around afterward, but he controlled it.

Once it had been a physical act, an effort of body and will to master that temper; now it was done so automatically that he couldn't recall occasions when it even threatened to flare any more.

"Look, Johnny, when we see Anne, let me handle it. Right?" Herb said. "I'll make it short."

"What are you going to do?"

"Give her an earful. If she's going to start pulling temperament on me, I'll slap her down so hard she'll bounce a week." He grinned happily. "She's had it all her way up to now. She knew there wasn't a replacement if she got bitchy. Let her try it now. Just let her try." Herb was pacing back and forth with quick, jerky steps.

John realized with a shock that he hated the stocky, red-faced man. The feeling was new, it was almost as if he could taste the hatred he felt, and the taste was unfamiliar and pleasant.

Herb stopped pacing and stared at him for a moment. "Why'd she call you? Why does she want you down, too?" She knows you're not mixed up with this end of it."

"She knows I'm a full partner, anyway," John said.

"Yeah, but that's not it." Herb's face twisted in a grin. "She thinks you're still hot for her, doesn't she? She knows you tumbled once, in the beginning, when you were working on her, getting the gimmick working right." The grin reflected no humor then. "Is she right, Johnny, baby? Is that it?"

"We made a deal," John said coldly. "You run your end, I run mine. She wants me along because she doesn't trust you, or believe anything you tell her any more. She wants a witness."

"Yeah, Johnny. But you be sure you remember our agreement." Suddenly Herb laughed. "You know what it was like, Johnny, seeing you and her? Like a flame trying to snuggle up to an icicle."

At three-thirty they were in Anne's suite in the Skyline Hotel in Grand Bahama. Herb had a reservation to fly back to New York on the 6 P.M. flight. Anne would not be off until four, so they made themselves comfortable in her rooms and waited. Herb turned her screen on, offered a helmet to John, who shook his head, and they both seated themselves. John watched the screen for several minutes; then he, too, put on a helmet.

Anne was looking at the waves far out at sea where they were long, green, undulating; then she brought her gaze in closer, to the blue-green and quick seas, and finally in to where they stumbled on the sand bars, breaking into foam that looked solid enough to walk on. She was peaceful, swaying with the motion of the boat, the sun hot on her back, the fishing rod heavy in her hands. It was like being an indolent animal at peace with its world, at home in the world, being one with it. After a few seconds she put down the rod and turned, looking at a tall smiling man in swimming trunks. He held out his hand and she took it. They entered the cabin of the boat, where drinks were waiting. Her mood of serenity and happiness ended abruptly, to be replaced by shocked disbelief and a start of fear.

"What the hell . . . ?" John muttered, adjusting the audio. You seldom needed audio when Anne was on.

". . . Captain Brothers had to let them go. After all, they've done nothing yet . . . ," the man was saying soberly.

"But why do you think they'll try to rob me?"

"Who else is here with a million dollars worth of jewels?"

John turned it off and said to Herb, "You're a fool! You can't get away with something like that!"

Herb stood up and crossed the room to stand before a window wall that was open to the stretch of glistening blue ocean beyond the brilliant white beaches. "You know what every woman wants? To own something worth stealing." He chuckled, a low throaty sound that was without mirth. "Among other things, that is. They want to be roughed up once or twice, and forced to kneel. . . . Our new psychologist is pretty good, you know? Hasn't steered us wrong yet. Anne might kick some, but it'll go over great."

"She won't stand for an actual robbery." Louder, emphasizing it, he added, "I won't stand for that."

"We can dub it," Herb said. "That's all we need, Johnny, plant the idea, and then dub the rest."

John stared at his back. He wanted to believe that. He needed to believe it. His voice showed no trace of emotion when he said, "It didn't start like this, Herb. What happened?"

Herb turned then. His face was dark against the glare of light behind him. "Okay, Johnny, it didn't start like this. Things accelerate, that's all. You thought of a gimmick, and the way we planned it, it sounded great, but it didn't last. We gave them the feeling of gambling, of learning to ski, of automobile racing, everything we could dream of, and it wasn't enough. How many times can you take the first ski jump of your life? After a while you want new thrills, you know? For you it's been great, hasn't it? You bought yourself a shining new lab and pulled the cover over you and it. You bought yourself time and equipment, and when things didn't go right you could toss it out and start over, and nobody gave a damn. Think of what it's been like for me, kid! I gotta keep coming up with something new, something that'll give Anne a jolt and, through her, all those nice little people who aren't even alive unless they're plugged in. You think it's been easy? Anne was a green kid. For her everything was new and exciting, but it isn't like that now, boy. You better believe it is *not* like that now. You know what she told me last month? She's sick and tired of men. Our little hot-box Annie! Tired of men!"

John crossed to him and pulled him around. "Why didn't you tell me?"

"Why, Johnny? What would you have done that I didn't do? I looked harder for the right guy for her. What would you do for a new thrill for her? I worked for them, kid. Right from the start you said for me to leave you alone. Okay. I left you alone.

You ever read any of the memos I sent? You initialed them, kiddo. Everything that's been done, we both signed. Don't give me any of that why-didn't-I-tell-you stuff. It won't work!" His face was ugly red and a vein bulged in his neck. John wondered if he had high blood pressure, if he would die of a stroke during one of his flash rages.

John left him at the window. He had read the memos. Herb knew he had. Herb was right; all he had wanted was to be left alone. It had been his idea; after twelve years of work in a laboratory on prototypes he had shown his . . . gimmick . . . to Herb Javits. Herb was one of the biggest producers on television then; now he was the biggest producer in the world.

The gimmick was fairly simple. A person fitted with electrodes in his brain could transmit his emotions, which in turn could be broadcast and picked up by the helmets to be felt by the audience. No words or thoughts went out, only basic emotions . . . fear, love, anger, hatred . . . That, tied in with a camera showing what the person saw, with a voice dubbed in, and you were the person having the experience, with one important difference, you could turn it off if it got to be too much. The "actor" couldn't. A simple gimmick. You didn't really need the camera and the soundtrack; many users never turned them on at all, but let their own imagination fill in to fit the emotional broadcast.

The helmets were not sold, only rented after a short, easy fitting session. Rent of one dollar a month was collected on the first of the month, and there were over thirty-seven million subscribers. Herb had bought his own network after the second month when the demand for more hours barred him from regular television. From a one-hour weekly show, it had gone to one hour nightly, and now it was on the air eight hours a day live, with another eight hours of taped programming.

What had started out as A DAY IN THE LIFE OF ANNE BEAUMONT was now a life in the life of Anne Beaumont, and the audience was insatiable.

Anne came in then, surrounded by the throng of hangers-on that mobbed her daily—hairdressers, masseurs, fitters, script men.

. . . She looked tired. She waved the crowd out when she saw John and Herb were there. "Hello, John," she said, "Herb."

"Anne, baby, you're looking great!" Herb said. He took her in his arms and kissed her solidly. She stood still, her hands at her sides.

She was tall, very slender, with wheat-colored hair and gray eyes. Her cheekbones were wide and high, her mouth firm and almost too large. Against her deep red-gold sun-tan her teeth looked whiter than John remembered them. Although too firm and strong ever to be thought of as pretty, she was a very beautiful woman. After Herb released her, she turned to John, hesitated only a moment, and then extended a slim, sun-browned hand. It was cool and dry in his.

"How have you been, John? It's been a long time."

He was very glad she didn't kiss him or call him darling. She smiled only slightly and gently removed her hand from his. He moved to the bar as she turned to Herb.

"I'm through, Herb," she said. Her voice was too quiet. She accepted a whiskey sour from John, but kept her gaze on Herb.

"What's the matter, honey? I was just watching you, baby. You were great today, like always. You've still got it, kid. It's coming through like always."

"What about this robbery? You must be out of your mind. . . ."

"Yeah, that. Listen, Anne baby, I swear to you I don't know a thing about it. Laughton must have been telling you the straight goods on that. You know we agreed that the rest of this week you just have a good time, remember? That comes over too, baby. When you have a good time and relax, thirty-seven million people are enjoying life and relaxing. That's good. They can't be stimulated all the time. They like the variety. . . ." Wordlessly John held out a glass, Scotch and water. Herb took it without looking.

Anne was watching him coldly. Suddenly she laughed. It was a cynical, bitter sound. "You're not a damn fool, Herb. Don't try to act like one." She sipped her drink again, continuing to stare at him over the rim of the glass. "I am warning you, if anyone shows here to rob me, I'm going to treat him like a real burglar. I bought a gun after today's broadcast, and I learned how to shoot when I was only nine or ten. I still know how. I'll kill him, Herb, whoever it is."

"Baby," Herb started, but she cut him short.

"And this is my last week. As of Saturday, I'm through."

"You can't do that, Anne," Herb said. John watched him closely, searching for a sign of weakness, anything; he saw nothing. Herb exuded confidence. "Look around, Anne, at this room, your clothes, everything. . . . You are the richest woman in the world, having the time of your life, able to go anywhere, do anything. . . ."

"While the whole world watches . . ."

"So what? It doesn't stop you, does it?" Herb started to pace, his steps jerky and quick. "You knew that when you signed the contract. You're a rare girl, Anne, beautiful, emotional, intelligent. Think of all those women who've got nothing but you. If you quit them, what do they do? Die? They might, you know. For the first time in their lives they are able to feel like they're living. You're giving them what no one ever did before, what was only hinted at in books and films in the old days. Suddenly they know what it feels like to face excitement, to experience love, to feel contented and peaceful. Think of them, Anne, empty, with nothing in their lives but you, what you're able to give them. Thirty-seven million drabs, Anne, who never felt anything but boredom and frustration until you gave them life. What do they have? Work, kids, bills. You've given them the world, baby! Without you they wouldn't even want to live any more."

She wasn't listening. Almost dreamily she said, "I talked to my lawyers, Herb, and the contract is meaningless. You've already broken it countless times by insisting on adding to the original agreement. I agreed to learn a lot of new things, so they could feel them with me. I did. My God! I've climbed mountains, hunted lions, learned to ski and water ski, but now you want me to die a little bit each week . . . that airplane crash, not bad, just enough to terrify me. Then the sharks. I really do think it was having sharks brought in when I was skiing that did it, Herb. You see, you will kill me. It will happen, and you won't be able to top it, Herb. Not ever."

There was a hard, waiting silence following her words. "No!" John shouted, soundlessly, the words not leaving his mouth. He was looking at Herb. He had stopped pacing when she started to talk. Something flicked across his face, surprise, fear, something not readily identifiable. Then his face went completely blank and he raised his glass and finished the Scotch and water, replacing the glass on the bar. When he turned again, he was smiling with disbelief.

"What's really bugging you, Anne? There have been plants before. You knew about them. Those lions didn't just happen by, you know. And the avalanche needed a nudge from someone. You know that. What else is bugging you?"

"I'm in love, Herb. I want out now before you manage to kill me." Herb waved that aside impatiently.

"Have you ever watched your own show, Anne?" She shook her head. "I thought not. So you wouldn't know about the expansion that took place last month, after we planted that new transmitter in your head. Johnny boy here's been busy, Anne. You know these scientist types, never satisfied, always improving, changing. Where's the camera, Anne? Do you ever know where it is any more? Have you even seen a camera in the past couple of weeks, or a recorder of any sort? You have not, and you won't again. You're on now, honey." His voice was quite low, amused almost. "In fact the only time you aren't on is when you're sleeping. I know you're in love; I know who he is; I know how he makes you feel; I even know how much money he makes per week. I should know, Anne baby. I pay him." He had come closer to her with each word, finishing with his face only inches from hers. He didn't have a chance to duck the flashing slap that jerked his head around, and before either of them realized it, he had hit her back. Anne fell back to the chair, too stunned to speak for a moment.

The silence grew, became something ugly and heavy, as if words were being born and dying without utterance because they were too brutal for the human spirit to bear. There was a spot of blood on Herb's mouth where her diamond ring had cut him. He touched it and looked at his finger. "It's all being taped now, honey, even this," he said. He returned to the bar, turning his back on her.

There was a large red print on her cheek. Her gray eyes had turned black with rage; she didn't take her gaze from him.

"Honey, relax," Herb said after a moment, his voice soft and easy again. "It won't make any difference to you, in what you do, or anything like that. You know we can't use most of the stuff, but it gives the editors a bigger variety to pick from. It was getting to the point where most of the interesting stuff was going on after you were off. Like buying the gun. That's great stuff there, baby. You weren't blanketing a single thing, and it'll all come through like pure gold." He finished mixing his drink, tasted it, and then swallowed most of it. "How many women have to go out and buy a gun to protect themselves? Think of them all, feeling that gun, feeling the things you felt when you picked it up, looked at it. . . ."

"How long have you been tuning in all the time?" she asked. John felt a stirring along his spine, a tingle of excitement. He knew what was going out over the miniature transmitter, the rising crests of emotion she was feeling. Only a trace of them showed on her smooth face, but the raging interior torment was being recorded faithfully. Her quiet voice and quiet body were lies; only the tapes never lied.

Herb felt it too, a storm behind her quietude. He put his glass down and went to her, kneeling by the chair, taking her hand in both of his. "Anne, please, don't be that angry with me. I was desperate for new material. When Johnny got this last wrinkle out, and we knew we could record around the clock, we had to try it, and it wouldn't have been any good if you had known. That's no way to test anything. You knew we were planting the transmitter . . ."

"How long?"

"Not quite a month."

"And Stuart? He's one of your men? He is transmitting also? You hired him to . . . to make love to me? Is that right?"

Herb nodded. She pulled her hand free and averted her face, not willing to see him any longer. He got up then and went to the window. "But what difference does it make?" he shouted. "If I introduced the two of you at a party, you wouldn't think anything of it. What difference if I did it this way? I knew you'd like each other. He's bright, like you, likes the same sort of things you do. Comes from a poor family, like yours. . . . Everything said you'd get along. . . ."

"Oh, yes," she said almost absently. "We get along." She was feeling in her hair, her fingers searching for the scars.

"It's all healed by now," John said. She looked at him as if she had forgotten he was there.

"I'll find a surgeon," she said, standing up, her fingers white on her glass. "A brain surgeon . . ."

"It's a new process," John said slowly. "It would be dangerous to go in after them. . . ."

She looked at him for a long time. "Dangerous?"

He nodded.

"You could take it back out. . . ."

He remembered the beginning, how he had quieted her fear of the electrodes and the wires. Her fear was that of a child for the unknown and the unknowable. Time and again he had proven to her that she could trust him, that he wouldn't lie to her. He hadn't lied to her, then. There was the same trust in her eyes, the same unshakable faith. She would believe him. She would accept without question whatever he said. Herb had called him an icicle, but that was wrong. An icicle would have melted in her fires. More like a stalactite, shaped by centuries of civilization, layer by layer he had been formed until he had forgotten how to bend, forgotten how to find release for the stirrings he felt somewhere in the hollow, rigid core of himself. She had tried and, frustrated, she had turned from him, hurt, but unable not to trust one she had loved. Now she waited. He could free her, and lose her again, this time irrevocably. Or he could hold her as long as she lived.

Her lovely gray eyes were shadowed with fear and the trust that he had given to her. Slowly he shook his head.

"I can't," he said. "No one can."

"I see," she murmured, the black filling her eyes. "I'd die, wouldn't I? Then you'd have a lovely sequence, wouldn't you, Herb?" She swung around, away from John. "You'd have to fake the story line, of course, but you are so good at that. An accident, emergency brain surgery needed, everything I feel going out to the poor little drabs who never will have brain surgery done. It's very good," she said admiringly. Her eyes were very black. "In fact, anything I do from now on, you'll use, won't you? If I kill you, that will simply be material for your editors to pick over. Trial, prison, very dramatic . . . On the other hand, if I kill myself . . ."

John felt chilled; a cold, hard weight seemed to be filling him. Herb laughed. "The story line will be something like this," he said. "Anne has fallen in love with a stranger, deeply, sincerely in love with him. Everyone knows how deep that love is; they've all felt it, too, you know. She finds him raping a child, a lovely little girl in her early teens. Stuart tells her they're through. He loves the little nymph. In a passion she kills herself. You are broadcasting a real storm of passion, right now, aren't you, honey? Never mind, when I run through this scene, I'll find out." She hurled her glass at him, ice cubes and orange sections leaving a trail across the room. Herb ducked, grinning.

"That's awfully good, baby. Corny, but after all, they can't get too much corn, can they? They'll love it, after they get over the shock of losing you. And they will get over it, you know. They always do. Wonder if it's true about what happens to someone experiencing a violent death?" Anne's teeth bit down on her lip, and slowly she sat down again, her eyes closed tight. Herb watched her for a moment, then said, even more cheerfully, "We've got the kid already. If you give them a death, you've got to give them a new life. Finish one with a bang. Start one with a bang. We'll name the kid Cindy, a real Cinderella story after that. They'll love her, too."

Anne opened her eyes, black, dulled now; she was so tight

with tension that John felt his own muscles contract and become taut. He wondered if he would be able to stand the tape she was transmitting. A wave of excitement swept him and he knew he would play it all, feel it all, the incredibly contained rage, fear, the horror of giving a death to them to gloat over, and finally, anguish. He would know them all. Watching Anne, he wished she would break then, with him there. She didn't. She stood up stiffly, her back rigid, a muscle hard and ridged in her jaw. Her voice was flat when she said, "Stuart is due in half an hour. I have to dress." She left them without looking back.

Herb winked at John and motioned toward the door. "Want to take me to the plane, kid?" In the cab he said, "Stick close to her for a couple of days, Johnny. There might be an even bigger reaction later when she really understands just how hooked she is." He chuckled again. "By God! It's a good thing she trusts you, Johnny, boy!"

As they waited in the chrome-and-marble terminal for the liner to unload its passengers, John said, "Do you think she'll be any good after this?"

"She can't help herself. She's too life oriented to deliberately choose to die. She's like a jungle inside, raw, wild, untouched by that smooth layer of civilization she shows on the outside. It's a thin layer, kid, real thin. She'll fight to stay alive. She'll become more wary, more alert to danger, more excited and exciting . . . She'll really go to pieces when he touches her tonight. She's primed real good. Might even have to do some editing, tone it down a little." His voice was very happy. "He touches her where she lives, and she reacts. A real wild one. She's one; the new kid's one; Stuart . . . They're few and far apart, Johnny. It's up to us to find them. God knows we're going to need all of them we can get." His face became thoughtful and withdrawn. "You know, that really wasn't such a bad idea of mine about rape and the kid. Who ever dreamed we'd get that kind of a reaction from her? With the right sort of buildup . . ." He had to run to catch his plane.

John hurried back to the hotel, to be near Anne if she needed him. He hoped she would leave him alone. His fingers shook as he turned on his screen; suddenly he had a clear memory of the child who had wept, and he hoped Stuart would hurt Anne just a little. The tremor in his fingers increased; Stuart was on from six until twelve, and he already had missed almost an hour of the show. He adjusted the helmet and sank back into a deep chair. He left the audio off, letting his own words form, letting his own thoughts fill in the spaces.

Anne was leaning toward him, sparkling champagne raised to her lips, her eyes large and soft. She was speaking, talking to him, John, calling him by name. He felt a tingle start somewhere deep inside him, and his glance was lowered to rest on her tanned hand in his, sending electricity through him. Her hand trembled when he ran his fingers up her palm, to her wrist where a blue vein throbbed. The slight throb became a pounding that grew, and when he looked again into her eyes, they were dark and very deep. They danced and he felt her body against his, yielding, pleading. The room darkened and she was an outline against the window, her gown floating down about her. The darkness grew denser, or he closed his eyes, and this time when her body pressed against his, there was nothing between them, and the pounding was everywhere.

In the deep chair, with the helmet on his head, John's hands clenched, opened, clenched, again and again.

The previous story fits anyone's definition of science fiction; this one does not, although at first sight it appears to have some of the same background material that science-fiction writers use. When the story appeared in print a few years ago, I received a letter from a woman who expressed sympathy that I had experienced the same situation she had lived through. In a sense this is true. Story ideas can come from single words, phrases, news items, personal experiences. . . . The New York Times in one day has enough story ideas in it to keep a writer occupied for his entire life. But the idea, or even the combination of ideas, is not the story. The story is born when the ideas coalesce and relate back to people, when the writer has "experienced" the events he then tells, and sometimes there is a letter that says it worked. At least, for this one woman it worked. The ideas? An eclipse, a very bright boy, and an overly helpful father.

When the Moon Was Red

WHEN the school officials first discussed Robbie with Shelley, she wasn't exactly surprised; pleased certainly, but with an inner feeling of vindication. Robbie wasn't quite eleven then and she had known for three or four years that he was mentally superior to his playmates and school friends. Not that he made any attempt to outstrip them in any way; it merely happened. When his cousin Stevie began collecting rocks, Robbie checked out half a dozen lapidary books and organized the collection systematically until Stevie gave it up in disgust. The collection was now quite valuable even though it did gather dust in the basement.

Frank had also got interested in rocks, and had made showcases for them which he regularly—for a time—exhibited to all callers.

And the year Robbie had his eighth-birthday party and had been given that hideous mud puppy. She had caught him carefully dissecting it with a razor blade on the kitchen table and drawing its insides on her monogrammed stationery. Frank had stayed the spanking she thought he deserved that time, and he had set up a regular operating table in the basement and proceeded to show Robbie how they had done it when he was in school. Robbie had sneaked away leaving him down there talking to the empty gray walls, looking foolishly at the mangled frog before him.

Robbie's stamp collection was under lock and key. "Good Lord, Shelley!" Frank had exploded when she protested, "the kid's stumbled across a sixty-five-dollar stamp! First thing you know he'll trade it for a BB gun or something."

"He didn't stumble across it, Frank. He did some hard trading to get it," Shelley said.

"When he's older he'll enjoy it more and appreciate it more. Just last night he knocked the whole book off the table when I tried to help him locate a violet Hamilton. He's too young for stuff like that."

Shelley looked at him calmly. "He didn't want any help. He didn't think he needed any."

"I still say he's too young. When he learns how to take care of it, that's time enough."

Shelley had given it up at that. Robbie was hardier than she was; he could fight it his own way. She had watched him fighting it his own way for all of his ten years, it seemed. He would start something, Frank would interfere, and he would wander away from it. While Frank was at his office, or on one of his business trips that kept him away nearly as much as he was there, Robbie's interests would reappear, still very much operative, but he filled in those other hours with other things. Robbie was very hardy.

Still it had come as a pleasure for the school authorities to recognize that he needed the challenge of the advanced program. He was not a genius, they were quick to declare, and that too she had known. But he was very intelligent, and under the present circumstances it was felt that the more intellectually able youngsters should be given the opportunity to develop their abilities.

Frank's reaction had been typical, she thought wryly. He had bought a new encyclopedia set for seven hundred dollars, had built bookshelves in Robbie's room and crammed them with books the saleslady had assured him were fundamental for a genius. So far Robbie had by and large ignored them, preferring to check out his own selections of dog-eared, smeary library books every Saturday. As often as not they included one horse story, one science-fiction adventure and one that ranged from mythology through King Arthur, poetry, riddles or puns. Very bad puns that sent him into howls of laughter. He never checked more than three, and never returned one unread. He could lie across his bed immersed in the world of print for hours. Or in the living room oblivious of the television and of Beatrice's attempts to draw him into a game. Beatrice adored him, annoyed and pestered him, and at times seemed to be his main source of amusement. Robbie was good to her, and his teasing was humorous rather than malicious. But most often he appeared unaware of her, and his gleaming black hair tumbled on his forehead as the greater part of him departed through the gate of words leaving the handsome well-built body that no one could distract.

Shelley half-listened to Beatrice sounding out the words in her first-grade reader, and really listened to the sounds emanating from the basement. "What, dear?" she asked at the impatient tug on her arm. "'Pleasant,'" she read and Beatrice continued chanting the adventures of Dick and Jane.

What could he be doing? Shelley wondered, as she absently corrected Beatrice. He had taken his old record player and the alarm clock from his room and disappeared to the basement immediately after dinner. Finally it was time for Beatrice's bath and bed, and she started down the stairs. Robbie met her at the bottom, grinning happily.

"Finished, Robbie?" Shelley hid the disappointment and started to retrace her steps.

He hesitated only a moment and then asked shyly, "Want to see what I'm doing?"

Shelley followed him to the workshop area and watched as he plugged in the record player. "I fixed it so it only makes fifteen revolutions a minute, and I took out the spindle. But I can put it back and speed it up again," he added hurriedly.

"What's it for, Robbie? The records won't play that slowly, will they?"

"No, I'm going to grind a mirror for a telescope on it. You have to make a parabolic curve in the mirror, and the book said to put the tool on a barrel and keep walking around it while you grind, but I couldn't find a barrel anywhere, so I thought this would give the same evenness."

"A telescope!" Shelley's mind flashed a picture of the observatory at that mountain in California and she shuddered involuntarily. "A telescope," she repeated weakly.

"Yes. I used my Christmas money for the kit. Ten dollars for the mirror blank and the tool and the pitch and all the grits and rouge. That's all right, isn't it? You said I could do anything I wanted to with it." His eyes, so deep a blue that they appeared black, fixed on her intently.

"But, Robbie, why didn't you mention it? When did you order it?"

"Last week," he said and became interested in the insulation of the extension cord he had connected to the record player. "I just forgot to say anything, I guess." His gaze shifted and concentrated on his toes, which immediately began to wiggle.

Shelley wanted to hug him to ease the ache that suddenly made her blink hard. Instead she said casually, "I suppose you have the instructions and books and everything in school, don't you?" He nodded without speaking and she added thoughtfully, "You know, your father will be gone the last two weeks of February. What a nice surprise this would be for him to find finished when he gets home then."

Robbie's quick look of gratitude erased any guilt she may have felt and she continued, "Why don't you put off your homework until after dinner for the next week or so, and you could spend some time down here after you get home from school every day. You won't be in your father's way if he wants to do anything down here that way." His smile of relief had to substitute for the kiss she halfway expected, and she reflected again on how fast he was leaving childhood behind.

They moved the record player to the table by her washer and covered it with an old sheet before they went upstairs, and when Frank returned from his bowling league they were in the living room watching television.

The grinding was slower than Shelley had thought possible, and several times she actually bit her tongue to keep from volunteering to help. Robbie stood over the revolving turntable rubbing the mirror blank back and forth over the protesting grit on the face of the tool until she felt she could cry for him. Patiently he explained that it would be a six-inch Newtonian type with a focal length of forty-eight inches, if all went well. He would need a tube, but he had located a source, if she could get it in the car for him—the man said they couldn't deliver just one aluminum tube. And he had the lenses for the eyepiece, but someday he'd like to get a Barlow lens. He hadn't figured out the clock drive for the mount, but that would come later after the telescope was finished. The mounting was the least important part of it because it could be changed any time, but the mirror, that was different. It had to be right the first time, or all the work was for nothing. Shelley listened and made sounds without meaning, feeling awed and not a little frightened by this serious-faced child of hers.

Beatrice was asleep and Frank still gone when Robbie called her to see the last flame test before he started the fine polishing of the mirror. She hurried down the stairs feeling almost as much excitement as there was in his voice.

"It's really working, Mom. Look!" The basement was in darkness but for the candle he held high for her. The mirror sat on edge, wedged by books so that it couldn't roll, and back from it about six feet stood Robbie holding the candle. It was like an ancient and slightly illicit rite of some sort, Shelley thought irrationally. "Watch," Robbie commanded.

He stooped on his haunches and moved the candle back and forth slowly until he was satisfied and then called her to kneel and look. "See," he said, "it fills the face of the mirror. One bright glob of light. Now watch." He moved the candle back perhaps an inch and it was reflected back to them inverted, a clearcut flame burning upside down. "Six feet!" he said jubilantly. "Boy! The book says that's good! It will come down another foot during the polishing."

"There's more?" Shelley asked as she straightened above the boy.

"Sure," Robbie said quickly. "You've got to polish almost as long as the grinding took in the first place. That completes the correct curve while it polishes. Then you silver it."

"How?" Shelley asked, forcing herself to sit in the chair and merely watch as he reverently lifted the mirror and replaced it in the special carton he had devised to keep it from dust, and Beatrice.

"Well," he admitted, "I won't do that part. Mr. Lindstrom said he could do it for me if I wanted him to."

"Oh, Mr. Lindstrom knows about it already." Shelley wished the words back before she finished them and she watched the guilty look flicker across Robbie's face. "Is he interested in astronomy?"

"Sure he is. He said if I hit a snag to give him a ring, and when I'm ready to silver it to bring it over." Mr. Lindstrom was his science teacher. There had been a period of several weeks when his name had cropped up every third sentence Robbie uttered until one night Frank had erupted.

"My God, what is this Lindstrom character? Some sort of high priest or something? If he's so good what's he doing stuck away teaching kids, why isn't he making a decent living like other men doing men's work?"

"Frank!" Shelley had exclaimed, "Stop that. Mr. Lindstrom is completely devoted to teaching. We're lucky to have him."

"Maybe," Frank said with his mouth full of blackberry pie, "but the way I heard it, a man takes up teaching after he's failed at everything else."

Robbie hadn't said another word, hadn't even given his father a reproachful glance, but somehow he gave Shelley the feeling that he had gathered himself in, had tested his muscles and, finding them insufficient, had decided to wait. That was the last time until now that he had even spoken Lindstrom's name.

"Do you have any cheesecloth?" Robbie asked abruptly, his attempt to change the subject painfully apparent even to him.

"I think so," Shelley said.

"Would you do something for me?"

Shelley mixed the jeweler's rouge with the correct amount of water and strained it through five thicknesses of cheesecloth as he directed, while he carefully cleaned off the thick glass tool in a bucket of hot sudsy water. He vacuumed the area fastidiously and wrapped his rags and old papers he used under the record player in newspaper. Feeling perplexed and stupid, Shelley watched without questioning him. Only after the tabletop and surrounding space was spotless did he inform her of the next step.

"I had to make sure none of the carborundum grit is around so it won't get on the mirror and scratch it. Now I have to melt the pitch and make what the book calls a pitch lap," he told her while he broke the pitch into a coffee can. "I have to pour the hot pitch on the tool, and when it starts to get a little cool I put the mirror on it to shape it to the curve. That's why I needed the rouge now. It keeps the mirror from sticking to the pitch."

Shelley watched him anxiously as he stirred the hot pitch melting in the can. She wanted to say, Be careful, darling, hurry. Your father is coming home tomorrow and he'll be home for the rest of the week and all weekend. Not again, she prayed, please not again. It isn't fair to Robbie. Absently he picked at his nose as he stirred, and she thought, he's so young. Too young to have to cope with it yet. They heard the footsteps overhead at the same time and Robbie turned suddenly stricken eyes to her as the voice called, "Hey, where's everybody? What is burning?"

Shelley ran across the basement to the stairs but Frank was already halfway down. "Confucius say," he boomed, "man who comes home early must be prepared to find wife unprepared.

But he didn't say she'd be trying to burn down the house. What's going on?"

"Frank, you're early. A whole day. Come on, let's find something to eat." Shelley tried to plant herself between him and Robbie, but his eyes swept over her head and he laughed.

"Hi, son," he yelled jovially. "Ol' Dad's back from the battles of commerce. What's cooking?" He laughed heartily and enwrapped Shelley in one arm as he crossed to the camp stove Robbie was using. "What's that?"

"Pitch," Robbie said in a small voice, not looking up from it.

"For God's sake, Shelley! Don't you know that stuff's dangerous to mess with!" He drew away from Shelley, who caught at his arm, pulled it free without another glance at her. "Back up, son, and let Dad have a crack at it. What's it for?"

"Frank," Shelley said desperately, "he's being careful. Come on up and tell me about the trip."

"Later," Frank said absently, paying no attention to her. "What's all that?" he asked, pointing toward the mirror and the turntable.

Shelley walked up the stairs with leaden feet. She tried not to listen to Robbie's monosyllabic answers to Frank's flow of questions, and finally, with the closing of the door, she no longer heard the words, but the echo of that deflated voice answering so low remained with her. She sat at the table twisting her rings, staring at the wall clock until they came up.

"You'd better get ready for bed, Robbie?" she said, avoiding his eye. "It's ten."

"Let's see now," Frank was saying, unaware of the silence of the boy, "I'll be off until Monday. Five days. I'll get the tube sprayed with black tomorrow, and while it's drying I'll run up to the university and see if any of the professors know anything about assembling it and getting it finished. Ought to be able to get hold of a good eyepiece in town."

"Frank," Shelley said quietly after Robbie had gone to bed and they were finishing sandwiches and coffee, "why don't you let him finish it? He's worked so hard on it."

Frank looked up from the instructions he was poring over. "You bet he has. Great kid, isn't he! Who else has a kid who'd think of building his own telescope? Boy, I'm telling you, he's some kid!" Frank was district sales manager for the entire midwestern block of states. He was a large man, dark and quite handsome, although starting to put on excess weight.

Shelley looked at him thinking, he's stupid, but she denied it as quickly as the idea came. Not stupid, simple. He continued to be a salesman in his own home, unmindful of the fact that his family hadn't been buying for years. He believed Robbie could do no wrong but that also he could do no right, without his, Frank's, help. She knew he saw himself as Robbie's only guide and idol, and in turn the boy's most trivial utterances became gospel for him. She had hoped the passage of time and Robbie's constant growth of interests would by sheer mass wear down Frank's overpowering interference. But Frank was an intelligent man and for his son he was quite willing to broaden his own scope by studying and by seeking help from experts in order to stay in the game. He was intelligent, Shelley reminded herself. He could be made to understand and see what he was doing.

"Frank," she said, "Just try to see it from his viewpoint. He wants to do it by himself. If he needs help, he'll ask for it."

"What do you mean? You know we always do things like that together. That's what's wrong with most kids, they don't have a father who's interested enough to go to a little bit of trouble for them. But, I tell you, Robbie's going to amount to something one of these days, and I'll see to it that when he gets a bug on something, he'll know he isn't alone. No sir, he knows he can count on his old man up to the end."

He stayed up for hours after Shelley went to bed, reading the books Robbie had collected on telescopes and astronomy. The next day he sent a special-delivery order for an equatorial-mount, precision-clock drive and tripod, to be delivered airmail. He located a camera that could be clamped to the eyepiece and spent several hours with the photographer who taught him how to use it.

"I know why he couldn't wait until I got home to get started on it," he explained to Shelley. "He wanted it ready in time for the eclipse of the moon next month. Boy, will I surprise him. I can't wait to see his face."

The telescope was completed and standing in the back yard two weeks later. Robbie had become withdrawn and subdued and refused to pose beside it for news photographers when they came to do a story about him and it. He didn't actually refuse, Shelley told herself; he just forgot to be home when they said they'd come. They settled for a picture of the telescope and an old snapshot of him. It was in the Sunday supplement. Frank ordered two-dozen copies and mailed them to his business friends.

"Mom," Robbie said hesitantly the afternoon of the eclipse, "if he falls asleep before time, do you think he'll wake up?"

Shelley shook her head, not trusting her voice for a moment. Then she said firmly, "I know he won't. We'll be quiet."

Robbie ducked his head back to his book without speaking again, but she knew he wasn't reading it. If only she could hold him on her lap, she thought, or even just hold him. She settled for an affectionate rubdown of his head, and he grinned as if he understood.

Robbie went to bed early, before nine, with his clock set to awaken him at twelve-thirty. He had laid out his lined jeans and a woolen shirt and his boots were standing at the back door, for the ground was still covered with the last snowfall.

Shelley read for two hours, pretending to be too engrossed in her book to answer Frank when he spoke. Occasionally she glanced at him and by eleven-thirty she thought he was going to fall asleep after all. However, he got up briskly and announced that he was going to make coffee.

Shelley followed him to the kitchen. "Frank," she said quietly, "will you please go on to bed and let him do it alone."

Frank turned to face her and an ugly frown passed over his features to be lost again in his perpetual bland half-smile.

"Honey, you're the one who should go to bed. You don't care about getting out in that snow."

"I don't intend to get out in it more than a minute, unless Robbie wants me to. That's beside the point."

"O.K., Shelley, let's get it out in the open. Just what is the point? For weeks you've been needling me about getting out of Robbie's way, and from where I stand I can't see that I'm in his way." Frank sat down at the table and lighted a cigarette, squinting a bit when the smoke curled up around his eyes. "Well," he prompted when Shelley remained quiet.

"Frank, don't you honestly see what it is you do? Every time he gets absorbed in something you take it from him and finish it yourself. It isn't his if you do it for him, and he resents it."

Frank was slowly shaking his head before she finished speaking and methodically he stubbed out the cigarette. "Shelley, baby, that isn't it at all," he said, oddly indulgent. "I've suspected it for a long time, and it's getting more and more obvious. You're jealous of me with the boy, aren't you? Don't you see there's no need for it. I love you more . . . This has nothing . . ."

"Frank!" she burst in angrily, "how dare you talk to me like that, as if I hadn't known about you and the others for years. I'm not concerned with what you do any longer. My only worry is for Robbie. I watched him with this telescope while you were gone. He's never been so excited about anything in his life. His eyes danced and he couldn't wait to get home and get to work on it; he'd run all the way from the bus stop and he brought home all his books and talked about it incessantly. Then you came home and took over. Is he excited now? Have you heard him say one word about it? He never even mentions it any more."

"So that's it!" Frank said and his voice was mean. "You just don't want me around at all. You want him all to yourself, don't you. I bet you had a good time trying to turn him against me while I was gone. By God, I should have seen it a long time ago." He jumped up from the chair and clutched at his hair as he did when angered. "Every time I come home he's a little more withdrawn. Oh, you've done a hell of a job on the kid. You must spend hours and hours brainwashing him to turn him against me. I can imagine the kind of stuff you must be filling his head with. But no more!" He was several feet from her as he spat out the words, and with each word he seemed to come closer and closer until his face was inches from her. "You hear me? No more. He's my kid and you can't split us up like that!"

Shelley stared unbelievingly at him and took a backward step and then another away from his large body crowding against her. "You know that isn't true," she whispered, feeling suddenly very cold and afraid, "I don't want to come between you. I just want you to see what happens every time he gets interested in something . . ."

"Stay out of my way, Shelley." Frank met her eyes evenly and repeated, "Stay out of the way. You're not interested in what he does, but don't try to interfere with me. I know you can't stand me any more. By Heaven, you don't even try to pretend. That's O.K. by me. But just stay out of my way! I won't let you turn him into a mama's boy and I won't let you get between us. He's going to have things that are good, not some cheap junk that he scrounges around for. I can afford the best for him, and by God, he'll get it. If you don't like it, don't look—or get out."

He turned from her and savagely yanked a cup and saucer from the cabinet. Shelley left the kitchen fighting off nausea and faintness, afraid of the full-blown hatred she felt for him that must have lain within her, dormant, unrecognized for a long time. She crossed the dining room and as she entered the living room she thought she caught a flicker of movement in the hallway leading to Robbie's room. "Dear God," she breathed, "let him be asleep. Please . . ."

At two o'clock Shelley made hot chocolate for them. She pulled on her boots and fastened the hood of her car coat tight around her neck and carried the thick mugs, steaming in the fifteen-degree temperature, out to the back of their yard where they were. She was walking carefully, feeling her way through the almost knee-deep snow, and without realizing it she was as silent as the night itself. Overhead the moon had turned into a ghastly dark brick-red ball and all about it the stars had come out once more. It had been brilliant out in the gleaming snow earlier, but now deep shadows merged with the bushes and flowed down into the ground, and the effect was weird and unpleasant. She paused to take a look at the moon away from the lights of the house, and before she moved again, she caught Frank's voice, urgent, spilling out words.

"You will love it, Robbie. We'll go up to Palomar together and see how real astronomers study eclipses and things. And we'll go to Disneyland every Sunday until you yell uncle. You've never even seen the ocean. Wait till you see, just wait till you see. And there are mountains just an hour's drive away, and the desert. Everything in one state."

"No!" the word formed in her throat and some of the chocolate spilled and ran down her leg, making her jerk and spill more. Matter of factly she told herself, "I'll kill him before I'll let him take Robbie away." She started walking again and called out, "Hey, fellows, hot chocolate! Any takers?"

They drank the chocolate, both silent and strained with her presence. Frank had been at the finder scope operating the camera and Robbie had field glasses trained on the moon when she joined them. He handed them over when he took the mug.

"It must be nearly over," Shelley said after one brief look. She didn't like the moon hidden and dark in the shadow.

"It isn't fully covered by the umbra yet," Robbie said. "That's still part of the penumbra. It'll get a lot darker. That's what the book says."

Frank chuckled. "And if the book says so, it's so, isn't it, pal?" He handed his mug back to Shelley. "We've been talking about some of the big observatories like Palomar, haven't we? We're going to see them all one of these days."

Shelley ignored the taunt, removed her glove and held her hand to Robbie's face for a moment. "Are you warm enough, honey? It's terribly cold out here." His face felt hotter than her hand.

"I'm O.K., Mom. I won't wait until it comes out of the shadow, just until totality. O.K.? That's not long."

"O.K. I'll have more chocolate waiting." She left them, the boy with the field glasses pointed toward the unfamiliar red moon and the man bending over the finder, clicking the camera button now and then. Back in the house she stood in the bedroom looking out the window. Very faintly she could still see them in the same positions as if they were carved. Beyond them, slightly behind them, the woods rose darkly, and off to the right of them Harrison's house lay dark and still in the morning hours. She'd put the hot-water bottle in with Robbie when he went to bed, she thought. He must be cold. There was a movement at the telescope and she turned to see them both running for the house. She met them at the back door and was nearly swept along with them.

"My gun, where is it?" Frank shouted and pounded down the basement stairs.

Robbie was dialing the phone with stiff uncooperative fingers. Frank returned jamming shells into the shotgun. "Put down that telephone! I said you are not to call Lindstrom!" he yelled at the boy.

"But he'd know what to do!" Robbie cried and continued working with the dial.

Frank nearly knocked him down as he shoved him away from the wall phone. "I know what to do, too!" he said harshly and ran out the door calling over his shoulder. "Call the police and tell them."

Shelley felt as though she were in a swiftly moving dream where she couldn't make herself heard or understood as she tried to stop Frank and then tried to get Robbie to tell her what was wrong. Now she reached for and caught Robbie as he started to follow after Frank, but he only pushed the door shut after he looked out. "For heaven's sake, Robbie, what is it?" she cried.

His face was hot and feverish-looking; there was an odd, fixed look in his eyes that didn't match the excitement he had shown only a moment before. Now he cocked his head as if listening, and slowly he appeared to become aware of Shelley shaking him. "He said he saw a spaceship or a flying saucer or something landing in the woods. He said now would be a perfect time for one, while everyone is either asleep or looking at the moon and they wouldn't be likely to notice something like that coming down. He said I should call the police and tell them. Do you think so?"

"Robbie," Shelley cried helplessly, "what are you talking about? Frank didn't see anything in the woods. I was looking all the time and there wasn't anything. Not a light or a movement or anything."

"I know it," he said with a tight little smile. "I'd better not say what he said to say. I'll tell them that he saw something and thinks they should investigate." The fixed look had returned to his eyes and Shelley's hands dropped from his shoulders letting him go. She watched while an anxiety grew and became almost uncontrollable. What was happening? Robbie spoke quietly into the phone and then held it out to her. "They want my mother or someone."

Shelley listened to the cool voice and answered it, "Yes, he took his gun and headed for the woods. I don't know what he saw." She told them where and hung up. Robbie was walking away from her toward the bedroom and she caught him and spun him around. "Tell me what happened out there, Robbie."

He patted her hand on his shoulder and said, "Let's see if we can see anything from the window." His boots trailed melting snow as he walked, and she felt a fear forcing her not to speak again yet. He walked stiffly as if unaware of what he was doing, as if his mind were far away.

At the window they stood side by side and strained to see what was happening. Nothing moved outside and it was darker than it had been. What had he called it? The umbra must be passing over the face of the moon. In the sullen red light that wasn't light at all they could see nothing. Suddenly Robbie spoke and his voice sounded very remote, as distant and cold as the red moon itself. "There was a round ship with glowing circular port-holes all around it. It came down without any noise and landed behind the stand of pines. I said I'd get hold of Mr. Lindstrom, and Dad began yelling that he'd go and see what it was and for me not to call in that flea brain. He thought he might need the gun." He stopped and his hand clenched hard on hers, squeezing tightly.

"Robbie! What is it? What's wrong?" Shelley cried, and abruptly the pressure on her hand eased and then she could hear the sound of guns and faintly, dimly, a scream of pain and fear. Without a sound Robbie fell to the floor at her side.

When the police came Shelley was rubbing his feet and hands alternately. She had wrestled him out of the heavy outer clothing and had managed to get him into his bed, but still he lay inert and limp, deeply unconscious.

"I'm sorry, ma'am, but we had to do it," the uniformed man said in a strained, shocked voice. "Your husband was yelling and shooting. I'm sorry, but he would have killed us both." Shelley could only stare in horror, and he stood twisting his hat looking everywhere but directly at her. Before the silence became unbreakable he replaced his hat and reached for the door. "You stay here with the boy, ma'am. They'll send an ambulance and a doctor and I'll tell him to come over directly. We won't need him out there."

Shelley mumbled something and went back to Robbie. She sat on the side of his bed and rubbed his hands, watching his chest rise and fall as he slept the deep sleep of the completely exhausted. Her eyes passed from his flushed face to the signs that covered one wall, signs and pictures. There it was, the circular saucer with the round portholes. It was the cover of a magazine he had saved. And below it the crazy sign that said, "Plan Ahead," and ran out of space for all the letters. And the one that said, "There Is No Problem The Mind Can't Solve."

She could picture vividly what had happened. What must have happened. It would take only a suggestion from Robbie and Frank would have to believe a ship had landed. And by mentioning Lindstrom's name Frank's decision to investigate had been assured. Thinking spacemen were there, probably terrified, he had shot at the first thing that moved, the county police.

Why had Robbie fainted before the shots? How could he have been so sure the shots would occur? She shuddered as her restless gaze roamed the room again and stopped on the sign that said, "Genius at Work."

My grandfather was a gentle man, a God-loving, God-fearing, proud man, a carryover from another era. Until he stopped farming, every year he returned to the government a check that was to compensate him for the tobacco he did not grow under the then new acreage-allotment plan. I think of him and those others like him who still survive in our midst as the gentle people, the ones who started life in log cabins, and finish it in their children's ranch houses, or chromium trailers, or "Homes." Their God is not dead, nor is He weakening. These gentle people thank God for their good fortune, and ask Him only for strength to meet their bad times. They believe in God's laws as handed down to Moses, and if love and the Commandments pull in opposite directions, a story is made. These proud, gentle people, a love that endures, and extraordinary courage: These are story ingredients.

Sirloin and White Wine

It was a tall house with tall windows now blankly eying the unkempt garden where weeds mingled with and overpowered all but the most robust of the perennials. Phlox heads, brilliant reds and whites, rode above the intruders, and the fence showed grayly through the sweetpeas with long windborne streamers that needed anchoring. Under a magnificent oak tree the grass had been erased, letting the earth shine through hard and white from five decades of being polished by softly rubbing feet. The glider was gone now.

Inside the house Frances Yeager sat quietly on a high stool and listened to the sounds of the moving men as they carried out a lifetime of memories. Their fourposter in sections, the chifforobe and doors in two trips, the out-of-tune upright piano that plinked dismally when they tilted it. She waited until they had the stove on the dolly and then she emptied the refrigerator, removing steak, salad and wine. Carefully she wrapped the wine bottle in many layers of paper. She had let it grow too cool, but the heat of the afternoon would compensate. The refrigerator had not been running, of course, since early that morning, but the cold had been enough, and the melting ice cubes in the salad would keep it crisp just right. She resumed her place on the stool when the men returned. With much grunting and not quite inaudible cursing they got the refrigerator out the door.

One of them came back and made a quick check through the house, his footsteps echoing up the stairs and through the rooms above, back down to the cellar, and once more into the kitchen. Now only the stool was left, and the man from the used-furniture store shifted from foot to foot before Frances realized the reason. Gravely she stood up and moved away from it; without looking directly at her, he picked it up and carried it out by one leg. Frances smiled slightly as the door banged shut. Men hid themselves poorly behind great noises. Likely he thought of his mother when he looked at her. The tears she had felt gathering retreated and she listened to the truck drive away with a grating sound of shifting gears as it climbed the hill from the house.

Without a backward glance at the bare kitchen she went out to the porch that opened onto it. Wry amusement crinkled about her eyes, for they had forgotten something after all. A folding chair remained on the porch along with the permanent swing that was firmly attached to the ceiling, and the portable grill that she had refused to part with. Mr. Steinmetz would send one of them back for the chair tomorrow, she thought, and the man would slam the door again even though the house was empty.

She rummaged about in a cardboard box until she found the meat grinder that she had kept. Humming softly she went back to the kitchen and fastened it to the counter, went back to the box for a sharp butcher knife, thought a second and carried the box itself to the kitchen. It contained the glasses for the wine—paper cups actually, paper plates and plastic "silverware" for the last meal, and the bottle of tiny white pills. She hummed through "Nearer, My God, To Thee," and when she finished the silence didn't seem to press in so close any more. It was fitting for the house to be so quiet, as still on their last night as it had been on their first. She thought of the day they signed it away.

The girl in charge had wanted them to come to The Home for dinner tonight, but she had refused saying, "Send someone about nine and we'll be ready, but our last supper should be at home to finish out the day, and then we'll start a new day somewhere else. Do you understand?" Would nine give them enough time? She was afraid to ask them to wait longer than that. The many papers they had finished signing lay between her and the pretty girl on the other side of the desk, and if this request were to be refused, she was ready to scoop them together and flee. Maybe she shouldn't have planned it for the last night, but she had to wait. Something might still turn up, she had argued with herself. Maybe Don . . .

The young lady smiled and said she understood, but Frances knew she couldn't. She was only twenty-five or so. She couldn't understand. The girl held the door for them, not noticing the look of annoyance on Harley's face or the abrupt stiffening of his back as she said, "I'm sure you'll both be happy here, Mrs. Yeager."

Harley took her arm and held it lightly as they descended the many stairs to the sidewalk.

Happy, Frances mused, cutting the meat from the bone and stripping it for the grinder. So many kinds of happiness. Like the kind that only comes once with the wedding, and the other kind when you know there's a child within you. And the kind that sees you past the first real sickness of your firstborn. And the little kinds like when your man brings a flower, just one flower, but because he thought of you when he saw it. That was a good kind; unexpected nice things stayed a long time.

She didn't grind the meat yet after all. It would grow too warm, she thought, and covered it again. She cleaned off the counter and returned to the porch. Harley would be back soon. He would have been watching for the truck to leave and then he would start down the street, dignified and straight, walking slowly, nodding all along the way to the neighbors, pretending there was no stiffness in his hip or tiredness in his legs.

It was harder on Harley; a man blamed himself when things piled up. He felt that he was failing her somehow. She sat and fanned herself for several minutes, swinging gently and not thinking at all. Harley returned then and joined her on the porch. He hadn't gone through the house and she knew he wouldn't. He loosened his tie and opened his collar, grunted as he settled down next to her on the swing. They were both dressed as if for church.

"We should look nice when we go," Frances had said smoothing down his handsome tie and giving it a final pat. She was wearing her pale lavender tissue faille—not as cool as it was cool-looking. She had tightened the belt so the new looseness wouldn't show too much. How much now? she had wondered, studying her model-thin figure. Fourteen, fifteen pounds? It didn't matter.

"Charlie's got a new boat," Harley commented, taking the fan from her and fanning them both alternately with it. "Outboard motor."

"I know; he mentioned it. Hot, isn't it?"

"Cool off when the sun gets behind the trees," he promised.

They sat and the swing moved softly and easily as the long afternoon—pungent with marigolds and carnations, heat and ever threatening showers, sibilant with bees and locusts—the long afternoon yielded and began lengthening and distorting the shadows, making their sources unidentifiable through them. Harley's head nodded and the fan first drooped and then dropped to his knees, and she thought back on other afternoons when he would come in from the yard or from his walk and alibi his yearning for a nap with a tale of hard labors over at Charlie's or out in the garden battling the persistent weeds. She sighed, recalling that more recently he didn't make excuses for his afternoon siestas, but simply disappeared for a while and reappeared two hours later in a bantering mood.

The sun dipped low and was eclipsed by the tops of the trees in the distant woods and she stirred herself, careful not to waken Harley as he dreamed. She ground the meat slowly and almost prayed the toughness was not in it, but rather a weakness in her arm. She had become weaker, would have less resistance; what if, after all, only she . . . ? She felt faint and clung to the handle of the meat grinder. The moment passed and her arm began cranking the grinder again as she fed into it the strips of sirloin. So foolish of Don to send them steaks when neither of them could chew steak any longer.

She quickly put aside the thought of Don, salted the meat and formed patties with it. She uncovered the wine and felt it testingly. She wasn't sure how cool wine should be, but it felt all right. For a long time she stared at it before she finally uncorked it and added the contents of the small bottle that cautioned, "two tablets every four hours—not to exceed eight a day." She had been saving them, patiently bearing the pain for weeks now because she knew she would need them—all of them. Her fear of the second just past faded as she watched them sink, bubbling. There were enough for both of them. She shook the wine bottle vigorously to dissolve the tablets and then held it to the window. A whisper of fizz escaped when she removed her thumb. It looked fine, not a bit like death.

Don had given them the wine also, how long ago, four, five years? A long time. "We'll use it someday when we're celebrating," she had said, and now, tonight, they were to have it. She wondered if Don would be deeply shocked. Don had enough trouble of his own without adding guilt on their account. Not that he was in any way to blame, but he might feel . . . Still staring at the wine she asked herself, will he feel guilt? Will he feel anything but relief? She had to shake herself then before she could break free from the thought, and she made herself hum again as she took her burden to the porch.

"Harley. Harley? Will you get the grill going for me." She didn't need to ask him to help, but she always did when she could. She didn't think of it any more, but automatically asked for little services that she could do just as well herself.

Harley yawned and pulled his watch from its pocket before he arose from the swing. "Six," he announced, "and I'm hungry. Those things take long to get done?" He adjusted the charcoal pan and lit the starter. In seconds the charcoal started to glow and he turned a pleased face toward her.

"They'll take five or ten minutes is all."

"Waste of good meat, grinding it up like baby food," he fussed, peering at the steak patties. "Damn fool."

She knew he meant Don and she pursed her lips. She hoped he wouldn't begin talking about Don tonight. Hurriedly she said, "Remember that time we took the children up Pike's Peak, and later broiled trout by the stream? Makes my mouth water now thinking about those trout."

"And Natalie got lost and you cried because you thought a bear might find her before we did." Harley put both hands behind his head and stretched his legs out before him when he sat down again; his mild, blue eyes were far, far away.

"And you fell in the water and nearly got pneumonia," Frances added softly, remembering. Her eyes grew moist, and more sharply than she meant to she asked, "Isn't that thing ready yet?"

"Yep," Harley admitted good-naturedly. "Put 'em on. No onion?"

"Harley Yeager! You know what onion does to your stomach."

He grunted and muttered something about onions doing more good for the soul than harm to the stomach and she relented and said the salad did have onion in it anyway. Then the hamburgers, sirloinburgers, were crackling and spewing out juices and they remained silent until she removed them and transferred them to the paper plates.

Harley poured the wine into the paper cups and sniffed at it suspiciously. "You sure this is good?"

"What can happen to sealed wine? Here, let me dip you some salad."

"It can get vinegary, I reckon." He sipped it tentatively and made a face. She tried not to look at him, but her eyes lifted up from the salad bowl, past the table and found his gaze on her. She blinked hard. "Must be good," he said finally. "Tastes too bad not to be."

"I know you'd rather have beer," Frances answered tartly and tasted hers.

"To us," Harley said and they touched cups and drank.

They ate in silence, burned the plates and "silverware," finished the wine and burned the cups, all in the grill, and as the flames died down and the light became dimmer they sat and let the swing fan them peacefully against the cooling evening air.

"Harley," Frances said, "it'll be all right. You'll see. Everything will be all right."

"Yep," he said heavily. "I'll jaw with the men and beat them all at checkers, and you'll gossip the hours away with the lady folk. It'll be fine."

The silence that comes between daylight and dark lay densely between them and only the swing murmured now and again. One of Frances' hands gripped the arm of the swing tightly and the other crept to her stomach and she could feel it there almost. After meals it was worse, but gradually it wore off and she could forget it for a while. Three times she had pressed her hand to her stomach and those times it had been to marvel at the life within, but this time it was death she carried in her body. The wine, and the pills in the wine, quieted it after a bit and her hand dropped to her lap in relaxation.

Now it was night-dark outside and the air was filled with the many voices of the sunless hours. The grill creaked loudly in cooling. Must be going on eight-thirty, she thought, and was startled that she had been dozing. Harley snored softly and his head touched her shoulder, resisted giving in, then lay there comfortably. She brushed her cheek against the fine, sparse hair and settled herself among the many pillows that belonged to the swing. Her hands lay open and easy in her lap and for the first time in months the pain was altogether gone.

"Mrs. Yeager?" asked a voice from the darkness and her eyes flew open.

She drew up sharply, not wishing to be caught asleep. "You're too early," she said in near panic. "They promised to let us be until nine."

"Aren't you ready?" he asked.

She drew a deep breath of relief. It was a young voice, very kind and understanding. Someone who wouldn't rush them, make Harley get up. Someone who could be talked to, who would listen politely, as long as she was able to talk.

"We have to wait for Harley," she said firmly. His breathing was shallow and a little mumble accompanied each outgoing breath. "He's resting."

"I see. We'll wait a bit, then."

Frances couldn't feel Harley's head against her shoulder, but she was aware of it and of his breathing. Please, Harley, she begged silently, this young man mustn't get suspicious. She said, "There's a folding chair over there. Why don't you sit a spell?" She felt odd, as if she were floating above the swing instead of on it and she had to reach out and find her voice, drawing it back to her so she could speak.

"Yes, ma'am," the man said and there were noises of a chair being opened and canvas being stretched, groaning in protest.

"I didn't hear the car," Frances explained, and it was almost as if she thought the words and listened to someone else saying them. "That's why you gave me a start when you spoke up. Sitting here swinging with Harley I almost forgot what night it was. Fifty-two years we been sitting here on the porch cooling off in the evenings." And this last night I wanted to say so much, so much to thank him for, to remind him of, all the good things to remember. But instead we both slept, she thought with regret.

"You've lived here ever since you married?"

There was a long pause and she feared that she couldn't mouth the words, and when they did finally come, her voice was little more than a whisper. "Harley built this house the summer he asked Papa for me. Everyone said he'd kill himself trying to get it finished, but he did and we moved right in."

"It's a fine old house," the young man whispered back, obviously thinking she was trying to let Harley sleep until the last moment.

"Raised three children in it. Used to keep chickens out back, but things changed and we had to let them go. Harley screened in this porch himself. Painted the house every four years regular until he had his accident. Broke his hip." Why was she rambling on so, she wondered, when it was so hard to make the words leave her throat? She remembered. Harley. He wasn't ready yet.

"Tough," the man murmured sympathetically.

You don't know how tough, she thought. "Four operations before he got so's he could walk again," she said dreamily. She recalled vividly Dr. Geraldin asking if they needed financial aid, and her own quick denial. He had been good to them and she was sure his fee had been much less than he usually charged. But the hospital and the specialists . . . It had been tough. That was the start of it, and the house had begun to yield its more than half-century-old treasures. And now it was bare. Maybe they had been too proud. "Pride goeth before destruction, and an haughty spirit before a fall," she quoted silently.

"I'm sorry," she heard herself saying, aware that he had spoken.

"I asked about the children."

"Oh. Well there's Natalie; she's the youngest. Married to a sergeant in the army. They're in Germany now, stationed there. I think they are having a vacation in Switzerland. Natalie had polio, you know, but you could hardly tell it now." Pretty Natalie who deserved so much now to make up for all the suffering . . .

"And there's Cecelia." She paused and waited for the flood of grief to pass before she continued. "She's a schoolteacher in Tennessee. Her husband was killed in Korea and she's raising three children down there. She always meant to come back here, but they had their house already . . . Anyway, she just stayed there and kept her job."

When she stopped, the silence in the air was broken only by Harley's breathing, now little gasps really rather than breaths of air inhaled and exhaled. Harley, she pleaded mutely, please hurry. I have to stop soon. He'll wonder what's wrong and call an ambulance or something. Please, Harley!

She was drifting and it was pleasant to close her eyes and float along unknowing, uncaring.

"And the other one?"

She was snapped back, frightened. "Yes, there's another one," the strange other voice said. "That's Don." She trailed off unhappily and had to think of Don at last. Her firstborn. Where had it gone wrong with Don? What happened? She said, "Don lives in California. He would help us if he could, but . . ." But he was paying three wives and supporting two families. "Don has needed help himself from time to time," she finished with dignity.

"I see," he said gently.

"We didn't tell any of them about giving up the house," she explained. "The girls couldn't do anything but grieve themselves. We should have thought ahead better, I guess."

"Mrs. Yeager," he said kindly, "it's really past time. There's no more for you to do here. We must be going."

Frances shut her eyes in a quick prayer and listened for Harley's breathing before she replied. She thought his breaths were coming farther and farther apart with very long pauses between them. With a great effort she said, "Just another minute. There's a whippoorwill that will be by soon."

"Of course," he agreed.

Frances made herself continue, "It's funny when you grow old. There's still so much you want to do, so many things you remember doing that you can't do any more that after a while it gets so most of the pleasure in life is in the memories of the years already gone. And the little things mean so much, little things that recall another time." She felt a warm blush spread across her face, reach down her neck to her chest, and she was grateful for the dark that hid it. She remembered with poignancy the time she and Harley had lain together out in the yard under the stars. A whippoorwill had sung that night. A ripple of sensuous pleasure rode through her and left again, bringing a smile that stayed. Imagine, almost telling him about that!

The young man remained silent for a long time after that and the quiet of the night crept over the porch and even Harley's breathing was stilled.

But all the memories weren't happy ones, Frances thought.

Don weighed heavily on her conscience, and abruptly his image merged with and became one with the long-forgotten picture of Jefferson Hendricks. She had been thirty-four and so tired of making do, of stretching money to make it go around when it simply wouldn't. And she had met Jeff, who could have given her so much and wanted to give her so much. "Harley, I'm sorry," she had said. "I don't want to hurt you, but he loves me and I'm going with him." And Harley, standing straight and proud, nodded, "I'll be here, Nance. Do what you have to." Nance. The seldom-used endearing name he had for her. The name that said he loved her and would be faithful, that he wanted only her happiness. She had cried, and before it was over he cried. That was the last of Jeff.

The end had come so fast, so without warning. A thing like a sewer assessment had brought them ruin. Three hundred seventy dollars. The mortgage didn't go through because they couldn't prove the title was clear to the land their house stood on. After fifty-two years they needed proof! Don sent the steaks, a whole carton of them, and a note saying he couldn't raise the money right away, but if they could wait until this deal . . . They didn't even consider asking Cecelia or Natalie.

We would have gone to The Home, Frances explained, but the voice was out of reach now and there were only the silent thoughts. We've not been afraid for all these fifty-two years, and we weren't afraid now, not if we could have been together still. They promised us that, but they didn't know about me, about this thing in my stomach . . . I would have found things for him to do, ways for him to help me. She was drifting, drifting, her mind a chaotic blend of consciously held thoughts and pleas and prayers. You've been with us, Lord. You were there when the children came and through the depressions and the wars . . . You know I couldn't go off and leave him to strangers. It wasn't for me. I wasn't afraid, but he would have been alone with girls who open doors for him and wouldn't let him be a man. He didn't know about it, Lord. Please don't punish him.

"Mrs. Yeager"—the gentle young voice cradled her softly and she drew back in fear, wanting to go to it, wanting to give in—

"it's time now," he said and she knew she must, but still she resisted. In the ash tree at the corner of the yard the whippoorwill sang.

Not yet . . . Harley . . . "Lord," she wept, "please . . . forgive me." Harley stirred and his hand was firm on hers as they lifted their heads together to listen to a voice that came through and over the whippoorwill,

"Come along, Nance, Harley. Come along. We'll talk about it."

"The reason most people refuse to accept extrasensory perception as a reality," said my husband, who is wise beyond his years, "is that it is not reliable. You can't predict when it will be operative; you can't count on it. It is magic." And what if you could? Why isn't the seer the richest man alive? The stock answer is that he can't use his powers to benefit himself, or he loses them. Magic. I am quite content to take either side of the ESP problem and argue it heatedly. Apparently this ambivalence goes very deep with me, because from time to time a story comes to the fore acknowledging that such powers certainly do exist, then comes one that is equally as strong in refuting them. When such a story comes to me, if I like it, I write it happily, always claiming the right to change my mind with the next one.

Perchance To Dream

BARNEY woke up, as much as he ever did, when the alarm screeched from across the room. He groped his way to it, knocking it off the chest of drawers, and then he had to open his eyes to find it. The shrill went through his head as if it had burrs on it, rubbing every nerve in the way until it went *boing*. He stumbled into the bathroom and doused his face with cold water.

"What did you dream this time?" Rosie asked from the kitchen door, wiping her hands on a towel. She was buxom and blond, but her voice sounded like a continuation of the alarm.

"Nothing," Barney muttered, spitting water.

"Why do you want to lie like that? I know you did. You tossed and talked and carried on all night. Warning you, keep it up, boy, and we'll get twin beds."

Barney wiped his face and looked at himself in the mirror—sallow, circles under eyes that were heavily pouched and tired, faint eyebrows that seemed to be questioning eternally, a drooping mouth, little round chin bristling with tan whiskers. He sighed at it. Rosie continued to talk at him, now and then raising her voice to imitate the alarm, and then subsiding to an almost normal tone. He paid no attention to the words, had long ago accepted the incessant noise as background to whatever was going on inside his skull. He ate his oatmeal and eggs and toast and caught no more than one word out of five that Rosie mouthed.

He was remembering the dream he had had after all. "There's going to be a bank holdup, that new black-and-white marble bank over by your mother's . . ."

"It ain't even open yet," Rosie said accusingly. She always made like a prosecutor when he started to tell her about the dreams, pointing out the illogic here, or the wrong fact there, making him wish he hadn't started to tell her at all, but he always did. He had to tell someone.

"I know that," he said, sopping up the last of the egg yellow with jellied toast. "It's going to be robbed anyway. I seen all their faces, jaws dropped, and money being shoved over the counter, guard caught with his pants down, getaway car waiting for the guy to walk out, get in, and leave. No one does anything for half a minute or more. Car gets to corner and makes the light, lost in the traffic by then. That's all."

"What about them new gadgets they put in. Paper's full of them. Cameras, automatic alarms that go off if the teller don't push a button or something, automatic doors that close and lock if anything goes wrong . . . What about all that stuff?"

He shrugged. "I don't know what about all that stuff. All I know is that it's going to be robbed, and the guy gets away."

"When?" she demanded. "You know so much, when?"

"I don't know," he admitted, then added, "summer. Women in shorts, hot outside, cool in bank."

Rosie shot him a look of scorn. "Summer," she said sarcastically. "This summer? Next? June? August?" He shook his head and she threw both hands up as if to beseech the ceiling for help. He finished the coffee and got up. She had made his lunch while he ate, and he picked up the paper sack and started to leave. "Dreams," she said bitterly. "Always dreams. What good are they? I ask you, what good are they? Look at the miserable dump! Work six days a week, live like a mole in this dump, and dream about holdups. Never dream anything useful, how to get a raise, or where to find a fortune hidden away. Not you! Dreams! What good are they?"

Wearily Barney left her still talking and walked down the four flights of steps, out into the cold April wind, and turned toward the corner where he caught his bus to work. As usual he wished he hadn't told her about the dream.

But he had to tell someone, he repeated to himself, waiting for the bus, not looking at any of the others also waiting. The dreams came once, twice a month, sometimes more, and like she said, what good were they? Like the time he had dreamed of the kids playing with a switch on the train track, and almost immediately, distorted out of real sequence by the quality of dreaming itself, the long snaking train had appeared, doing seventy, and had hit the open switch. He had watched the cars roll down a bank, into the river below, and he had been helpless to do anything about it either then in the dream, or later. When he saw the picture in *Time*, he knew it was the same train. It had been derailed in France.

The bus came and he was elbowed out of the way as the others crowded inside. By the time he boarded there were no seats left, and the straps were already being clutched. He braced himself and swayed back and forth with the motion of the bus. Other dreams had been about things like the last play of a football game, and a long look at the final scoreboard, where he could see that the home team had sixty points and the visitors seventeen, but no indication of what teams they were. And horse races where he could see the finish and the odds posted, but where, at which track, when? He usually couldn't tell. Sometimes there would be headlines, with date and all, things like, FATALITIES ZOOM OVER SIX-HUNDRED MARK FOR HOLIDAY, or, ECONOMY DRIVE BY WHITE HOUSE. What good were they?

He got off the bus and went to the department store where he sold shoes six days a week. He had worked in the same store, in the same department, for nineteen years, never varying his schedule of arriving at 9:10, having his sandwich and apple at

12:45, leaving for the day at 5:30. He prided himself on his work. Not bad for a dropout, he would say to himself totaling his weekly sales, ever hopeful for the bonus that went with topping the quota set by the store's newest efficiency expert. Sometimes he actually did top the quota, and that buoyed him for weeks afterward, made him even more hopeful knowing the goal was not unattainable. He caught his bus home at 5:40 that day, as every day, and he swayed and jerked with the bus's movements.

At the corner where he and Rosie had to transfer to get the subway to visit her mother, he felt himself being pushed toward the door of the bus by an oversized man carrying two shopping bags. He didn't resist the push, and found himself in the street, heading for the subway, as if that had been his intention all along. It would add half an hour to his trip. Rosie would start to worry about him; he never was late . . . He would tell her he had a customer who dawdled. He caught the subway and again was squashed between other commuters until he left it. He walked past the bank, not staring at it exactly, but noting the opening date boasted of in great fancy lettering: April 30, two weeks away. The outside was finished, and from the appearance of the inside, all there was done except some detail work and the installation of desks and things like that. He nodded. It was the same bank. Then he returned to the subway and went home.

Rosie had stuffed cabbage for supper, and there was a letter from their son Jimmie, who had joined the Navy when he was seventeen; Lucille had been there, the daughter with an infant of two months; the television needed a tube or something . . . He dreamed that night of his son Jimmie. He could see the boys in their uniforms standing at a bar, Jimmie with them, guzzling beer. A big fan overhead went around in slow motion. Girls came in and the boys went with them. He watched Jimmie with the girl and then woke up. Rosie said sleepily, "What's wrong with you, Barney?" She giggled then at his touch. He made love to her and went back to sleep thinking that some dreams he just couldn't tell her.

On Sunday they visited her mother and walked past the bank. It looked ready to open then, Barney thought, clean and shiny new inside and out. They didn't speak of it, but he knew that Rosie was looking also. That night, eating strudel, watching Ed Sullivan, Rosie said wistfully, "I wish only once you'd be able to say when something is gonna happen, so's I could be there and see."

There was a special dust-bowl show at ten and they watched that also, feeling that Texas was in another world, if it actually existed at all. Neither of them had been farther from home than to Jersey. They agreed that they didn't like Texas with all that empty land, and the dust devils, and all.

The dust devils swirling up from the ground made Barney think about his dreams. It was sort of like dust devils, he decided. Like time was whirling about in front of them, and sometimes something got tossed out of the spinning mess, and he got to see it. Only when they went through it, it was sorted out like, with a before and after, so's you could tell when anything was. But being tossed out of the storm, there wasn't no before, and there wasn't no after. There just was it, whatever the *it* happened to be: sometimes a long sense-making scene, sometimes a snatch, a snapshot glance. Then when he really got to that piece of time, the bit he'd already seen was in place where it belonged. He thought of his dreams much as he did of his memories; neither was more real than the other, and no less real.

They had started when he was only a kid, and he had told about them then. His pa had whacked him a good one for telling them. Things like seeing his sister having a baby, and the one about the apartment house down the street burning down. He'd learned not to talk about them. Then his first wife—he had told her, and she left him when she tried to cash in and found that the no-dating system made a monkey out of her and her schemes. She'd bet on Honeyboy the day before he won, or she'd stand on a corner all day waiting for an accident that didn't happen for another month or two, and she'd be left owing the bets she'd made. A real gambler that one had been. She had lasted only seven months and was gone. Then Rosie came along, and she didn't believe in gambling; he'd made sure of that before they got married.

Rosie had been a looker all right when they got married, big, chesty, blonde. The night he met her, he dreamed of her and him old together, her still big and still blonde; he knew they were meant for each other, and he proposed. That was the first dream he never told her; there had been others, but not many. Usually he shared them, at first causing wonder and excitement, and then nothing but the questioning D.A. routine she began assuming in the past few years.

"I been thinking," Rosie said, during the commercial before the news, "maybe you should tell someone at the bank . . . You don't have to say you dreamed it," she said quickly, knowing he wouldn't stick his neck out for that. "You could say you heard a couple of hoods in a bar, or something."

"Rosie, Rosie, what could I tell them? It's gonna happen, just like I dreamed it. Tell them, don't tell them, that don't make no difference. It'll happen."

"I don't know," she said. "It just don't seem right to know something like that and not try to do something about it. It just don't seem right to me." She looked at the screen and the newscaster, but then said, "Makes you sorta wonder about things like free will and all, don't it?"

"Rosie!"

She shrugged, still not looking at him, but not seeing the newscast either. "Why'd it happen to a guy like you? Why not one of them university men, you know, someone who'd do something about it, or make some use of it, or something. Seems such a waste somehow."

They had talked once about his going to the university and telling someone there about it, but he hadn't. Who'd he tell there? A history professor? He thought of it as a special sort of history, not happened yet, but meant to happen, and Rosie said no, it had to be someone who knew about what happened in your head, a doctor or something. In the end, he had gone to no one. He remembered the whack his father had given him, and how his first wife had walked out, taking everything she could carry with her. He imagined the sort of conversations he would have: And then I saw the plane sort of turn over . . . What kind? . . . I don't know . . . I ain't seen one like it . . . But you said . . . Yeah, but that was in the dream, it ain't here now . . . Where was it? . . . In the sky somewheres . . . Yes, but over what country? . . . I don't know . . . Blue sky . . . Was it an American plane? . . . I don't know . . . You're sure the wings swept back like that? . . . Yeah . . . Mr. Peterson, have you had access to . . . Never mind. . . .

It would be just about like that, he knew. Things he dreamed he had no business knowing, and they wouldn't believe how he knew. Finally he hadn't gone to anyone.

Rosie said, "Maybe you could just warn the bank with a note in the mail."

He said, "Why'd you think they installed all those safety gadgets? They expect someone to try to rob them, that's why. What good would it do for me to say what they already expect." He stood up. "I'm going to bed."

The next time he walked past the bank again, it was the grand opening. They were giving coffee and doughnuts to new depositors, and toys to the kids, and there were pretty girls standing at attention in front of the door, and a red carpet from the bank door to the street. It was all very happy and not very banklike. Barney walked right on past. That night the paper had pictures, and names of important people who had opened accounts there. That was Wednesday.

On Friday Barney always did the weekly shopping in the department store's grocery section, getting a 15-percent discount on the things he bought. He had his list in his pocket and the green-and-white-striped shopping bag Rosie had made when he went to work; he stuffed the bag in his raincoat pocket. The weather had turned warm and there was rain moving in from the ocean, probably be raining hard by the time he did the shopping and went home. During his morning coffee break he bought some thread that Rosie's mother wanted, and he decided to take it to her during his lunch hour. He didn't want to go out after supper in the rain and deliver it, be tied up all evening, and then again on Sunday. He liked Rosie's mother, but once a week was enough. When he went to the subway he had his raincoat on. It had turned much warmer, summery, and the rain was still holding off the coast somewhere, but coming. He could smell it coming. The sun was making him perspire, but in the subway it was cooler, and he didn't remove the coat. When he left the train, his way led past the bank, and across the street from it he stopped, shivering suddenly. This was the day.

The sudden change in weather had brought out summer clothes, shorts on a couple of women, sleeveless blouses; there was the same woman pushing a baby carriage that he had seen before in the dream. He looked about wildly for a sign of the getaway car and saw nothing that remotely resembled the one that should be there. It had been green, dark green, and very plain, no trimming at all on it anywhere. Probably had a souped-up engine, he thought, remembering the plainness of the body. He backed into a store front and stood there for the next five minutes waiting for something to happen. Nothing did. The woman with the baby carriage had stopped to chat with another woman, this one in shorts, and farther up the street there were some teen-age girls ambling along this way. He remembered them. When they got to the bank entrance . . .

His eyes searched the pattern of traffic for the green car, and his feeling of panic grew. He might be able to stop it even then, he thought. He might make them alert and ready for a robbery. He shrank back against the store, afraid to cross the street, afraid any moment the green car would pull around the corner and the desperate man would step out, hand in pocket holding a gun, his eyes wild. . . . Another five minutes passed. Where were the girls? He saw them again; they were window shopping, following the lines of the windows as if attached to them, going inside the glass display alcoves, back out again, on to the next, slowly, not going anywhere in particular, taking plenty of time. Barney could stand it no longer. He left the building front and the wind whipped his coat, billowing it, the shopping bag slipping from the pocket. He fought the coat back down and, clutching the bag, hurried across the street. He felt in the other pocket and found the shopping list there and held on to it nervously.

Inside the bank the air was cool and quiet; it smelled of new wood, new, clean wax, new carpeting. He hurried to the first window, where a teller was using an adding machine. She was a middle-aged woman, thin, gray, with a black silk string on glasses that had no stems. The very one!

"Quick," Barney said, leaning close to the bars, "the manager. There's going to be a robbery!"

The woman stared at him, turning as gray as her hair, and she reached through the opening under the bars and slid his shopping bag inside, her eyes never leaving his face, only her hands aware of what she was doing. Barney couldn't speak then, fear and horror blotting out all thoughts as he remembered the dream. He had seen her exactly like this! When she pushed the bag back toward him, he took it and backed away three steps, then turned and walked out of the bank. A cab was disgorging a passenger and Barney stepped inside it as the man finished paying and walked away.

"Where to, bud?" the cabby asked, pulling away from the curb, making the corner before the light turned.

"The subway entrance, three blocks up," Barney said. The cab was a green private car, with a meter installed. It smelled of paint.

"Careful of that left door, bud," the driver said. "'S'wet. Didn't even have time to paint in the taxi sign yet. . . ."

Barney punched back in at work at exactly one o'clock. In the cab he had taken off the raincoat and folded it carefully, placing it on top of the money. He carried the bag to the stockroom behind the shoe department and put it down.

"Finished shopping already?" the section manager asked. "Looks like you have a load to carry home." He went out. Barney didn't look at the money. He worked the rest of the afternoon in a semidaze, and when he totaled his book that night, he had exceeded the quota by seven pairs of shoes. The section manager patted him on the back. "Gonna buy champagne and celebrate?" he asked jovially.

Barney smiled shyly. He went straight home from work and told Rosie what had happened. For once she had nothing to say when he finished. In silence she poured coffee for both of them, forgetting about her chops that were burning on the stove until the apartment suddenly was full of smoke.

She turned off the gas, raked out the burned chops and opened the window. A cold, rain-laden wind swept through the kitchen, and its touch on her skin seemed to waken her.

"What are we going to do?" she asked then, returning to sit across from him.

"I don't know. I don't even know how much there is. . . ." Together they counted the money, and when they finished Barney felt weak. "Ninety-seven thousand dollars!" he whispered unbelievingly.

"The paper! It should be in the evening paper!" Rosie said. She snatched up her raincoat and ran out of the apartment, returning in ten minutes with the paper. Barney hadn't moved while she was out.

"A payroll, that's what it was," she said. "You robbed them of a payroll. . . ." Her face was awed, and she kept raising her eyes from the page to look at her husband. "The teller says you were so desperate that she didn't dare do anything. She could see the outline of a gun through the raincoat. You were squeezing it until your hand was white. . . ." She looked again, blankly. "A gun?"

Barney shook his head. "The shopping list. I told you."

"Witnesses say there were three men. . . ." Rosie read on.

"The man leaving the cab," Barney said helplessly. "Those girls, what did they see?"

Rosie looked on down the column, her finger running back and forth on the lines of print, "Here it is . . . three girls agreed that the bandit was tall and dark, young, no more than thirty, handsome. . . ." She stopped again and stared at him. "They saw *you?*"

"Garbage," Barney cried. "What else?"

"They say you winked at them. Barney, did you wink at those children?"

"Rosie! Will you stop this cross-examination? I go to jail maybe, and you wonder if I winked at fourteen-year-olds?"

"Sixteen," she said coldly.

For a minute or so she continued to read, her lips moving, her finger following every word. Then she put down the paper. "I don't know, Barney, I just don't know. Who's right? They say a black car, you say green. They say young, dark man, you . . . look at yourself. They say gun, you say list . . . I tell you, I just don't know."

They continued to sit for the next fifteen minutes. Then Barney said, "I'm a bank robber, Rosie! Next year I should retire, and I'll be in prison instead. A bank robber! What will Lucille and Jimmie say?"

Rosie reached across the table and patted his hand. "So they don't catch you, Barney. So we don't let them catch you. We leave the country maybe. . . ." His hand trembled under hers and she rose and came around the table to sit right next to him. She put her arm around his shoulder and drew his head to her large breast. "Barney, Barney, you didn't mean to. Look at it like that. You were innocent, only wanted to help. Did you plan such a thing? Did you draw maps and keep charts of times and things like that? That's what bank robbers do. They know where there's going to be a payroll, and they have guns, and charts, and maps, and cars waiting with motors running. Did you do all that? You are as innocent as a baby, Barney. So we say your uncle Herbert died and left you some money. That's what we say to Lucille and to Jimmie."

"I ain't got no uncle Herbert," Barney said.

"So? Do they know you ain't got no uncle Herbert? You didn't know it yourself until this minute." She squeezed his shoulder reassuringly. "Did we ever tell even one little lie to Lucille, or to Jimmie? Did we? Honest, that's what we always been with them. So now it pays off. Honest we been, honest we still are. They know. You'll see. Your uncle Herbert left you all this money, and who's going to doubt it?"

"Uncle Herbert that nobody's ever seen, or heard of. Not even a letter?"

"So? He's from . . . Texas. That's it. He's been in Texas all these years, pumping oil and oiling down the dust devils. So who has time to write?"

Three weeks later they were in Spain, and as the days wore on under sunny skies, with the blue ocean lapping quietly by night, and the days filled with sight-seeing, the fear of being caught and put in jail faded, and one night Barney confessed to Rose that he had dreamed of such a place long ago. A place where they would be old together.

"And what did you dream last night?" she demanded, her hands on her hips, her voice sounding like the almost forgotten alarm clock, carrying through the thin walls of the pension into the next apartment where an elderly Spaniard turned to his wife and shrugged saying, "Americans! Crazy Americans!" He wished that the little American husband would speak in a loud enough voice so he could hear about the marvelous dreams that the wife insisted on sharing, but he never did.

Some writers can build a story much as a mason can build a wall, starting with one small part, adding more and more units until it is done. I can't do that. I discover stories the way one might look down and see a patterned carpet underfoot. The story is the entire thing when I see it. It is like a memory in that there is a unitary whole, and also there are the separate parts that can be examined in any order I choose. Like an unbidden memory, a story can present itself in a piece at any time, any place. This one came to me as I stepped into the bathtub. I wrote the first sentence then, and the next day I wrote the rest of it. I take a notebook and pencil with me to the tub unless I am in a terrible hurry, but it really isn't necessary. The story remembered doesn't go away any more than incidents from the past go away once remembered. I was there; I felt it; I remember how it was.

How Many Miles to Babylon?

HEAT lay over the land, turning the marsh forests into casseroles forgotten in an oven. It was still, heavy heat, pressed down by a lid of sun, and walking through it was like wading submerged in a calm, hot ocean. Marley's feet were weights that dragged in the sand of the road, and at each step she stirred whirlwinds of dust that rose to form clouds. Each dirty cloud hung in the air briefly, then sank straight down, back to the road.

Her mother had named her Marlene after seeing *The Blue Angel* three nights in a row and bearing a girl child on the fourth. Later she admitted she should have saved the name for Marley's sister, who was a long-legged blonde. Marley was also blonde, but sturdy. As she walked, she crooned to an infant she snuggled close to her breast. *How many miles to Babylon?* The no-see-'ems buzzed about her face, dirt stained by the dust sticking to sweat, and she sang in a curiously sweet, childlike voice.

She thought about being twelve again, in the first uncertain phase of womanhood, which shamed and thrilled her. The father had been dead for almost a year, and there were four younger ones in the family: the sister who should have been Marlene, and was eleven, and three brothers. The mother put coupons in an envelope along with a grocery list and thrust it at Marley.

"But you said this time Lucinda would go with me!"

"She has a headache. You know how upset she gets. . . . You are strong enough to bring them alone. You can get a candy bar," the mother said.

"I don't want to go! I have to every time! It isn't fair!"

"Oh, Lord," the mother said, casting up her gaze. "Oh, God, what have I done to deserve it all?"

They felt that one day the Lord would answer her, but He didn't that day, and Marley went to the grocery store nine blocks away. A freezing rain started to fall as she went. If you pretend no one can see you, pretend hard enough, maybe they can't, she thought, and concentrated on pretending. She hummed to herself as she walked, watching her feet. The Riley boys didn't notice when she passed their house. Other times they had thrown snowballs. "Yah, yah! Charity babe!"

She deliberated over the candy counter while Mr. Strothers filled the order, and finally she selected a bar that was at least half an inch longer than any of the others. She unwrapped it carefully and turned it over and over counting the nuts that showed before she allowed herself the first bite.

"Do you have any idea of how much dried milk one nickel can buy?" Mrs. Strothers' sharp voice jolted her, and guiltily she let her hand drop to below the counter height.

"Leave her be," Mr. Strothers called from behind the meat counter. "I'm givin' the kid the candy bar."

"You have enough to do to feed your own family without taking in every relief case that comes through the door," his wife said, staring hard at Marley.

Slowly Marley raised her hand and laid the untasted candy bar on the countertop. She turned and walked to the window and stood looking out the space between a box of bananas and a bin of potatoes at the world being wrapped in an ice blanket.

Mrs. Strothers made an angry sound. Watching her reflection in the window, Marley saw her take a scrap of wrapping paper, lift the candy bar with it, and drop it into the trash can.

Marley pulled the wagon home, slipping and sliding and humming all the way, invisible to the world, the world invisible to her.

How many miles to Babylon? Five score and ten, she sang liltingly, and did not see the steaming, tangled woods at each side of her, saw only the stretch of road directly before her eyes. Once there was a rattler twenty feet ahead of her and she came to a stop, waiting for it to move. It lay somnolent in the dust, its body larger around than her arm. She backed up ten feet and, adjusting the infant carefully, reached down with one hand and felt in the sand for rocks. She threw four or five of them before she hit the snake, and it struck immediately, lashing out at the air. She threw again and this time it began to move, slowly, crossing the road, slithering into the undergrowth and out of sight. She went on.

Another time she was forced to slow her pace when for a panicky moment she thought she might have heat prostration if she didn't get out of the midday sun. *How many miles to Babylon?* It was four miles from the farm to town. She fixed the thin shawl about the infant to keep the no-see-'ems off it, to keep it shaded, and she crooned softly, bowing her head under the white-hot sky.

The first time she had seen the road had been by the headlights of the truck Jim had bought. It held all their possessions and rattled and bumped along, in time, it seemed, to the impromptu singing that came from the front seat.

They arrived at the farm at almost midnight. In horror they stared at the view caught in the beams of the headlights. The land had been filled above the level of the swamps and a few trees had been cut to rot where they fell. The underbrush was head-high as far as the light reached. Marley felt scalding tears on her cheeks; Jim started to curse, and somewhere along the way he was cursing not only the company that had sold him the land but also her.

They slept in the truck that night and for the next six weeks. And at the end of the six weeks Marley knew she was pregnant.

In the beginning he had tried to get his money back, but he couldn't. He decided to make it into a farm, like the ad said. "Don't I work hard enough!" he yelled at her when she asked if they couldn't give up and go back home, back to their jobs. "Don't I! You always say hard work is what it takes. By God, I work hard enough! It's my land and I'm going to stay on it, and so are you. You're my wife, just like this land is mine, and you'll do what I say! Damn you, shut up with that talk about going home! *This* is home!"

When he learned she was pregnant: "I thought you said you knew what to do. We agreed, no kids. You lied to me, you little slut! You told me you knew what to do!"

"I'm getting old! I want a baby now, while I can still have it. Wait, Jim, just wait. You'll love . . ."

He hit her before she could say anything else, and minutes later he overcame her as she was running up the road toward town, away from him. "Marley, I'm sorry. I'm nuts about you. You know that. Tell me you know that."

He lifted her and carried her back to the newly finished cabin, to their pallet on the floor, and he made love to her until she promised, sobbing, never to leave him again.

How many miles to Babylon? She had to rest. The four miles had become part of a suntime nightmare, and the endless road was a treadmill she would pace forever. She shivered and knew the flash of terror, and the shiver, came from weakness; the child had been born only a month ago. The road was higher than the surrounding ground and was sun-baked, and sun-bleached, and sun-crumbled, but to step off it into the shade was to step where the land oozed and made sucking noises, and where the snakes were as silent as moving air. She shifted the infant in her arms and held one hand to her forehead, straining to see past the water mirages on the road, straining to see a bit of shade cast by an overhanging tree. Reluctantly she turned and looked behind her and saw without surprise that she had passed through such a spot only minutes ago. The dust clouds were still hanging in the air in front of a spot of shade. She turned back and went through them and sat down in the sand, laying the infant on her legs. She kept the shawl in place over its face and head. The insects were on her the second she stopped her motion and she put her head in her arms and hunched over her child, closing her burning eyes.

Will I get there by candlelight? At home it would be cool now, and at night a blanket would be needed. The air was different; you didn't have to suck it in, but rather it flowed easily through and through a person and left him feeling clean. She raised her head and wearily brushed the insects away from her wrists and face. She pulled the shawl closer about the baby. The infant had welts on its arms and legs where the insects had got to it before. No matter how hard she tried, since its birth, she hadn't been able to keep them out of the crude, one-room lean-to Jim had built. Her arms and legs were covered with welts and old sores caused by scratching the bites, and scratches from the underbrush that grew faster than they could chop it out. Back home the air was chilled by now. Kids would have their sweaters on these days.

She had quit school. The truant officer came to her house, and her English teacher came. "It is criminal to make her leave school," they said. "She is certain to get a scholarship." The mother sat blinking back tears and called on God to help her. The English teacher looked at Marley with impatience. "You understand what it means to have an education. Don't you?"

That year Marley failed every subject except Art and Physical Education, and when the principal called her to his office for a talk, she sat staring out the window and pretended he couldn't see her, nor she him.

How many miles to Babylon? She put her hand under the shawl and felt the infant's incredibly tiny, clenched fingers. *Five score and ten. Will I get there by candlelight?*

For seventeen years she worked in the canning factory. She worked six days a week and on Sunday she took her mother to church and did the ironing in the afternoon. Lucinda graduated and married a lieutenant in the army. The boys graduated and two of them went to college. At night she read books from the library, or went to a movie once in a while; she learned to sew, and she kept her mother company. After a few years she believed she could do no other work and pretended she couldn't see the factory; or the other girls who came worked a few years, married, then left to have babies. She managed to teach her hands to do the work without supervision, and she carried out her task as if she were blind. In her blindness she was invisible.

She wasn't aware of it when they replaced the aging foreman, who had been there as long as she had, until one day Jim sat next to her in the cafeteria.

"I've been watching you, wondering how long it would take you to notice me," he said, unwrapping his sandwich. "Forever, I guess."

She looked up from the book she was reading as she ate, and she saw a man as lonely as she was, a big, powerfully built man with coarse, black hair, and a scar on his forehead.

Months after that he said to her, "You're so much above them all. You don't even see them and all their little meannesses, ready to take a guy home and get him drunk so they can go through his pockets, and then the back of their hand to him when someone new comes along."

She knew he had been hurt by a woman, and her heart cringed at the thought. It was a physical tightening in her chest, and for a moment she was afraid she was having a seizure, such as her mother often had. When it had passed, he was holding her hand and looking into her eyes. "You do like me, don't you, Marley? Look how you're shaking. Say you like me."

Like him? Helplessly she admitted to herself that she adored him. Through her long years of virgin spinsterhood she never had dreamed falling in love could change her so much; she never had dreamed of falling in love at all. For the first time in her life she saw spring come to the city that year, softly, whispering quiet, too sly to be caught, adding a color splash here and there when eyes were turned away, hiding and laughing in the newly awakened flowers. She looked at herself and saw the same softness come to her face, touching her skin with fairy fingers, leaving a glow, sprinkling her eyes with fire sparks. She looked at her body and saw that it was firm and untouched-looking and, unnoticed, had gone on by itself to develop full breasts and a narrow waist and rounded hips. Her pale hair responded to her first trip to a beauty parlor and she walked out with her head high and gleaming; lightness was in her feet and a smile on her coral-colored lips.

She wrote to Lucinda: You and the boys will have to take care of Mom from now on. I have for twenty years. Then her freed spirit took the pen and dashed off line after line about Jim and the farm in Florida. I love him, she wrote. She put her head in the crook of her arm and wept. She was thirty-six and she loved him with the passion of a girl half her age.

She blinked at the sun-drenched road. Reluctantly she gathered up the child again and forced herself from the spot of shade. She hummed and sang snatches of the words to her child, *How many miles to Babylon?* The last time she had walked to town had been five days before the child was born. She had gone that time to see Doctor Silvers, too. "It'll be fifty dollars," he said, looking at her shrewdly. She was wearing one of Lucinda's pretty hand-me-down maternity dresses. She nodded mutely. Fifty dollars! " 'Course, if you can't pay," the doctor added, "we won't turn you away."

She smiled. "We can pay," she said. And she wondered why Mrs. Strothers had thrown away the perfectly good candy bar. She walked back the four miles unaware of the heat and the dwindling distance that separated her from the farm. At the turnoff she stopped and looked blankly at the sky. It was late; Jim might even be in from the clearing that occupied all his time. She set her shoulders and went on to the house of rotting logs.

"Where the hell you been?"

"I went to see a doctor."

"For God's sake!" He turned from her and stalked to the truck that no longer would run, but which served as a safe place for their food since the rats hadn't managed to find a way to get into the cab yet. He pulled out a piece of salt pork and cut off a chunk. The stove was in the front yard, and viciously he shoved another stick inside it and slammed the pork down on a skillet. She said nothing. Her legs were burning and she wondered if she were running a temperature; the world shimmered before her eyes. She heard Jim distantly when he said, "I told you, no doctor! I told you and you had to go off and find yourself one first chance you got, didn't you. How the hell do you think we can pay a doctor? I told you Toogie's wife can take care of you. You and that Goddamned baby!"

Only once had he touched her during the past month, since she had to stop working at his side every day. And that once had been an open-handed slap that sent her across the cabin into the wall. She closed her eyes when she saw him coming near her, and she thought, "He's going to hit me again. He doesn't know how scared I am."

She closed her eyes, and, magically, he couldn't see her and went past her into the cabin, bringing out with him the black coffeepot, which he banged down on the wood stove.

How many miles to Babylon? Five score and ten. Will I get there by candlelight? She remembered the cypress tree that she was nearing. Its knees sticking up from the black water of the marsh were rafts on which water moccasins rested, coiled and looped or stretched out full-length. She stayed in the center of the road, grateful for the shade of the spreading branches; her eyes followed the movement of her feet and refused to see the horror of the protruding cypress knees. She was only minutes from town now. She knew she couldn't have walked much farther. Her skin was hot, and large black dots swam before her eyes. She stopped, swaying, and rested in the shade for a moment.

She was in labor for two days before Jim found Toogie's wife and brought her to the lean-to. She was a monstrous woman, black with greenish-black eyes and the facial bones of an Indian. She had one finger missing from her right hand, and the stub frightened Marley.

She never knew there could be such pain. The black woman did things to her and she screamed until she lost consciousness. In the void she heard Jim's yell, "For God's sake, can't you shut her up!" The black woman cradled her and she sobbed against her massive breasts. Then the child came, and she was blonde.

"Missy, you take your man, go away from this here place," Toogie's wife said before she left. "This here place kill all you. Kill him first."

Marley studied Jim that night. The infant lay against her side and she was too weak to lift her head, but whenever Jim came into her range of vision she studied him and she saw that the black woman was right. He was wild and strange, as if somehow Jim had been replaced gradually by a being alien to all she knew. He cursed and hit her when he was angry. The sun and the never ending work of trying to force back the jungle had changed him into something she feared. He brought her tea made from herbs furnished by the black woman and he held up her head so she could sip it. Then his hands were running over her flabby-flat belly and suddenly he was pushing the infant off the pallet, and his voice was thick and blurred. She fainted.

After twelve days her milk stopped, and the baby cried weakly all day until Jim came home. He refused to go to town that night. The next day the child's cry was weaker; Jim made love to Marley before he walked into town. He brought two cans of evaporated milk back with him.

Her strength was returning, and he said she had to clear the space around the cabin so they could have a garden. She was afraid to leave the baby inside and she couldn't put it on the ground outside, so she put it in the cab of the truck and covered the open windows with threadbare toweling. She worked for two hours before she had to stop. The baby never stopped crying, and when she looked she saw that mosquitoes had got inside the truck and the infant was a mass of red bites that were swollen and hard.

She wept as she bathed the child and applied baking-soda paste to the bites. The child screamed until it fell asleep from exhaustion. Jim took her to the pallet and she wept again. "God,

help me," she prayed. "I love him. I can't help it. I love him."
The infant screamed and no longer could open its swollen eyes.

*How many miles to Babylon? Five score and ten. Will I get
there by candlelight? Yes! And back again.* She left the shade
and walked into town singing her song to her one-month-old
infant. She held it tight against her breast. She was wrapped in
her invisibility as she made her way to the doctor's office. She
saw none of the patients in the outer office, but carried her child
past the emptiness into the examining room. The doctor came
into her field of vision, and she had to pretend hard before he
would go away. He took the child and laid it on the table. She
kept her eyes on the baby when he unwrapped the shawl and
stood staring

"Ma'am, where's your husband?" The voice came from the
emptiness.

"I hit him with the pickax."

Her eyes never left the infant with its twisted neck and the
large, livid imprint of a hand that had barely begun to turn
black, covering the side of its face.

How many miles to Babylon? she hummed, and tears continued to course down her dust-caked cheeks, making a shiny
trail from her blind eyes to her chin.

For me the intellectual dissection of a story into its various parts is always a post mortem. First there are the images, the scenes, the people moving about doing things, saying things. Translating this extremely visual whole into words is the process by which daydreams are turned into stories. I remember a recurrent daydream I had years ago in which I stripped a Gothic horror story of its trappings: the brooding mansion, the swirling fogs, the flickering candles, the ghostly sighs, the mysterious past. Then this story revealed itself to me, and sometime after it was written I realized it had its origins in that particular daydream. I haven't given any thought since this story was written to that daydream again.

The Downstairs Room

VERA answered the telephone with one hand and tried to fasten Jeff's hood with the other. "Yes, I'll be there tonight. No, I don't think . . . Jeff, hold still . . . Sorry. He has to leave. . . . Look, call me back in fifteen minutes, okay?" She hung up and, jerking Jeff to her, finished the strap.

"So long, Mom." That was Jerry, the oldest of the three and in junior high school. The door slammed.

"Mother, where's my history book?"

"On the table."

"It's not on the table! Jeff took it!"

"I did not! I didn't see the stupid book!"

"Look under the table," Vera called irritably.

"Got it. 'By, Mother." Susan slamming the door was no less emphatic than her older brother. She was ten. Vera shut her eyes until the reverberations ceased.

"Jeff, you'll miss the bus. Where's your lunch box?"

"I don't know."

"You had it a minute ago. Where did you take it?"

"I didn't take it. Susan took it."

"Never mind; there it is. Now get!" Jeff wetted her cheek with his jellyish kiss and the door slammed for the third time—no, the fourth time that morning; Hank was a door slammer also.

Vera sat down and let her head rest between her hands several minutes and then got up to pour coffee. Why, why, why couldn't they get out every morning without the shouting? Every day it took a little longer for the knot to untie itself just below her throat. The telephone rang before she finished the coffee and she took it with her.

"I'm sorry, Edith. You know, the morning madness. What was it?"

She listened with a sense of sinking. Another P.T.A. festival. When she hung up she had committed herself to baking a cake, taking a batch of candy, and supervising the cakewalk for two hours on the evening of the festival. Her coffee was cold. Why wouldn't they leave her alone? She thought with envy of all the mothers who never got mixed up with the extracurricular activities. She didn't know how they stayed clear of it all.

Later, while the clothes were washing, she finally went into the room downstairs. For ten years they had been planning on finishing it, turning it into a television-recreation room, and finally the dream was becoming an actuality. It didn't look very basement-ish any longer. A skeleton of a built-in booth suggested meals down there, out of the impossible kitchen where only four of them should sit and eat at one time, and five did.

Cream walls, she thought, and narrowed her eyes seeing them, and brick-red tile flooring, yellow plastic chair and bench covers. She sat on a ladder rung sipping her coffee. It would be warm and homey, a nice place to be, a place where no one shouted and bickered, but played together amicably, where the telephone peal didn't penetrate. For dancing they could push aside the twin couches that she wanted, and there would be only fire-light—like the place Hank used to take her to before they were married. Soft dreamy music and a pretty, swishy dress, dancing for hours . . .

"Hey! Vera! You down there?"

She jerked her head at the sound and looked about her bewildered.

"Vera! Where are you?"

"Hank? Down here. I'm coming."

"You going deaf or something?" he asked, not looking up as she emerged from the stairs. "Look what I ran across this morning." He was busy opening a large box and didn't see her face as she stared at the clock over the refrigerator.

Twelve-thirty! It couldn't be!

"Hank, what time is it?" she asked.

"I don't know. After twelve. I'm on my lunch hour. Why?" Without waiting for an answer he finished ripping open the box and pulled out a tile. "Look! Three cents each! How about that!"

Vera forced her eyes from the impossible clock and stared uncomprehendingly at the tile he held. The tile was purple.

"Well?" Hank demanded.

Vera shook her head. "Purple?"

"Mauve, that's what the man said it is. Mauve and white, green or blue or pink, they all would go with it."

"But we agreed on red," Vera said slowly. She felt confused and disoriented, and again her eyes flashed to the clock.

"I know, but this was such a bargain. I've got to run, but think about it, will you? Look at these designs and just think about it." He brushed her cheek with a kiss and left. She winced when the door slammed.

In her hand she was still holding the coffee cup, and in it there was still coffee. Dazedly she put it down. There was a number she could call. Jerry had written it down somewhere. Her fingers felt cold as she dialed and listened to the mechanical voice repeating, "The time is now 12:35."

Halfway through dinner she remembered that she hadn't written up her minutes for the Women's Alliance meeting and she rushed to do it, upsetting her own and everyone else's meal. It was nearly ten-thirty when she returned home from the meeting. Jerry was still up.

"Go to bed," she told him shortly and turned to Hank. "Why don't you make him go to bed when I'm not here?"

"He was, just as soon as this show is over," Hank said.

Jerry went grumbling as she continued to frown at him, and then she inspected Jeff and Susan. Jeff had his socks on. She came from his room carrying them. "Really, Hank, didn't he even have his bath?"

"Sure he did. He said his feet were cold. What difference does it make if he wanted to sleep in his socks? Sit down, honey. You're tired. I don't know why you go to all those things when you don't want to. You always come home in a mood."

"It's not that. I never go anywhere any more, and when I do go out I never know what to expect when I get home again. Jerry still up, Hank in his socks. And who left the crayons out?"

"Susan was trying out tile designs. We were all trying out designs. Want to see?"

Hank pointed to a pile of drawing paper and watched her face as she glanced at them. The purple, brash and undeniable with the crayons, seemed almost a personal affront. She shuddered and turned from them.

"Honey, what's the matter with you? If you don't like it, say so, and we'll get something else."

"No, it's all right. I guess I am tired." She forced herself to look through the designs and found that she did like one. "Look, Hank, whose is this?" The purple and white blocks made an odd pattern that was rather like an optical illusion in that first she found her eyes tracing the white tiles as being predominant, and without knowing when the switch came she was following the dark ones. They made curved diagonal lines of alternating purple and white.

"Yours truly, madam," Hank said modestly. "Genius never fails to find recognition."

"You nut." She grinned at him and he rose and put his arm around her shoulders and surveyed his artwork with her. Arm in arm they walked to the kitchen and ate cookies and coffee before going to bed.

She helped him lay the tile during the next week, but she

didn't go into the room again during the day or when she was alone. Only after the last piece was in place and the mastic was dry was she even tempted. Then, as the other time, she was washing, and also a load was in the dryer. She stood in the doorway looking at the floor. There, without too much light, the dark tiles didn't look so purple, more black than anything. Black and white was always nice. The pattern had to be seen from the doorway to grasp it. Laying it down she had kept referring to the diagram they used, but the whole had been lost in the various parts, and now it emerged again. It resembled arcs of circles like emerging waves of dark and light from a distant, not visible, source, somewhere over there in the corner. Her eyes traversed the rings to the corner, where they converged into the heart of the purple—It was solid purple over there. The purple crept out from under the restraining white lines . . . crawled, oozed, and with each emergence grew stronger, wider, more impelling . . . but there, she lost them and was again on the white lines. With a gasp she pulled her eyes away and stood trembling against the door jamb.

Determinedly she turned from the room and unloaded the dryer and started to fold the clothes. The door held a fascination, and finally she piled the clothes in the basket and nearly ran up the stairs.

Several nights later Hank questioned her. "What's wrong, Vera? Did I do something?"

Guiltily she looked up from the magazine she was holding. "Why?"

"You know why. You missed the Red Cross meeting Tuesday, and tonight is Civil Defense night. You're staying home. Are you sick? What's been wrong with you?"

"Nothing," she said shortly. "I'm tired of all those meetings. I admit it. That's all."

Hank crossed the room and sat down next to her. He took her hand between his. "Look, honey, I know you. Remember? Something's wrong. Tell me about it."

"It's nothing," she repeated helplessly.

"Why don't you run over to Doctor Felton's tomorrow and

have him take a look? Maybe you're anemic or something."

Vera looked at her hand in his and, suddenly irritated, asked sharply, "What should I tell him? That you decided something was wrong? I feel fine."

"You're jumpy. You yell at the kids over nothing. You sit and stare at nothing and you don't hear me. You haven't left the house in over a week. You aren't sleeping. You're up and down all night."

She looked at him quickly and shifted her gaze before he could trap her into admission. "It's nothing," she said. "You're imagining things." She was looking beyond him and she saw a long web hanging from the ceiling, and another stretched from the top of the floor lamp to the wall. How did they come back so fast? She'd vacuumed only . . . When? She looked at the rug . . . not for several days.

". . . and it didn't just happen," Hank was saying. "For months you've been getting more and more jumpy. Will you go over and let him check you?"

Vera looked at him in genuine amazement. Months? She almost felt like laughing. Not for months. Just since . . . since . . . At the questioning look on his face she said, "It's enough to make anyone nervous the way the children squabble all the time. You don't realize how much of it goes on. And someone's always calling up wanting something. I guess my nerves aren't what they used to be."

"The kids don't squabble any more than they ever did, and not as much as a lot of kids do. And you don't have to feel guilty about turning people down once in a while. It's not that."

He left it there, however, and she realized that he expected her to have the doctor examine her, to go over for a going over. The phrase repeated itself in her mind, like a TV jingle. Slyly she thought she would let him keep thinking she would go. She hadn't said one way or the other.

That night the dream returned.

She was high up in an empty theater that was shrouded in shadows, descending from the uppermost reaches of a steep balcony that overhung a void. The black beyond the rail was impenetrable with no stage, or seats, or walls or floor showing. Each night she came closer to the rail, wanting more than anything to see what was under it, and feeling a paralyzing terror as she neared the edge. So many steps, zigzagging downward, barely outlined by a pencil-thin line of light that edged them, so many theater seats aligned evenly, each covered with a velour that was first rough and then smooth. She ran her hand over the backs as she descended past them, and they were like velvet, but smoother than any velvet made. She pressed her hand down into the softness and it sank vanishing, and still, even while sinking into the stuff, it glided over the top of it and found no place to hold. Then it came out and she went down the next step and ran her hand over the next seat. The seats were all up, like knees pressing against chests . . . With each step downward her terror grew and she could feel her eyes widening until they hurt. Her mouth was open but voiceless, her hand swallowed up in the smooth softness of the velour, and before her the darkness of the void that would swallow her whole person just as the chair backs took her hand—take her, giving her nothing to hold onto, take her and drain her and finally reject her and let her fall forever. The steps smoothed out and became a glasslike incline and she was slipping, clutching at the chairs, at the velour that smothered her hand and wouldn't hold it. The purple . . . Her feet scrabbled for balance but she slipped and slipped, and the void was purple like the chairs. And she was falling into the purple. . . .

She awakened, trembling and cold; her eyes ached and her throat was dry as if she had been screaming. She crept from the bed and sat in the kitchen drinking water. The dream that had yanked her from sleep was gone, leaving only the feeling of utter despair and fear that had no substance.

"It's too dark in here," she complained to Hank, rolling paint on the smooth wallboard several nights later. He looked up from the trimwork he was doing and stood for a minute examining the room.

"Dark!" he said finally. "Four lamps and a ceiling light, plus white walls. I don't know what else we could do to lighten it, do you?"

"No," she admitted reluctantly. "But it always seems too shadowy. I miss windows, I guess. I'll get used to it."

"Sure you will," he agreed and went back to painting around the door.

She filled her roller again and returned to her wall. But she could feel the shadows now. If only she hadn't admitted them. That was it. She mustn't give them life by saying them. She smiled at the wall and stroked furiously. For over a week now it hadn't grown simply because she refused to mention it. But if she looked . . . She knew it was there in the corner. The dark sun, she called it to herself, recalling the moment she realized what it was.

"Jerry, what's the sun?" Susan had asked mischievously.

"It's a star, goofball."

"What's a star, then?"

"Burning gas."

"What's gas?" Susan was nearing her triumph and she squirmed all over her chair. Vera started to tell her to sit still, but she bit her lip and stole a glance at Hank. He wasn't even noticing them.

"Knock it off, goofball. I'm busy," Jerry grunted and picked up his schoolbook.

"Gas is what I have in my hand," Susan chanted. "And I don't have anything. Nothing. Gas is nothing. And the sun is nothing. The sun is nothing. The sun is nothing."

"Susan, shut up!" Vera felt them all staring at her and ran from the room muttering about a headache.

The dark sun was in the corner of the room, a dark sun with compelling concentric rings about it, dark, quavering bands and dark shadows. She painted vigorously and pretended the corner didn't exist. Suddenly she was jerked away from the wall and swung around.

"Vera, for God's sake, what's wrong with you?" Hank was staring at her with fear in his eyes.

"What did I do?" she gasped.

Hank took the roller from her flaccid hand and replaced it in the pan. "Sit down, honey," he said quietly. He sat opposite her in the incomplete booth and let his eyes examine her carefully. "Did you go to see Dr. Felton, or was that a lie?"

"Of course, I did. I told you. I need more rest. That's all."

"What did you tell him?"

"What could I? Just that I was tired and didn't feel like doing as much as I used to. You were right all the time; I let myself get involved in too many things."

Hank closed his eyes for a moment and she stole a look behind her, at the corner. It was the first time she had been willing to sit down in the room since the morning she sat on the ladder rung. It was there, but not growing. The bands shimmied like heat rising off a highway. She watched them in fascination until Hank's voice recalled her.

". . . like right now. You haven't heard a thing! What's wrong?"

"I'm sorry," she said quickly, fearfully. "Hank, I am sorry. I was thinking."

"Vera, do you realize that you stood over there and rolled an empty roller for at least ten minutes in one spot? Do you remember doing it?"

She shook her head. Her feet felt so cold. They might be on one of the rays! It would be like dry ice, so cold that it would burn, right through her shoes, into her feet, up her legs. She shivered, her eyes fastened on Hank's face. Her feet felt numb, as if they would slip out from under her if she were to stand. She would slip and fall, and if she fell on one of them, she wouldn't be able to rise again. She would grow cold and numb all over, and the terrible dark sun would expand until it reached her. . . .

"Vera!" Hank jumped to his feet and hauled her up also. "Come on, you belong in bed. I'm staying home tomorrow and taking you over to Dr. Felton's myself. Come on."

With his rough touch the spell was broken and she looked at him in a puzzled manner, not quite knowing why he was so concerned. Upstairs she balked at being put to bed.

"Why are you watching me like that?" she asked angrily as his eyes followed her movements about the kitchen making tea. "If you look closely enough you'll see everyone doing foolish things once in a while. My mind was on something else, that's all."

She stood at the stove waiting for the water to boil and he came over to stand behind her. "I didn't mean to stare, honey. I've just been so worried."

If he touched her, she'd scream. She waited stiffly for his hands, but he went past and opened the refrigerator. She felt the stiffness melt, leaving her alone and cold. He'd had no intention of touching her in the first place. She glanced at his back and the thought formed, how she hated him! He thought he owned her, could handle her or not as his whim dictated. She was the one who had to conform to all his preferences; she had to please his taste, serve the dishes he liked; she had to be there when he called, satisfy his needs. What a convenience he bought when he purchased the marriage license: a housekeeper, errand boy, laundress, cook . . . He could use her as he used a tool, knowing when he put it down, it would remain and be waiting when he returned. The water was boiling briskly and she lifted the pan and poured it over the tea leaves in the pot. Like right now, she had to make the tea, wait on him like a servant . . . He even wanted her to open her mind to his prying.

With a stifled cry she dropped the pan, turned and ran from the kitchen, tears blinding her. She locked herself in the bathroom and wept for almost an hour while he pleaded with her at the door to let him in, to tell him what was wrong. When she came out, he met her in the hallway and stood blocking her way.

"What was that all about?"

"Leave me alone! Just leave me alone! I'm going to watch the late movie."

He looked at her a minute, then swung about and went into the bedroom, slamming the door behind him. With the banging of the door, all the hate went out of her and the tears flowed again. With a wordless cry she ran after him and clung to him.

"Hank, forgive me. I don't know why I acted like that. I'm a terrible wife. I don't cook any more and I don't clean the house and your shirt has a button gone and nothing goes right any more. I don't see how you put up with me. Please, forgive me." She sobbed in his arms and tasted the bitterness of her unworth. His reassuring words never even registered in that area that knew how vile she was.

The next morning she was bright and forcefully cheerful. She laughed at Hank's renewed vow to take her to the doctor.

"You dear nut," she said with a smile. "I promise you I'll go. And I'll even pay him and bring the receipt back if you insist. It's a lot of nonsense, your staying home to take me. Probably it's my eyes. You know how the thought of wearing glasses rubs me. They remind me that I'm getting old. But," she added quickly before he could speak, "I promise you I will go."

Hank called from his office that afternoon and she sat down to talk to him. "Yes, dear. Of course, I went . . . absolutely nothing. I have an appointment for an eye examination next month . . . I know, but they work that far ahead. I couldn't get an earlier appointment . . . Yes, dear, see you later."

Her hand was clenched so tightly about the telephone that it was numb and only gradually became tingly when she released the phone. Get out more! Go to afternoon classes somewhere! Dance! Have fun! What kind of a doctor was he? She was tired to death and he told her to do more! She felt her eyes throbbing, and slowly she went into the bedroom to lie down until time for Jeff and Susan to come home from school. That crazy doctor! People like her didn't have nervous breakdowns. What had she to worry her? The kids? Money? A chasing husband? Nothing! She pressed her hands into her eyes and the thought came, if only she could sleep! Oh, God, if only she could sleep through one night! She looked with disgust at the prescribed pills and with a sudden motion threw them against the wall. She didn't need tranquilizers. She needed something to busy her up. She was tranquil almost to the point of unconsciousness now.

She lay quietly staring at the ceiling, and suddenly voices at the front door brought her out of her mindless reverie. Susan and Jeff? She looked at the clock and jumped to her feet. Four-thirty! She ran to the living room and grabbed Jeff by the arm, causing him to drop a small bag of candy.

"Where have you been? Why didn't you come home with the bus? Did you get off at the shopping center?" She shouted at the frightened child, digging her fingers into his arm, and when he didn't recover enough to answer immediately, she slapped him and pushed him away from her. "Get in your room!" she screamed. "You can tell your father about it!"

Jeff was screaming too by then and he ran away from her, but at the door he turned and yelled, "I hate you!"

Vera started to go after him, but Susan was crying also, and she turned instead to her. "Well, what's wrong with you?"

"We were at the festival. The bus didn't bring us home early today. It's always late for the festival." Susan lost it in convulsive, choking sobs and she ran out.

Vera stared at the closed bedroom doors and for an instant she felt dizzy, as if she were falling headfirst from a great height. Hesitantly she started toward Jeff's room, but she stopped and pressed her knuckles against her teeth until they hurt.

When Hank came home Jeff's cheek was no longer red and the swelling had been greatly reduced by ice packs held in place by Vera. She kept looking at the child with fear in her eyes.

"I was so worried," she tried to explain. "It kept getting later and he didn't come. I just didn't think about the festival and the bus being late. I saw the candy and I thought . . . You don't understand how afraid I was. I thought all sorts of things might have happened . . . I forgot about the . . . Going to the doctor and upsetting the day made me forget. Hank, say something!"

"Honey, it's all right. Calm down. Now forget it; he isn't hurt. Anyone would have worried. I don't blame you for getting upset. It was natural."

She jerked away from him and her eyes were burning. He knew! He was just trying to soothe her. He knew! Angrily she cried, "It's your fault! You made me go see that stupid doctor. That ruined my whole day and all for nothing. You know no one else would slap a child like that. Only a monster would hit a child enough to leave a mark! How can you say it's natural?" She took a deep breath that didn't ease her breathlessness. "You know what the doctor told me? That I'm tired! Is that what you wanted to hear? You hoped he'd find something serious, didn't you? You believed it, didn't you? You wanted me to be sick! But I'm not! I'm tired. Can't you understand that? *I am tired!*"

"Stop that! Stop it!" Hank's hands were on her shoulders shaking her, and she clamped her lips together and let him hold her quietly.

"I feel so ashamed," she moaned. "I hit him and I couldn't stop myself. It's so terrible! I'm so ashamed."

"Go lie down, honey. I'll put on some soup or something. Go on and lie down. After the kids eat, we'll talk."

She let him baby her, and the sounds of pans clinking against the stove, the gurgle of water and, soon after, the percolating coffee, all brought peace to her. She closed her eyes and a deep sigh escaped her lips.

But she hadn't been worried about Jeff. She hadn't even thought about him. She shook her head against the pillow; subconsciously she must have been worrying about him. That was it, her subconscious had been worrying and too late translated the worry into the hasty slap. She brought the idea into sharper focus and convinced herself that it was so. And she must have been dozing when Jerry had come home and changed. He said she told him okay to play ball. She must have been dozing or she'd remember. Poor Hank. He was so good to her and deserved so much better than he got. He had the children downstairs so their noise wouldn't bother her. That suited them fine; they wanted to be away from her with her tempers and scolding and slaps. It wasn't fair to Hank to have to come home and prepare his own dinner while she lay on the bed and watched the ceiling and tried not to think about the dark sun.

The dark sun! They were eating down there with it behind them. Instantly she sat upright, and for a second the fear enveloped her like an impenetrable fog. Then she relaxed again. It didn't bother them; it was waiting for her.

None of them noticed how the white bands were being pushed and squeezed out. They didn't realize how the dark rings grew; they fairly leapt out at her whenever she entered the room. She couldn't follow the white stripes more than halfway into the room now. She would try and try to make her eyes follow the white to the place where the purple converged into the dark sun, but it had swallowed them up. The way it would swallow her if she let it.

What if it reached out for one of them? For Jeff? She stiffened and sat even stiller on the side of the bed. What if it had done it already? She listened. The house was unearthly quiet. Hank couldn't keep them that quiet.

Silently she crept down the stairs and advanced to the door, her head turned to one side so that she might hear, if a sound should come. None did. She stood by the door listening for a long time, and finally she touched it and it opened without a revealing squeak. Her eyes were drawn instantly to the floor, and the dark sun was more than halfway out. As she looked it advanced another foot, and the white was merely a tracing of light that more sharply defined the threatening purple.

Suddenly a loud blast of music shattered the quiet and there were shrieks of laughter and normalcy returned. Hank was standing before her carrying a tray laden with dishes.

"Hi, feeling better? Unless you want to watch that crazy puppet show, you'd better settle for your dinner in the kitchen." He grinned at her, and past his shoulder she could now see that they were sitting before the television, the rest of the room darkened and shadowed. She led the way to the kitchen holding her breath, running up the stairs. It was the first time it moved like that as she watched!

She hardly heard Hank's small talk designed primarily, she knew, to put her at ease. Her problem was not being tired, she thought clearly. It was that room, and no normal person was afraid of a room. That damned purple floor! Breaking into Hank's words she said suddenly, "Dr. Felton gave me the name of a specialist, a psychiatrist. Perhaps I'll go talk to him."

Hank reached across the table and squeezed her hand. "I'm glad, honey," was all he said.

Her appointment was for the following Thursday, and she knew she had to keep out of the room until after she talked to him. It was the purple, she decided. Sometime, somehow it had come to mean something to her that was more than she could stand. It had to be. Otherwise it was something that had been within her all the time, and a dark, unknown part of her being was merely using the purple floor to crush her. Vehemently she denied that thought as soon as it formed.

She still didn't sleep much, and when she did, the terror-ridden but afterward forgotten dream intruded, bringing her shaking out of her sleep. Apathy was now a part of her and she lay across the bed trying not to think of it, and the harder she tried, the more often the dark sun was before her, swinging in and out of her line of vision wherever she looked. Had it grown more? Was it to the door yet?

On Wednesday morning Edith dropped in. "We missed you at the festival. I had the devil of a time filling in for you at the cakewalk," she said accusingly. Then very quickly, "Have you been sick?"

"No," Vera answered sharply. "A cold, but it's better."

"Oh? Well, take care of it; 'flu season, you know. But the reason I stopped by is that darned teachers' breakfast coming up week after next. Will you be available to take over in Miss Howell's room?"

Vera felt her nails biting into her palms and she shook her head without speaking.

"But you're the room mother!" Edith protested in alarm. "I thought it was settled."

"I can't," Vera muttered. "I'm sorry, but I can't. I'm having my eyes examined that day."

"What day?" Edith asked. "We didn't decide the day until the Board meeting yesterday. How did you know what day I would say?"

"Stop cross-examining me!" Vera flared suddenly. "I can't come."

Edith became very cool and disdainful and pulled on her gloves, glancing about the room with upraised eyebrows. "Well," she said rising, "I'm sorry I bothered you. I can see that you have lots to do."

After she was gone Vera looked about the room curiously.

How had it become so messed up? The couch pillows were strewn about and magazines were half on the tables, half on the floor. The rug was covered with lint, and dust covered the furniture. She shuddered once and closed her eyes. What did she do all day? Had she been going back down there without remembering about it?

The thought overwhelmed her with terror and she crouched back against her chair as if resisting a force that compelled her to go down the stairs. How long she sat pressed against the chair she didn't know, but finally she heard the telephone ringing insistently.

"Oh, Georgia. How are you? . . . No, I'm all right . . . Oh, Edith called you. I see. I guess she caught me on one of my bad days. I'll call her and apologize . . . Sure, I'm fine. I'll go over for the breakfast. I don't know what made me think it was the day for my eye examination . . . She said what? . . ." She couldn't control the trembling of her hands and she let the telephone fall and watched it dangle from the coiled wire as if it were a snake.

She ran to the bathroom mirror and examined her face in it. Edith even saw it now; the purple was on her, had reached out somehow and marked her, and, by marking, claimed her. Wildly she pulled at her eyes, clutching at her skin, trying to rip off the purple circles that were spreading down her cheeks as she clawed at them. With a cry of despair she ran down the stairs to the door. It was waiting for her as she had known it would be.

Without struggling further, finding sudden relief in the cessation of struggle, she stepped on the glass-smooth incline edged with white and slid down it finding nothing to hold onto as she fell with unbearable terror into the purple sun and was swallowed up by the nothingness of it.

If I had a patron I would demand from him a yearly travel allowance, justifying my trips as part of the continual data-gathering process each writer undergoes. I have never tried deliberately to force a story into a particular locale, nor have I tried to find a story that would reveal a place where I have visited. But every trip I have taken, every new place I have seen eventually appears as the only place a certain story could have happened. I like to think the geographical necessity adds depth; I know many of these stories would not have occurred to me if I had not been there at one time. In my future there lie stories set in Texas, in Arizona, and in these lovely Pocono Mountains where I live now. I don't feel anxious about them; I know one day one of them will swim before my inner eye, and it will be right for the location. Then another, and another. I can wait. When this happens something in me reminds me of how the wind smelled there, how the sun felt, how the ground looked in the distance. In this story it was Florida revisited.

Countdown

STAN stepped out his door as the low-slung MG pulled to a whiplash stop at the curb. He called goodby to his wife spooning Pablum into the baby and she answered and another day was begun. He stepped into the day at T minus sixteen hours and thirty-seven minutes. He never thought of it beginning until he left the house; inside it there was no new day, no job, no endless games of hearts, no countdowns. He stiffened his shoulders and strode the length of the yard and climbed into the car, his knees uncomfortably high in the bucket seat.

"Hi, boss," Ken greeted him and jerked the gearshift, hurtling the little car into high speed before Stan was braced for it. "Sorry," Ken grinned. The MG was his third car that year, and the month then was only April.

Neither of the men glanced at the sky, which had been swept clean of clouds during the night. A high-pressure area poised over Tennessee assured the day would continue brilliant and sparkling, the wind at ten to fifteen knots. Stan breathed deeply; the scent of orange blossoms was riding the unaccustomed north wind. Ken stopped at the end of the street and held back the car, crouched ready to spring into the first opening in the steady flow that made the causeway appear to be one long showroom of used cars. For a moment Stan had the impression that he was being floated past the lineup, that the stream was not moving at all. The moment passed as Ken manipulated the gearshift and pressed hard on the accelerator. Then they were part of the eddy surging toward the Cape.

The tires whined over the grating of the drawbridge. The causeway widened again and became landborne, and on either side of the road houses grew thicker than a forest, houses, shops, bait stores, joints . . . another bridge. The rivers were restless that morning, sparkling with choppy waves under the steady wind. Ducks dotted the Indian River, and beyond them mullets flashed from the water tirelessly. On the other side of the causeway, fishermen wearing waders were already cursing bait-stealing puffins and feeling a crust form where the briny waters of the Banana River splashed on them.

"Just like yesterday, or last month, or last year," Stan commented, giving up trying to light a cigarette in the wind.

"And tomorrow and next month and probably next year," Ken agreed.

Stan nodded; he hoped so. Ken concentrated on driving and Stan thought about Sue. She was going to take the baby to the beach, she had said. He'd give her a call at two, after she'd returned and the baby was sleeping. He hoped the wind wouldn't be too chill for her to swim.

The line of cars came to a halt and he succeeded in lighting the cigarette he still held. They sat for fifteen minutes before the flow again started. During the break Ken talked about the new dancer at the Cocoa Palmetto Grove Club. He had a date with her for that night—if all went well. Stan half-listened. Neither of them was really interested in continuing the small conversation.

They moved again, past the jetties and the dock; the shrimp fleet was gone, leaving the area desolate and forsaken, with only the off-balanced-looking pelicans gliding effortlessly over the waves of the high tide. At the Cape gates the traffic was all but halted completely as the guards made a minute examination of every identification photograph. They were waved on and Ken finally parked the car less than a quarter of a mile from Stan's office. Ken waved his goodby and hurried toward the Section 7 building where he had to punch in, and Stan turned toward the Administration Building.

A briefing had been called for, scheduled at 10:15, and was actually held at 10:45. Until then Stan had no pressing work and he sat behind his desk and glanced through papers without paying much attention to any of them. They would have to be gone over again, of course, and as it was he signed nothing, nor authorized anything, nor countermanded anything. He killed the time without thinking, consciously not thinking.

Stan was a very minor cog in the administration, being the superintendent of the parts-coordination unit, which did little more than ascertain that the parts ordered were in fact the same parts that were delivered, and later in the course of events, see that the parts delivered were in fact the parts needed for assembly. Secretly he called himself a glorified file clerk. He was satisfied to be nothing more. The biggest wheels had had their briefing the day previous, and were now dispensing the information down to the lower echelons, among which Stan was counted.

The briefing was about what Stan expected. A phase had ended, and what had been a private unverified certainty now became a semi-publicly-admitted fact. All administrative and supervisory personnel were to remain on the Cape until after countdown, and they were to assign skeletal standby crews to remain on duty. There were to be no leaks. Stan's mind skittered away from the sepulchral tones the president of his company always assumed when speaking of matters of grave import. The president was to be in Washington at the actual time of firing and was now giving the usual pat-on-the-back treatment deemed so necessary to maintain morale. Vaguely Stan was wishing Sue had gone to visit her mother, the idea he had first suggested and then ordered, and ultimately abandoned.

The loudspeaker hissed and the quiet voice announced, "T-minus-fourteen hours, twenty-six minutes and holding."

The president of the company looked annoyed momentarily and then continued from his prepared text. Stan did some rapid figuring and realized that he would be on the Cape all night. With this one, shooting by night would be as effective as a daylight firing. It would make little difference. If the count picked up soon and no further holds developed, it would go at about one in the morning. The baby had been born at one-thirty, he recalled.

He roused with a start when the meeting broke up, and joined the men pressing silently toward the door. The company president was climbing into a black limousine to be whisked away to Patrick Air Force Base, where a private plane waited. The count was still holding, and lunch only fifteen minutes away. Might as well make quitting time no earlier than two—if they were lucky.

Ken joined him in the cafeteria and they loaded their trays and carried them to the end of the room where the others were already gathered. Ken dealt and Stan studied his hand carefully. He had the Queen of spades along with the Ace and Jack of hearts and three other high leads, but with eleven men playing and two decks in use, he knew he had no chance of shooting the moon. He picked his cards carefully and passed them to the man on his left, and in turn received almost identical cards from Ken on his right. The play continued and he amassed seven points and tossed a nickel and two pennies in the pot. The faces of the players were serious and concentrative and the many cards flew around the circle speedily, each man bolting down his lunch and following it hurriedly with coffee or milk without looking at the food, speaking of nothing but the game in progress.

They all froze when the loudspeaker hissed and the quiet voice announced, "T minus fourteen hours and twenty-six minutes and counting." The hold had lasted one hour and forty-nine minutes.

They finished the hand and added the score quickly; Stan was twelve cents loser. He caught Ken's arm and asked, "Is that a heavy date for tonight?" Ken shrugged. "Come on around at quitting time and I'll buy you a cup of coffee," Stan continued. Ken's eyes gleamed brightly for a second and again he shrugged, nodding.

"She'll keep," was all he said.

Stan shuffled through his papers again, this time having his secretary—shared with the superintendent of office supplies—make notes as he went through his work. He sent her out at two and called Sue.

"Hi, honey. How was the beach?"

"Wonderful! Every bit of thirty degrees," she answered laughing. "How do you convince a baby that a seashell isn't an appropriate toothing ring?" Sue knew the call was being monitored, but her voice was light and quick.

Stan laughed also and soon after hung up, a smile fading slowly from his thin face. By two-thirty he had finished the work on his desk and reached for his ringing telephone as the loudspeaker hissed into action again. He waited for it, holding the phone by the mouthpiece.

"T minus twelve hours, fourteen minutes and holding."

"Robertson," he said into the mouthpiece.

"Delaney here, Stan. Part HG9647LS. Sent a replacement over."

Stan listened without comment as Delaney filled him in with what had gone wrong. He repeated the number and hung up. They had to go through him for every part. The written memorandum would follow shortly, but he had to see that the replacement for the replacement was in stock, and see that the records showed why two of the gidgets had been used from the stocks. For that he didn't need the memorandum. It took him fifteen minutes to satisfy himself that he had fulfilled his duties. At three-ten he went to his company's warehouse, one of many such small buildings scattered out among the palmettos on the Cape.

Here it was business as usual today, and even as he riffled

through a sheaf of orders a truck arrived and began unloading. Ken entered the loading area and waved to Stan. He checked with his men and then approached Stan, a serious, intent look of concern barely visible on his handsome face. Stan reminded himself that he wanted to write a letter of commendation about Ken's work soon. He wondered how much the younger man knew about what was going on there that day. He guessed Ken knew everything. Ken had a way of ferreting inside dope that was pretty uncanny.

"Stan, was the wafer that bad? Did we cause the hold?" Ken asked after glancing about cautiously.

Stan studied him curiously. Ken's face had the stricken look of a parent whose child has broken a showroom window. He felt old and out of touch suddenly. One time he had been that eager, he was certain. That had been when the company was primarily engaged in putting men in orbit and everyone who breathed the same air on the Cape felt a personal pride. Now he couldn't seem to recapture the mood.

"It was the wafer," he said quietly. "Not really bad, questionable. They bent it testing the transistor."

"Goddam!" Ken grunted. "Clumsy bastards!"

Stan shrugged. They both turned and looked back over the Cape where the missile stood against the sky, surrounded by the tightest security guard that had ever guarded a missile before firing. It stood as big as a building of fifty stories, and was almost as broad at its base as that same building. A modified Saturn, clustered engined, aswarm with men probing its innards. No slim beauty this, but a beast of burden, ugly and utilitarian, the end product of eighteen months of preliminary shots and tests. "It's a beast," Stan muttered, more to himself than to be heard and answered.

"It sure is," Ken agreed, with an altogether different inflection. Stan looked at him quickly. The younger man's face held subdued excitement. He looked abashed momentarily, then defiant. His voice was almost sullen when he said, "Well, anyone who thinks at all knows what it is."

Stan said nothing for several moments and then murmured,

"I wouldn't think about it too much if I were you, Ken. Not too much."

Ken seemed to dig himself into the ground, to brace himself, but Stan said no more, turning and walking away toward the transportation pool jeep he had commandeered.

At five-fifteen Stan called home once more. There was a note of fear in Sue's tone when she recognized his voice. No one else would have caught it.

"I think I'll grab a bite down here, honey. Got behind in paper work," Stan said lightly, knowing he didn't fool her.

"All right. Will you be la . . . I mean, do you have your key, or should I leave it open?"

"Lock up, honey," he said gently. "I have the key. How's the little bit?"

"Great. Ate a whole jar of squash! Can you imagine anything human liking squash?"

After he cradled the phone he sat with his hand on it for several minutes, as though it were the head of the little squash lover. The secretary looked in to announce that she was leaving, if he had nothing else. . . . He waved her off. Ken was there by then and they went down to the cafeteria together. This time the game of hearts was for a nickel a point and made up of mostly supervisory personnel. Stan lost one dollar twenty cents. The game went past the dinner hour and into the night shift. Intermittently the speaker advised them of the progress of the shoot, and just before the last light of day faded away, Stan excused himself and walked outside.

The sky was streaked with high, multicolored stratus clouds, shimmering radiantly against the background of deep, luminous, greenish blue. No stars were visible as yet. Stan could make out the jetties and the dock where the shrimp boats had homed for the night. He counted them slowly, nine; all of them had come home safely. Across the finger of water from them, the electronically outfitted cutter was ablaze with light, floating serenely past the fleet of ancient high-masted boats, as a ballerina would move past silently disapproving grandmothers condemning the world from the safety of a secluded porch. The wind had a chill to it now that the sun no longer contributed heat, and Stan shivered. Slowly, reluctantly, he let his eyes turn to the gantry where the vapor-wrapped beast continued to be held forcibly with the umbilical and the gantry cables. The searchlights were already on it, assaulting it from all sides, as though the beams were responsible for its upright position. Stan stared at it several seconds before he became aware of a second presence.

"It bugs you, doesn't it, Stan?" Ken's voice was low and not the voice of a subordinate but of a friend.

Stan tried to imagine them in a boat on the St. John's, with plugs tugging at their lines as they reeled in waiting for the big one to lunge. In that capacity Ken was his friend; here, on the Cape, Ken was one of the others, one of those who found glory and pride in the beast. Stan shrugged and muttered, "It's a beast."

He would have re-entered the building that housed the cafeteria, but Ken's fingers were on his arm and he waited.

"Just be a realist for a minute, will you, pal?" Ken pleaded. "I saw the look you gave me a while ago. You think I don't know about it? I know what's going upstairs tonight as well as you do, even if I don't qualify for the briefings. We all know. And it's a cold, hard fact that it has to go and it has to be successful. You know *they* rendezvoused in space just ten days ago. And since then, not a peep. Just what do you suppose they're doing up there? Making borsch?"

The sky had darkened perceptibly during the few minutes they had been out, and now the last lingering light flickered red on Ken's face. Deep frown lines shadowed it, turning the boyish contours into deep valleys and high, flushed ridges. Stan smiled grimly and reminded him, "I said, don't think about it, fella. Come on, let's raise the ante to a dime a point and see if we can't liven up that game inside."

At nine-thirty the voice intoned, "T minus seven hours, fourteen minutes and holding."

Stan finished the hand he was holding and paid out his last quarter. He left the game to call Sue for the last time that night. She was reading a mystery.

"Don't sit up with it too late, honey," he said. "You know how you get carried away."

"I'm half through it," her voice came back, "and I don't see how I could put it down now. There have been three murders already and it's beginning to look like there won't be enough characters left for . . ." Her voice stopped and quickly she changed the subject. "I forgot to tell you, there's a letter from Mother. She'll be here the first week of June."

"Hey, that's great! I'll make a note to call Johnny on the Pelican. We'll charter it one day while she's here. Let her see some real fish."

"She'd love that."

He told her goodnight and they exchanged silent kisses and he hung up. Sue was a good kid, he told himself emphatically. Really a good kid.

He left the building and climbed into the jeep. The count had resumed after half an hour this time. It was three miles to the partially buried blockhouse just above the high-tide mark on the beach. There was a feeling of activity even on the outside of the concrete structure. Stan stepped inside and waved to an Air Force colonel, who came forward and clapped him on the shoulder.

"Hi, Stan. Come on outside. I've been in and out of this so much tonight that the mosquitoes are advertising me as a cheap thrill ride. Look at 'em swarming tonight."

"It's the north wind," Stan said. "Brings them down from the groves on Merritt Island. Come on down to the beach. They won't be so bad down there."

The colonel waved a vile cigar about him, smoking the insects away as they walked to the edge of the water. "Nice night here," he said and put the cigar back between his teeth.

"Yeah," Stan agreed. "Wanted to tell you, Sue's mother is coming in June. You and Thelma want to help finance a charter boat for some deep-sea fishing?"

"Say! That sounds pretty good! Remind me when the time comes."

They stood together, their backs to the Cape and its activities as if they were unaware of it. The cigar burned down as they stood, and finally the colonel took it between his thumb and index finger and flicked it out over the water. It vanished without a trace or a sound. "Not what we dreamed of ten years ago, is it, Stan?" the colonel said softly.

Stan grunted and kicked at the sand.

"It's a hell of a night," the colonel said bitterly and turned to retrace his steps toward the blockhouse.

At midnight Stan was kibitzing a game of chess between an army major and an electronics engineer from one of the other companies. The disembodied voice proclaimed the hour adding, "T minus four hours, fourteen minutes."

The major checked the engineer and cursed when the engineer countered with a queen move that ended the game in mate. The three of them moved toward the coffeemaker and sat down again with steaming mugs and talked about women, cars, kids and the dock strike back in New York.

Three A.M. Stan sat behind his desk in the darkened office and he smoked. "T minus one hour fifty minutes," the voice said. Sue would be curled slightly, on her left side, her left hand under her pillow, her right hand on the spot where he should be. Stan could see her. And he could see the little likeness of her, on her knees, toes crossing, hands holding down the crib, one thumb conveniently near the rosy lips that mewed now and then in sleep. Tomorrow—today—they would go to Lake Poinsett, and Sue would conceal her fear of the giant rattlesnakes, and they would fish and later he would fall asleep out in the open, under the sky, and she would read and warm the milk for the baby in the contraption that plugged into the cigarette lighter of the car. Then he would wake up and she would smile and tell him how his line whistled through the water as a big bass carried his plug to the bottom of the lake . . . and most important, her eyes would be filled with love, and there would be no reproach in them.

Stan ground out his cigarette and left the office. He walked toward the blockhouse. Very faintly he could hear the voice say, "T minus one hour, thirty mintues."

The mosquitoes whined and buzzed and bit with stinging ferocity. He slapped at them absently and walked on. A guard stopped him once and told him to get somewhere right away. T minus one hour. The blockhouse was filled almost past capacity. Beside the main control bunker, it was the one most advantageously situated for a good view—even using the television, as all of them would do, since the view slits had been covered for this one. Ken pushed his way to the door when he sighted Stan. His eyes were very bright with excitement.

"God!" he said, "let's get out of here until the last minute. The lousy air conditioning wasn't meant for three thousand people crammed in the place."

They went to the beach and sat on the hard-packed sand. The mosquitoes were kept back by the breeze coming from the dark, hissing waters. Stan told Ken about the fishing party and invited him to be the sixth and last member of it.

For perhaps five minutes their conversation was about fishing, and then they became silent. Behind them the voice reached out to remind them, "T minus fifteen minutes." Ken rose and brushed the sand from his pants.

"Coming?" he asked.

"In a minute," Stan said. Ken left him alone.

"T minus ten minutes and holding," the voice floated out.

The sky was lightening slightly and Stan watched a dim star grow dimmer until it faded altogether. Far out on the horizon he could just make out the beginning of a sunrise, a sliver of paleness in the deep blue that promised the sun would rise again, just as it had yesterday and the day before, and the day before that. He watched the sliver widen and become vivid rose colored and the voice said, "T minus eight minutes and counting." Slowly he rose and brushed the sand off and turned his back on the sunrise to enter the bunker. He remained by the door until the last minute when the guard closed and secured it. Then he leaned against the rough concrete wall and closed his eyes to the ordered confusion that was everywhere in the crowded room. He couldn't see the television screen, nor did he want to.

"T minus one minute," followed by the familiar, inexorable backward counting of the seconds.

In Sue's eyes there would be no censure, no reproach. The building seemed to quiver and then came the blast of noise and the roar and a great shout.

When they left the bunker, it was full daylight outside. The sky was boldly blue, beautiful—and polluted. Silently Stan, followed by Ken, accepted a ride back to the parking lot with four others who were also silent and thoughtful now. Stan settled himself back in the bucket seat of the fiery MG and closed his eyes, not to open them again until they stopped outside his house. Surprisingly, Ken cut the motor and got out also, walking behind Stan into the yard, onto the steps and into the house. Sue stood holding the door for them, and there was no censure, no reproach in her eyes, only love. Stan took her hand and held it tightly for a moment.

Ken walked past them and very quietly opened the door to the room where the baby slept. He didn't enter the room, but stood looking, and then just as quietly closed the door and came back to the living room to stand before Stan and Sue. His face was no longer young and handsome.

"My God, Stan," he whispered, "what have we done?"

"Go on home, Ken," Stan answered tiredly, regretting that Ken had taken the step from immaturity to adulthood and was even now mentally staggering under its immeasurable burdens. "Get some sleep," he said. "We'll be out at the lake later if you want to join us. Go on." He closed the door on his friend, on the world that existed outside and couldn't be allowed to enter. And then he turned again to Sue. One day, he knew, he would return and her eyes would slide past him to fasten on the baby and she would also ask, "What have we done?" One day . . . He held her, his eyes wide open and staring. He very much wanted to weep.

Above them, above the earth in a nearly circular orbit whose aphelion and perihelion didn't vary more than seven miles, rode the nose cone of the rocket, and inside it, just one push of a finger away, nestled the Bomb.

*Sometimes there is no explanation. I tell you this because—
I want to tell you this. Perhaps I had become bored with
statistics. I don't remember if that preceded the story. Possibly it did. Perhaps I merely got tired of seeing a whole
economy, an entire civilization, geared to a thing that doesn't
even exist: an average man.*

The Plausible Improbable

JAMES Jeffrey Wentworth Moore knew when he was going to
die. Also he suspected how. James Jeffrey Wentworth Moore, at
sixty-two, also knew he was a living refutation of all the argu-
ments, hypotheses, and proofs of determinism. In time his very
presence would have sufficed to scrub every theory of causality.
Proponents of the school of probability, moreover, had reason to
shudder as his name became known to them, for he was both
the exception to and undeniable proof of the rule of the statistical norm. Things happened to James Jeffrey Wentworth
Moore that were uncaused, things that ranged far beyond the
chance of probability, and yet, strangely, gave it credence.

His very birth, he was wont to think, had been an improbable
feat. At fifty-two, Mrs. Moore had long since denied herself the
questionable pleasure of counting days when her weeks on the
calendar failed to divide her years into a pattern of twenty-eight-
day cycles. Thus it was that she suddenly became aware of the
child within only after he had been there and growing some
four months. Time running its due course brought about the
necessary development of the foetus and he became James Jeff
. . . But enough of that.

In the first five years of his life James had every conceivable
childhood disease; some of them he repeated once or twice; some
of the things he had a modern virologist would be hard put to
give a name to. The casual reader will shrug and mutter, so do

a lot of brats. But consider: James was the only child of an aged couple who oversheltered him, clasping the sickly child to their bosoms until they must have been as filters through which all bacteria and viruses necessarily had to pass. From what source then the measles, mumps, whooping cough, etc., but improbable or no, they did pass. Dr. Spock could have researched this one child and, using this data alone, produced a tome double the volume of the one extant, which would have been enough reference book for any mother to diagnose everything that resulted in fever and bed, for every subsequent infant born.

From his sixth birthday to the date of this telling, James never had another illness. It was as if a statistical table with the figures of so many hours of bedridden illness had been consulted and in the shortest possible time had been complied with. Suppose one did a week's sleeping at one time, fifty-six hours, and then remained awake the remaining one hundred twelve hours. So it was with the hours, days, weeks, years that a normal person is confined to bed. James was normal; he merely got all his in early, you might say.

Accidents are another matter, of course, and more of them later.

Such was the pattern of his early life; if the book said that the average child had so many teeth by such and such an age, he sprouted the teeth, but only at the last minute. If the average child grew two inches in the year between his fifth and sixth birthday, so did James; however, he grew the two inches during the week preceding the said birthday. There was no area in which he failed to conform to the norm.

When he was seventeen the pattern was strained to a point just short of total collapse. Both his parents were accidentally killed and he became the recipient of a large fortune, being the beneficiary of two double-indemnity policies. Vaguely superstitious, he devised a method of investing the money: He threw a pair of dice and then ran down the daily newspaper listings of stocks and bought into each company that corresponded to the numbers on the cubes. It took quite a few companies to consume the entire one hundred thousand dollars, but each company prospered and within ten years James found himself a major stockholder in the most important, fastest-growing companies in the country. Wisely, knowing nothing about business himself, he left his money alone and let it grow.

Naturally he married, and the girl he chose loved him deeply, bore him a son and a daughter, and continued to love him through the years. But the statistical tables came to bear once more, and, according to the figures, the average man has one-point-seven affairs before his marriage has reached the tenth anniversary.

It was the point-seven affair that turned his luck. It was with a girl he hardly knew, and it was consummated in the back seat of his car. And worst of all, despite his elaborate precautions, it resulted in pregnancy. Had he been aware at that time that the average man sires two and eight-tenths children, he wouldn't have been so surprised when the child was born and diagnosed as subnormal. It was, as near as James could make out from the various conferences with the doctors, about 80-percent normal. His wife and the seven-tenths mistress got together somehow, and between them and their two and eight-tenths children he found himself pauperized. Since his years of wealth were fewer than his accumulated years of near poverty, it is safe to assume that his lifetime average income was precisely that.

After the divorce he joined the army and was almost immediately wounded in Fort Smith, Arkansas. During the next several years he found his true vocation. He learned that he could count on drawing to an inside straight, that he could hold a pair and draw the other two, that he could plunk down a ten-spot on the worst horse in a given race and take home a bundle. After the first mild flutter of excitement at this discovery, he accepted it as a way to make a living, but it was not the thrill that gambling seemed to be to others. Games became harder to locate as his name preceded him, and he became the special target for a gang of roving cat-burglars who seemed to sniff out his trail with uncanny accuracy after each big win. After being cleaned out down to his soiled socks for the third time, he decided winning by gambling was becoming too expensive a way to support himself. Boredom he could have tolerated, but the ennui brought on by witless wins, followed by thorough thieves, was too much.

He renewed his search for that something that would make his life less a matter of things happening and more a matter of taking fate by the handle and giving it a hefty twist. It was then that Professor Limnitz found him.

The professor was an investigator in extrasensory perception for a large privately endowed university, and he seized on James as a trout seizes on the first dry fly of the season.

It took him the better part of two years to convince himself that James had no special talent for clairvoyance or telepathy; however, during those two years James made a discovery. He liked learning.

At the age of forty, then, James entered college. His grades fluctuated erratically between brilliant and exceptionally poor so that when he received his degree four years later he had an average score, the only on-the-nose average score the college had ever graduated. That didn't deter James; he went for his higher degrees with a determination that was fearsome to behold, and in exactly three years four months he received his certificate that proclaimed him Doctor of Philosophy, and he accepted a chair with the very university where Limnitz was still watching with bated breath while students, housewives, and assorted persons were engaged in divining the spots of cards.

Again life appeared orderly and settled, and for several years James really believed he was no more different than any of the other professors. He wrote a short book about his gambling days that overnight became a best seller, and followed it with another that, his publisher wrote scathingly, sold exactly four copies.

In a four-year period he had seven serious accidents, making the total now what any man might expect in a lifetime. Life seemed paradoxical at all times during this period. He was either being honored at the dean's polished table, or reposing sadly in his doghouse. Periodically he indulged Professor Limnitz and submitted to a new test, always run at least two times. He was ready to believe fate finally had forgotten him. But he was wrong; the table of statistics said no. This time James actually caused his own downfall. He published his thesis proving that behaviorism and determinism were flip sides of the weary page that said flatly, I don't know. He was thoroughly castigated, and, even though he had used his own life as proof of his theme, he was denounced as a liar and invited to answer questions at the next session of the Academy of Psychologists and Philosophers.

Surprisingly, it was Professor Limnitz who leaped to his rescue, but since he was discredited by the very nature of his work, his graphs and charts and batteries of tests were held unacceptable. Screaming, he danced up and down on the stage, pointing to his well-prepared Rorschach Test and answers, to his personality-trait charts, his standard revised Stanfort-Binet Intelligence Tests and the Wechsler-Bellevue Intelligence Tests. He had the Alpha Aptitude Tests and others of his own devising, but the members yawned or even grinned openly, and in disgust he fled the stage, first shouting vengefully, "You'll see! This man isn't an individual! He is the personification of the statistical norm! You'll see!"

They twisted James in his own words; they used logic on his statements which were consequently shown to be words without meaning; they brought the science of semantics to bear and proved that he spoke in tautologies. Then the psychologists began, and one by one they proved that he was insane, that he had a delayed Oedipus complex that colored his entire life, having never resolved it satisfactorily, that he was suffering from Freudian repressions that ranged from sexual to sexual; since each and every one of them seemed to return to that point, James was almost convinced that his entire thesis had been the result of the seven-tenths mistress and the consummation of his desire in the back seat of the car rather than in a bed. They pointed out the results of his intelligence tests, ranging from genius to imbecile, his personality tests ranging from the innermost introvert to the outermost extrovert, to the aptitude tests that proved, first, that he had the deft touch of a surgeon, and then again, that he couldn't be trusted to carry one quart bottle ten steps without breaking it on the way. James felt himself flushing hot and then draining out completely and shivering with cold. He alternated between the two until the man seated next to him moved, muttering about the management and drafts.

The last speaker of the evening was Dr. Witheringspoon. The venerable old man made his way haltingly to the center of the podium and stopped, rocking back and forth, not speaking until his rocking motion came to a halt, as if afraid the expulsion of air with words would be enough to overbalance his precarious hold of gravity and topple him backward on the stage.

"Gentlemen," he said finally in his fine, quavering voice, his silver hair flowing about his face angelically, "there is only one way to settle an argument of this nature. Either Dr. Moore has told the entire truth and these tests do prove conclusively that he is indeed the statistical norm, or else he is endeavoring to perpetuate a hoax on this learned assembly. As far as the evidence is concerned, it is obvious that he has lined up convincing proofs." There was an angry rustling in the audience and he held up his veined and one-molecule-thick-skin-covered hand for silence. "Gentlemen," he chided gently. "Gentlemen!" They became uneasily silent. "First, he has documentary proof of his childhood illnesses. Unfortunately, I am not a statistician, but it would seem highly improbable that one child in that environment would have been exposed to such a complexity of illnesses. But in itself that isn't enough." He coughed and sipped his water apologetically before he continued. "Then step by step he has taken us up through his extraordinary life, and you must admit that he has fulfilled each and every requisite of the ordinary, normal, statistical man in every respect, even down to the number of positions he has held and the number of children he has fathered. And each of these . . . ah . . . accomplishments has been methodically and singly achieved."

It must be added at this point that James was thoroughly honest in his self-appraisal and omitted nothing, which may be why the men comprising the audience, albeit they were men of science and medicine and such, were secretly resentful, for obviously to achieve the statistical norm it follows that in order to arrive at the figure of one and seven-tenths affairs before the tenth anniversary, it must be true that some of them had gone over, and how far over is left to the individual conscience, and others must have failed miserably to live up to this goal-on-paper. There were many uneasy glances exchanged that night when this very minor point continually cropped up in dissertation after dissertation.

The good doctor was continuing in this manner: "Dr. Moore has shown that he has fulfilled his obligations insofar as illnesses are concerned, positions, marriage, accidents; in fact, every contingency that might arise has been met on the very last minute that it would still be applicable. I might add, although it is self-evident, that even his physical appearance is precisely that of the statistical man." His smile, turned full on James, was pitying. "Now, gentlemen," he proceeded, "having perused Dr. Moore's monograph repeatedly in advance of this meeting, I have come prepared to submit the final proof by demonstration that this assembly would consider properly conducted and validated." There was an outburst of applause and he smiled gently at his flock.

"Gentlemen," Dr. Witheringspoon concluded in his silvery voice when the adulation became less openly demonstrative, "it remains only for Dr. Moore to die when he is exactly sixty-two years and four months of age."

This time the applause was in the form of a standing ovation and James found himself joining it, swept up by the tide of irrepressible emotion that carried the others. Gradually the full meaning of the doctor's words stilled his hands and slowly he became aware of eyes turning to him speculatively.

"But, gentlemen," Dr. Witheringspoon said, his voice sounding rather like tarnished silver at the moment, "Dr. Moore can't die! He has used up his quota of accidents, and also he has already suffered through all the time allotted the average man for illness." He smiled sweetly at James and bowed very slightly. "Thus," he finished, "I refute Dr. Moore."

James picked his way through the crowd thronging about the aged philosopher. He heard snatches of humorous comments about his possible demise: ". . . impossible for any of the ordinary means of expiration—heart attack, thrombosis, cerebral hemorrhage, cancer . . ." Laughter. "No illness, no accident. He may be forced to be immortal!" Laughter. "Or," almost hysterically, "suffer death from an act of God!" "Or perhaps the very molecules in this room will separate and he'll succumb to anoxia."

James froze where he stood, hearing no more of the wall-shaking expressions of mirth. The uncaused cause; the unrandomization of molecules; the most improbable event of which he could conceive. He left the building in a run and found his colleague from the physics department sitting in his apartment wiggling his toes and drinking vodka from a water glass.

"Possible," that man of science grunted. "Anything's possible. Odds. One in a trillion. Why not? Nothing makes 'em diffuse. Law of Entropy. Name it even if we don't know the bastard. Name everything."

"But has it ever been observed?" James demanded in an unsteady voice.

"Lab scale. Limited quantities, closed space. Fluctuation of density," the physics man said, bored.

James considered it throughout the night: anoxia—deprivation of oxygen . . . closed space . . . limited quantities . . . The next day he resigned from the university and started driving west. He kept all the car windows open until, on the third day, he located a site he regarded as ideal. It was a windswept piece of prairie in the shadows of gaunt mountains. There he pitched his tent, screened on three sides, and, with a sigh of contentment, settled in to live the life of a hermit until he had bypassed the sixty-second year, fourth month of his life.

The days were uneventful: He saw no one, and even air traffic was negligible, represented only now and then by a quickly dispersed white contrail ribbon. Because the wind howled incessantly, keeping the air turbulent all the day and night, he failed to notice it at all on the eve of his departure date. He retired as usual when the daylight failed and the mountain shadow swallowed his car in the distance and advanced toward the tent. When he closed his eyes he thought: two hours, all that remained of his self-imposed exile. He fell asleep instantly.

The first raindrops that leaked through the tent brought a wry grin to his sleep-relaxed face, but abruptly he sat up and consulted his watch. It was eleven forty-five. With shaking hands he lighted his lantern and looked at the top of the tent, now sagging badly, drops forming, dropping, faster and faster. The noise outside didn't even sound like rain, but rather as if somehow he had been moved, tent and all, and put under a waterfall. He sat on his cot, a drop of water on the end of his nose, and he knew that for the first time in his sixty-two years and four months he was about to get rained on. He swung his legs over the cot, and when he found the water already up to his knees he didn't even bother to pull his feet up again.

There is a chilling short story by Jerome Bixby called It's a Good Life. *In it people are forced to keep that phrase uppermost in their minds, and continually remind each other, "It's a good life!" What happens to cause a man to climb a tower and start shooting bystanders? It's a good life! Why does another man engage in wholesale manslaughter on the street? It's a good life! And another to use his automobile as a lethal weapon? Or yet another to make bombs with loving care and leave them in phone booths? Or assassinate a president? It's a good life, brother. It's a good life. It's . . . a . . . good . . . life!*

The Feel of Desperation

MARGE was hungry. She had used her lunch hour to pick up some plastic dolls for the P.T.A. Fall Festival, knowing she would have time to eat between two and three-thirty, before the bank reopened for the Friday evening rush. Now it appeared she was going to have to wait for Mrs. Ashton to come and collect the dolls.

Ralph, the other teller, grinned commiseratingly at her and left. The manager, Mr. Redmon, stood by the door, waiting for the minute hand to click into place, but before he could set the lock, two people appeared. Mrs. Ashton pushed her way to the fore. A tall slender man in a windbreaker followed her closely. Marge sighed her relief.

"Marge, my dear," Mrs. Ashton began at the door and continued with no change in volume as she crossed the floor. "You don't know how I rushed to get here before you left. Did you get them? I've lined up six mothers to make dresses. Did you ask Warren?"

Marge pointed to the carton near the door. "Fifty of them," she said, "forty-five cents each," and realized that she had done it again. Warren had been half-asleep when she returned from the

P.T.A. board meeting last night, and she had been too tired to start the annual argument about the parents' show.

"Fifty?" Mrs. Ashton was saying. "At two dollars, that will bring one hundred dollars. That's fine. I'll just give you a check for these now. Right place for it, isn't it?" She laughed, and began scrawling out the check.

The man in the windbreaker was still standing at the wall desk, thumbing through a small notebook. Marge wished he'd make out his deposit slip, or whatever, and get in behind Mrs. Ashton. She really was hungry.

Without looking up, Mrs. Ashton asked, "Will Warren play for us?"

"I didn't get a chance to ask him yet," Marge said; at the quick look of reproach, she added, "I'm sure he will." He'd swear and have her on the defensive for a day or two, but in the end he would play.

"That's fine! I'll put him down." Mrs. Ashton beamed.

The stranger at the desk was just standing there, probably listening to every word. Marge wished Mrs. Ashton would hand over the check and leave. She'd call home and tell Annie to let the children eat early, then broil a steak for Warren and herself later. He liked to have time for a leisurely martini. That would be the best way . . .

Mrs. Ashton waved the check back and forth, drying it. "Will you be home tomorrow? I have some extra tulip bulbs . . ."

It was ten past two when she finally left, with the dolls. Mr. Redmon locked the door behind her and glanced impatiently toward the last customer.

The man looked up and for the first time Marge saw his face. His features were clear and strong, almost boyishly sensitive, but he was unsmiling. He was taller than Mr. Redmon, probably six feet plus an inch or even two, but that might have been an illusion caused by his slenderness. He wore a gray hat and slacks and a tan windbreaker over a white tieless shirt, and he carried a case that looked more like a toolbox than a briefcase.

The two men were coming toward her. She started to smile, but didn't. Mr. Redmon looked frightened. She noticed for the first time that the other man was keeping his right hand inside his jacket pocket. She felt her face stiffen. Deep-blue eyes held her own.

"Don't get panicky, honey," he said softly, "but be careful, very, very careful." He pushed the black bag across the countertop.

It was as if she had been emptied of all thought and there was only a hollow dread within her. It was happening here at her bank! Her fingers fumbled opening the drawer and then were pushing money into the case and her eyes remained locked with his. It was forever—an instant—timeless—and he was reaching for it.

"That's fine, honey," he said. "Now just as carefully walk around the end of the counter and come out. Bring your purse."

She shook her head and took a step backward, away from him. For the first time she saw the gun pointed at the very still figure of Mr. Redmon. He nodded at her to obey. She walked around the counter and the three of them went back to the small office. The man taped Mr. Redmon's mouth and tied his hands and feet, fastening him to his heavy mahogany desk. He lifted the phone from the receiver.

"Listen, both of you," he said slowly. "I've been thinking of this for a long time, and I'm not going to be stopped. You tell them I have her with me." Mr. Redmon's eyes pleaded and he shook his head violently. The man ignored it. "I don't want to hurt her, but it will be up to them. And tell them," he added distinctly, "the only way they'll get me is dead. Just tell them I said that." He turned to Marge and motioned toward the door.

She didn't move, seemed unable to move. He took her arm. "Look at him, honey. He knows I mean every word."

She looked from him to Mr. Redmon and she found herself walking, the case dangling from her hand where he placed it. Using her keys, her car that was just outside the bank, he drove several blocks to an above-the-street parking lot with four decks. The car wound around the ramp to the top, along the narrow passageway to the rear.

"Come on, honey. We change here." He made her slide under

the wheel to get out by him. He unlocked the door of a blue Ford and she crawled in without being ordered. He reached behind the front seat and pulled out an overnight bag, putting it on the seat at her side before he got in also. "You've been very sensible so far," he said tightly, his gaze darting around at the other cars. "Just a little more now and you can go. Put this on." He handed her a pink blouse, and when she didn't move he edged the gun out of his pocket. "Look, honey, you do exactly as I say or I'll knock you out and dress you myself." The edge to his voice was more frightening than the gun.

She had trouble with her trembling hands as she unbuttoned her blouse, but finally handed it to him and put on the pink one. It was a little loose, not noticeably. At his command she handed him her earrings and stared at the blond wig he took from the suitcase. Impatiently he thrust it at her and she got it on also. Then he put her things and his windbreaker in the case and pulled on a coat that matched his slacks, and added a tie. It all hadn't taken more than three or four minutes.

"What are you going to do with me?" she asked.

He began backing out. "Just do exactly as I say and you'll have an adventure you can tell your grandchildren about."

"They'll catch you. They always do."

"No!" he said intensely. "For once I get to state the terms and I'm not including being caught in them. Either I make it with the money, or they kill me. But they won't catch me!"

Marge shuddered and moved closer to the door.

"There's a sweater and a purse on the back seat. Get them." She was straightening up again when he stopped and tossed a half dollar to a white-coated attendant.

When they drove away, she was shaking visibly, the first reaction of shocked, frightened obedience crumbling. Why hadn't she screamed in the lot? She felt as though she were coming out from a deep dream, only now being consciously in control of her actions. He couldn't act quickly enough to stop her if she could jump from the car at a stop sign or a red light. They were out of the downtown area and she looked out trying to remember the next red light. About three blocks. If she could work the door handle . . . Cautiously she maneuvered one hand behind her back. She couldn't halt her gasp of dismay when he turned from the street into a side street, and then into an alley. He stopped the car and pulled on the brake without turning off the ignition. Hope flooded her. Maybe he'd put her out there.

Casually he said, "I was in a prison camp in Korea and one of the guards taught me a kind of cute trick." His hand reached out and took her wrist as he spoke and his fingers moved up and down as though feeling for a certain spot. Her eyes followed his fingers and then he was bringing her arm up behind her, her hand up to the shoulder blade, and higher. Pain exploded in her shoulder and she screamed. He released her and massaged her back as she wept. "Every day he'd do that until I screamed. Sometimes he'd throw it out of joint, sometimes not. I never knew. Got so I screamed before he touched me. That seemed to please him." Marge sobbed into her hands. He waited until she stopped and then he said, "Sorry, honey. I didn't want to hurt you, but you might as well understand that this isn't a game. Your manager knew I meant it, and you might as well admit now that you do too. If I have to remind you again, you'll not use that arm for a long time. Keep off the door!" He flicked on the radio and drove out of the alley toward the turnpike.

They were on the toll road before the announcer cut into the music. "We interrupt this program . . ." He turned it louder and she listened to a recount of the robbery, complete with their descriptions. Marge stared dully ahead. They were looking for her car, for a man in a windbreaker, and a woman with dark-brown hair. She was a blonde beside a man in a conservative suit traveling in a car filled with vacation luggage.

The music resumed and she said, "You thought of everything, didn't you? But they'll find my car and get your fingerprints from it. They'll call in the F.B.I."

He laughed. "They'll lift smudges from your car, just as they did in the bank. I was very careful." He glanced her way. "There will be roadblocks and license checks; you remember to be just as careful and there won't be any trouble."

"Where are you going to take me?"

"You stay until I think I can make it alone."

Her shoulder ached and there was a tightening in the back of her neck that she knew would bring on a violent headache within hours. The miles changed at an alarming rate, and her expectations of an early pursuit faded as the monotony of the wind-filled ride wore her hopes to nothing. There had to be something he had overlooked. She leaned her head back against the seat and shut her eyes, trying to think.

At four-thirty he pulled off to the side of the road. "I have sandwiches," he said pleasantly as if out for a Sunday picnic, "and a thermos of coffee. You did miss lunch, didn't you?" His voice was low-pitched, naturally soft, the sort of voice that was never heard in a group larger than three.

The headache had arrived by then and she nodded briefly. While they ate, he studied a road map. "There's a tollgate ahead about four or five miles," he said. "They'll probably be looking over all cars. Now listen. We are Mr. and Mrs. Robert Thorne, from Gary, on our way to Raleigh, North Carolina, to visit your parents on our vacation. They might search the car, but I don't think they'll go through the luggage unless they get suspicious. So," he looked at her levelly over the paper cup of coffee, "if you want to get back to your husband and those two children again, don't make them suspicious." He watched as she sipped the steaming coffee. "What's wrong? You sick?"

"Headache," she answered.

He reached across her to the glove compartment and found a bottle of aspirin. It was half-empty. He shook out two and handed them to her, watching until she swallowed them.

When she finished her coffee, he put the thermos on the seat between them. "Gives us a real homey touch, doesn't it?" He worked the car back into the traffic, heavier and slower now. "They're stopped up there, all right," he said, grimly satisfied.

Marge felt herself tensing and she worked her hands together, feeling the palms moist and clammy.

"What's your husband do?" he asked and she started at the sound of his voice. "Ease up, honey," he murmured. "Tell me about your husband."

"He's a classified salesman for the telephone company."

"Away a lot?"

"He travels in the state."

"Make good money?"

"Yes," she said sharply. "Why?"

"Just wondered. Announcer said you were the mother of two kids. If he's such a hotshot why are you working?"

"That's none of your business!"

"Granted. Own your home?"

"Please," she cried. "Leave me alone! I can't talk!"

"Oh, yes you can," he snapped. "I asked if you own your home. You talk if it chokes you."

They were driving at twenty miles an hour in spurts, and on both sides drivers were honking their horns and hanging out the windows trying to see what was happening ahead. Marge's rigidity had decreased at the persistent questioning and she understood why he intended to keep it up.

"We have our own home," she said.

"Keep talking. Tell me all about it. When you got it, how much, what kind of furniture."

His hands gripping the wheel showed white at the knuckles, and a stab of fear went through her. What if he should panic? He might start shooting, or might try to break through the roadblock. She had seen it on television and in movies, and they always got killed. Almost hysterically she chattered about the house. It was four years old, split-level with hemlocks and junipers. The lower level was the workroom where Warren once made some lawn furniture that they didn't use. Joanne had a birthday party on the terrace last week. She was ten; Larry was eight and played Little League ball, first base unless Hank showed up, and then he played in the field.

The car in front of them was moving again and he jerked their car as he followed. Marge's voice faltered. What had she been saying? They stopped in sight of the tollgate and she thought, Now! The police would recognize her. She had to be ready.

"Split-level!" he snorted in disgust.

"What's wrong with split-levels?" she said, staring at the car ahead, willing it to move on. The line moved like a measuring worm gathering itself in, inching forward, stretching out again. A uniformed officer approached the car in front of them and spoke with the driver. On the other side another trooper glanced in the rear.

"Goddam it! I didn't say anything's wrong with split-levels—if they are on hillsides!" The robber yelled and the officer at the rear of the other car turned to look.

Marge stared at him terrified. She started to speak, but her tongue was frozen and nothing came out. He said, still in a loud, rough tone, "If you have to have a split-level, dammit, have it! But don't expect me to like it!" The policeman was within a few feet of them and she knew he could hear every word. "Now if you'll just shut up about split-levels for the rest of this trip. . . . Sorry, Officer."

"O.K., Mac. License, please." He studied the license and compared the statistics to the man before he handed it back. Briefly he glanced at Marge, and she trembled with anticipation. He must see that something was wrong! She felt tears forming in her eyes and inside she was screaming, I'm Marge Elliot! Look at me! See the wig! But he turned from them and flicked his eyes over the thermos and the luggage and fishing gear in the back, and waved them on. She would scream! She'd make them notice! She felt his hand tighten on her wrist and she went limp.

They picked up speed almost immediately. She felt weak from frustration. "You think you're so damned smart! I hope they catch you and let me testify. I hope you rot in jail for the rest of your life. You'll never get to spend a cent of the money."

"Wasn't planning to anyway," he said cheerfully and began to whistle, "Oh, we ain't got a barrel of money . . ."

"You've had good luck, but it won't last," she continued, oblivious of the song, knowing only her rage at the stupidity of the troopers, at the clever way he manipulated her, making her play along with the grim farce, at her own cowardice.

"What's the name of your subdivision?" He was ignoring her outburst as if she were a petulant child.

"Pleasant View," she said.

"Oh, my God! Pleasant View!" He grinned broadly at the flush that raced across her face.

It was the first time he had smiled and it made him look incredibly young and vulnerable. Marge shivered at the thought. Him vulnerable! She thought of Warren, and irrationally she wondered if he would give Larry and Joanne their dinner on time. They liked to eat at five. What would he tell them? Mother is going for a ride with a bank robber; eat your pork chop. She shook off the thought. They were with Annie. He would be with the police somewhere, waiting to hear, smoking too much and swearing viciously, his face unshaved-looking by now and dark with anger. Had he sworn so when she met him? She couldn't remember. Probably not or she would have been shocked by it. Yea, though I walk through the valley . . . She pushed that aside also. That was her mother speaking through her mind, the conditioning of her childhood, behind her and meaningless now. It shouldn't be; she was very active in church work. She wished passionately she could return to the time when she knew someone would be there to take care of things when there was trouble. For so long she had been self-sufficient, needing no one; where was that strength now when she did need it?

She was roused from her thoughts by the slowing of the car, and reluctantly she opened her eyes. They were stopping at a filling station. She kept her eyes turned away from him so he couldn't see the sudden hope that bloomed in them.

"Forget it!" he said in a whisper. "You're not getting out, so relax." He told the attendant to fill it and they sat side by side as the gauge clicked and the bell rang, as the spray covered the windshield and was wiped off, and they were again on the highway. The attendant had not looked at her once.

Marge felt that suddenly everything about her was too tight; her necklace was choking her and she pulled at it, finally taking it off and putting it on the seat between them. Her fingers twisted her rings around and around and she became aware of the moistness of her hands, and the heat of her girdle against her body. Her skirt was too tight, the band cutting into her waist, and her watch was uncomfortable on her wrist. She knew her feet were swelling; she felt herself swelling all over. The diamond on her finger caught the light and flashed as she turned it, and impatiently she pushed it around so only two narrow gold bands showed. There were red marks on the palms of her hands where she had gripped with her nails. She looked at the watch and compared it to the car clock, not believing it was running at all. It was Warren's Christmas gift from five years ago. "Go buy yourself a watch. Have it inscribed and everything. Pick out a nice one." In spite she had picked out an exceptionally nice one and now she stared at it dully, and ran her finger under the band, relieving the pressure of it on her skin.

"Are you all right?" His voice startled her and she jerked reflexively. "There's a rest park ahead," he said. "We'll get out and walk up and down a few minutes. Don't faint on me now!"

Had she been near fainting? She thought probably she had. The tightness had gone into her chest by then and breathing was a labored business. The car stopped and they were walking briskly, his hand firm on her arm, his steps setting a fast pace. Another car pulled into the small park and he was stopping her before a rustic brown outhouse.

"I'm going to stand right here," he said curtly. "Don't get cute!"

There was nothing there. Nothing. Rough log walls, a smooth wooden seat with two covers, paper . . . Tears filled her eyes as she looked about wildly, and she felt defeat once more. She remembered her watch and yanked it off, leaving it on the seat. The newcomers were exercising a small dog, the man whistling cheerfully, his wife throwing sticks for the dog to retrieve. Marge walked back to the car, at his side, keeping her eyes on the ground. His grip was painful on her arm; the two other people ignored them, and they were driving away again.

"What did you do?" he demanded after they were again on the road. His fingers clamped on her wrist in a brutal grasp.

"Nothing."

"You're lying! I could see it on your face. You were scared and pleased with yourself. What did you do?" He was holding his anger under tight control, but it showed in the way he gripped the steering wheel, in the working of his jaw muscles, in the steely fingers that paralyzed her arm, abruptly letting go and flinging it from him. He said no more until the park was out of sight and the emergency lane was clear of cars on both sides of the road. Then he pulled out of the driving lane and stopped the car. "Tell me!" His eyes burned into her and she thought he was going to bring out the gun and shoot her.

"Nothing," she whispered. "There wasn't anything in there! I couldn't do anything!" She felt her heart beating as though it were going to stop completely after a last wild adagio of its own. Without reason or forethought she twisted in the seat and began to fumble with the door. She had to get out! He pulled her back and slapped her, snapping her head back. She fell halfway across the seat with her face pressed down against the plastic of the covering. "Please," she cried, "let me go! Please let me out. Tie me up, or knock me out, or anything. I have to get out! I can't stand any more!" She sobbed violently until there was nothing left in her, and she again became aware of him, of the futility of her hysteria. Wearily she pulled herself up and groped in the purse for the handkerchief she had seen there.

"You've been saving that for a long time, haven't you?" She raised her eyes at the quiet of his tone. He sat smoking calmly, not touching her or even looking at her. His anger was gone, leaving his thin face thoughtful and withdrawn, almost resigned-looking. "What's the matter, honey, can't a woman have a cry once in a while in a split-level in Pleasant View?" It was as if he weren't talking to her, or even thinking of her, but of something far away. The car came alive and rolled back onto the highway.

"Leave me alone. Just leave me alone."

"Sure, honey. How old are you? Thirty-one, thirty-two? Doesn't matter. Your type I know," he said expressionlessly. "Out of school, into the marriage parlor, a few trips to the maternity hospital and presto, all through being a woman. Soon as the kids are old enough to start school you go to work, and for the rest of your lives you're as independent as hell. What makes you so damned afraid of being a woman?"

She was too tired to protest. It was pointless to argue with a man who had a gun in his pocket.

He told her to fix her makeup. She obeyed silently. Then he said, "We're leaving the toll road the next turnoff and I want you to lie back with your eyes shut. You're a mess. I don't know how serious it was letting you out back there, and maybe I'll have to make you tell me about it. So be good to yourself and do it my way now."

The phrase "might have to make you tell . . ." droned through her mind. She wouldn't tell him. He couldn't make her tell. She moved her shoulder imperceptibly, and the instant stab of pain made a mockery of her resolution. She couldn't remember ever being hurt deliberately before. To be hurt and made to cry out and cower before him like a common whore—the word flashed into her mind, startling her—just because he was big and had a gun . . . She hoped she'd see him chained and helpless. She would sit in the witness chair and tell them how he hit her and she'd be the calm one and he'd know he was going to prison because of her. She wouldn't tell him! Not even if he did hit her or twist her arm . . . She cringed at the remembered pain, and at the thought of breaking again under his will. She couldn't humble herself again to him! She couldn't!

She was too afraid to lie outright. He'd know. He might even kill her if she lied now. At first she had been terrified and it had worn off, and then he had hurt her and frightened her again, not the same way. She had become afraid of the pain and the humiliation of being hurt, not of being killed. Now she thought she might not live to see Larry and Joanne again. She felt her throat constrict but she had no more tears, no more emotions to spend. She lay with her eyes shut, trying to plan.

"Why did you do it?" she asked after a long silence. "You said you weren't planning on using the money."

"That's right. But I needed it."

"Most people don't take up robbery. Most people are willing to work for the money they need."

"Work!" he said contemptuously. "You mean most people dream up ways to steal it without running the risk of arousing suspicions."

Marge swallowed her quick retort and said meekly, "I thought it might help if we talk. I won't try anything, I promise."

"I bet."

"About the rest park . . ."

"Later," he snapped. "There's the tollgate. Be asleep!"

She tried to look dead. The car stopped and change was jingled and he asked about a good restaurant. Inwardly she could almost laugh. Him asking about a restaurant like the average tourist! He was so clever, not overlooking a thing. And she had outsmarted him. When they caught him, she'd get the credit for keeping her head and giving them a lead.

He turned on the car lights and reduced speed as they approached the town. "About the rest room?"

"I left my watch in it," she said defiantly.

"I see. With your name on it, no doubt."

"My first name," she said. What if the woman merely kept it? Or if she handed it in and the police merely put it way down in a lost-and-found drawer? Just Marge and Warren on it; who would comment on that, or connect it to the robbery?

Music blared from the radio and he turned it down.

"Well?" Marge said. She turned away from his blazing eyes.

"You want a medal? I don't believe you!"

"What do I care whether or not you believe me! I've done nothing wrong!" She took a deep breath and said more calmly, "I told you I'd cooperate and I will. Not because I want you to get away with it. I just don't want to be hurt again and I don't want anyone killed. I hope they catch you and execute you!"

"And you'd testify?"

"Gladly."

He laughed abruptly, stopping it almost as quickly as it started. "O.K., that's fair enough. We know where we stand. I'll try not to hurt you so you can return home and send your kids to school so they can grow up to become good substantial citizens like their parents. The boy can be like his father and the girl like you, making the same meaningless tracks on the same endless treadmill."

"That's insane!" Marge cried. "You make it sound shameful to be normal." She shook her head angrily. He had no right. He made her life sound hopeless and without purpose or meaning. Desperately she said, "You're sick. You said you were in a prison camp. They did something to you. They must have brainwashed you without your realizing it."

"Let's drop it," he cut in rudely. "The news is on."

They listened silently to a summation of the day's happenings and a brief rehash of the robbery, with another description of both of them. Her car had been located and had given no clues that could be termed helpful.

No mention was made of her watch.

They stopped at a drive-in and had hamburgers and coffee. Besides the coffee they drank, he had the thermos filled for later use. Then they were speeding on the highway again.

Away from the turnpike she became aware of the mountainous nature of the countryside and wondered vaguely where they were. It didn't seem very important. They had been driving over eight hours and she was too tired to care. Before the silence became too heavy to interrupt she asked, "Are you married?"

"Isn't everyone?" he said cynically.

Marge followed it up quickly. "Do you love her? Is the money for her?"

"A kid gets taken out of college and told to kill or be killed," he said instead of answering directly. "Finally he comes home and there's a girl he kissed in another lifetime smiling at him holding a ring in one hand and her panties in the other. Bang, he's married and has a family. No time to think or wonder what the hell it's all about. I don't know. Maybe I did love her, maybe I still do. I don't know. It doesn't matter. I had to get out of it. She'll use the money until she finds a new guy to conjure it up and hand it over in exchange for the privilege of being told what to do. It's not her fault," he added, sounding sad. "She does what she has to. I guess we all do."

"If you didn't like it, you could have changed it without this. Others do."

"Do they? Or do they just change partners and go on dancing to the same tired music?"

"That's going to sound pretty stupid when they put you in prison."

"I'm not going to jail. Remember, honey?"

She felt a chill at the sureness of his voice. "I suppose," she said quickly, "you'll issue bulletins from time to time telling the rest of us about the better life, now that you've found it."

"People could use them, don't you think?"

"The first step, of course, is to rob a bank. A man can't just run off; he has to provide for his family."

"Honey," he said mockingly, "don't you realize that's all most men are doing now? Providing. How long since you thought of your husband as a man and wanted him?" His laugh was harsh when she sucked in an indignant breath. "Bulletins!" he said. "That's an idea. First I'd kick out all that extra junk—P.T.A. meetings every week, ladies' auxiliaries, socials, and I don't give a damn if they are for the church, charity or your old Aunt Suzy. A man gets tired of having his wife just coming in, or going out, or too busy on the telephone committee, or plain too tired. And every time a woman used sex as a club, she should be knocked up so she'd have nine months to meditate on its real meaning. There'd be damn few women able to hold jobs. Sex wasn't meant to be a club or a reward, and every time your men lose another round, you despise them a little bit more."

"Stop it!" she cried. She bit back her denial. She wouldn't give him the satisfaction of arguing with him. Why was she even listening to it? What did he know about her and Warren? After fourteen years no woman got excited . . . She clenched her fists and drew up the image of Larry and Joanne, but her own plan to broil steaks and have martinis kept intruding. She knew Warren would have taken her afterwards, and then she would have told him about playing the piano for school. And the robber had heard back in the bank. He knew.

"I'm through. It's no good anyway," he said tiredly, the mockery and bite gone. "We're all on the same merry-go-round and it's going too fast to see beyond the next horse, too fast to realize that the same paths that lead to it can take us away. Once you're on and the music starts, you don't get off again."

She glanced at his brooding silhouette. You did, she thought. They drove and she became numb with fatigue. She put on the sweater and tried to arrange her legs so she could be more comfortable. She must have dozed, for suddenly he was awakening her. She was dizzy with the motion of the car.

"Want some?" he asked, offering her coffee. She shook her head and huddled against the seat. "It will warm you," he insisted.

It wasn't worth quarreling over and she drank it even though it was sweetened and bitter. "We'll stop in about an hour," he said. "There's a city about forty miles ahead and we'll find a motel." She stiffened and drew herself up and he laughed bitterly. "Don't be a damn fool. After I get some rest, you're out of it."

"What do you mean?"

"Just that. There were sleeping pills in the coffee. They won't take full effect for an hour or so and you'll sleep about eight hours. By then I'll be gone." He sounded very tired. "When we get to the motel I'll help you in. Don't start yelling or anything if you wake up and find me helping you. If we have to pull out because of anything you do, I'll kill you." His voice, desperate in his weariness, sounded of truth.

Sleeping pills, she thought. It would look perfect. A man and his wife not able to keep driving. He'd help her and no one would notice anything. Occasionally she took sleeping pills and rolled about for hours before they had any effect on her. What if he overdosed her? If she could vomit them up . . .

"Relax, honey," he said, almost gently, and one of his hands covered hers in her lap. "Don't be scared now. You've been very brave really. I couldn't tell from watching you a few times how you'd take it. I thought I might have to keep you out cold the whole trip, but you've been fine. You can be proud of yourself. Someday you'll look back on it all and wonder if it really happened. You'll be a hero, on television, in the newspapers. Maybe a national magazine will buy your story. All the women in your subdivision will be jealous."

He continued to talk quietly, keeping her attention for a long time before her mind began to wander away. "No one should have to take pills to sleep," she murmured when his words ceased.

"I know." His fingers pressed her hand.

She was drifting along a wooded path, feeling alive with excitement at what awaited her at the end . . . It was so nice not worrying or planning, knowing someone was taking care of things. Her hand rested passively under his, the warmth of it spreading through her body. She sighed and let her head relax against his shoulder.

She felt his hands on her and she was walking, haltingly. "Does this look all right, honey?" She made the effort to mumble, "Fine." "O.K., just put the bag down there," he said to someone else and she drooped on his arm. She was unutterably weary and her time sense was gone. He put her down on the bed and pulled a cover over her.

"I'm sorry," she started thickly, and subsided when his hand removed the wig, stroking her hair, pressing her head back down.

"It's all right," he whispered. "Sleep."

The dream returned. They were very far up the path and the merry-go-round was nothing, a blur in the distance. He was close to her and the excitement was a glow that enveloped them both and she slept deeply wrapped in his male warmness.

"Marge! Marge! Are you all right?" Someone was shaking her and shouting. She was too heavy and tried to pull away. Another voice, "Take it easy, Mr. Elliot. The doctor's coming." She climbed up through layers of mist that held her back and rough hands hauled at her and cold wetness shocked her face. "Darling! Wake up! What did he do to you?" She moaned softly and worked at opening her eyes. "It's all right, Marge," Warren said. "They got your message. They're chasing him right now. He won't get away." He was sitting on the side of the double bed pulling at her.

She stared at him and shook her head. "They won't catch him."

"Snap out of it, Marge! You're safe now. Listen!" There was a distant, lost sound of a siren somewhere in the gray dawn, and as Warren shook her, Marge heard the rapid, faint reports of guns firing. They sounded once more. The siren's wail stopped abruptly and the morning became silent again.

She slipped from Warren's hands and lay back on the bed. She was fully clothed and very, very cold.

"Where is that Goddam doctor?"

Outside someone was shouting, ". . . over the cliff . . ."

Marge squeezed her eyelids together but couldn't contain the tears behind them.

"Don't cry, Marge. Please," Warren said helplessly. "It's over now. You heard. He's dead. You'll forget when we get back home, back to normal. Please, don't . . . Did he . . . did he do anything . . . ?"

She shook her head blindly, unable to speak. When he leaned down and touched her, she jerked away from him and buried her face in the pillow where the man's head had rested.

It happens occasionally that I don't know what one of my stories means until it is done. I will know everything that takes place in it, how the people feel and react with each other, what parts of it need emphasis, what parts need understatement, and still if I were to try to sum up the statement being made, I would be unable to, or wrong. This story is one of those. It felt right. It played right when I visualized it from start to finish. I had done all I could to translate the scenes I saw into words, and on rereading, the words evoked the same scenes. But I didn't know why the parts were right for it. My husband, Damon Knight, says there is no such thing as a story. There is the story the writer believes he is writing, and there are the stories the readers think they are reading. They might not all be the same story, although they are the same words. I hope readers will find the same story in this one that I found after thinking about it for a long time. It is one of my favorites.

A Time To Keep

HARRISON had been with the English department of the university for twenty-five of his fifty-five years, and for twenty-two of those years he had been a widower; beyond that no one seemed to know anything about Harrison. He had a penchant for turning the conversation from himself, not as if he had anything to conceal, but rather as if there never before had been anything to be discussed.

He was, away from the university, like a policeman out of uniform, seen with only partial recognition by his fellow faculty members, and never noted at all by his students. In a vague, semiconscious manner he was aware of his own insignificance and once even tried to grapple with it by volunteering to serve on a faculty committee investigating intramural gambling. His contribution to the study lay in a prominent position on his desk for several weeks, then less prominently on an easily accessible bookshelf, from there to a file, and finally was burned, uncalled for and unread. He never volunteered again.

He was sitting at his desk, grading papers, when Miss Frazer knocked lightly on his door. She knocked a second time and thrust her homely face around it. "I said, do you want a lift across the bridge? It's raining."

"Thank you," he said looking up quickly, almost guiltily. "Are you leaving now?"

"Fifteen minutes or so. Don't hurry." She checked his clock over the door with her watch and added, "I'll be in the faculty lounge."

Harrison clipped together the papers he had finished and slid them into his briefcase along with his books. It was four twenty-five. The wind drove the rain against his windows in violent, erratic flurries of activity and he sat watching it for a few seconds, thinking it was kind of Miss Frazer always to remember him when the weather was bad. No one else ever had.

He closed the venetian blinds on the windows then and flicked the wall switch, shrouding the small office in deep shadows with only the rectangular, elongated streak of light that shone through the transom to relieve the darkness of the early October evening. Harrison grasped the door handle and opened the door. . . .

. . . He was walking against the driving rain, his head ducked low in an effort to catch most of the onslaught in his hat brim. The bridge stretched endlessly before him, bare of traffic, devoid of light, only the faint wavering house lights on the far side to show that it did indeed have an end. He felt the cold rain seeping into his shoes, pressing his trousers against his legs in a clammy embrace. His chest cringed back into itself as the frigid water soaked through his suit coat, into his shirt and plastered it tightly against his body. He could feel himself shivering deep inside and lengthened his stride, watching his feet slosh through rivulets of forging water that covered his shoes. The lights seemed as far as ever from him, he thought with a mild thrill of surprise, when he raised his eyes again. Now his thighs felt warm and tight with the strenuous pace he maintained, and incredulously there was a tingle of excitement that ran through him. He lifted his head and let the rain sting his face with immeasurably fast, icy needles. It felt good, and he walked head up in the furious rain. The house lights shone brightly as the wind ebbed, only to fade and become ghostlike as a new curtain of water obscured them once more. Their distance didn't seem to have changed. Harrison walked steadily, unthinking, face on into the rain.

He heard a cry of fear and pain ahead of him before he could see anything in the lightless dusk. Then he did see figures: two youngsters, teen-agers, and an elderly man. One of the boys was nearly six feet tall, looked as if he belonged on the campus football team; he was holding the old man by his arms, smiling. Harrison tore his eyes away from that incongruously sweet smile of the boy to look instead at the other one. Shorter, lighter than the one holding the man, he was rifling through his pockets rapidly, but thoroughly. When it appeared there would be too little to be of consequence, he began to swear in a vicious, tremulous voice and his right hand lashed out to swipe again and again at the pain-contorted face of his victim. The man groaned and went limp, his arms outstretched in the hands of the tall, athletic youth. The boy let him go and very slowly he crumpled to the concrete. Water swirled over his hands, made a rust-colored eddy about his head, was dammed up by his body. The boys turned together and looked at Harrison. The tall one was still smiling, and he looked like an angel discovering the delights of heaven. Harrison turned and ran. There was a door . . .

He slammed the door behind him and leaned against it trying to catch his breath. He turned from it, dazed and blinking in the cold daylight of the fluorescent rods on the ceiling of the hall. His clothes were dry, but he shivered still and his heart was pounding thunderously in his ears, shaking his entire body with its force. Instinctively he looked at his watch and it was four twenty-seven. He drove home with Miss Frazer.

Characteristically, he made an early appointment with his doctor and during the next weeks he managed to push the memory of the frightening hallucination back, behind other memories whose edges were long since blunted with polishing.

The next time was during the Christmas holiday. Snow lay in deceptively soft-looking piles everywhere, and where the streets and sidewalks appeared swept clean there was a glistening overlay of ice. The telephone lines sagged with its weight, the wires encased in half-inch translucent tubing. Trees dipped their branches to the ground and in the night silence the burdened branches cracked and splintered with nerve-shattering rifle blasts of noise. Long icicles pointed pale witches' fingers over every window and gathered in conspiratorial clusters at every corner of the eaves. Harrison sat staring out his study window, looking through a melted spot in the fairyland of frost tracings on the pane. He could see the tops of the university buildings in the distance across the bridge, looking as if they were hung from the indeterminant sky by thin ribbons of smoke from their chimneys. He wished that the holidays were over, had never even begun.

For nearly an hour he sat quietly, his book on his lap unopened, and when he turned his gaze once more to the window the small melted spot had frosted over. He held his hand against the window for a minute or so and looked again. The sun was still diffused to the point of nonexistence by the colorless, formless clouds, and the light had an unreal glow to it.

He had some early term papers to read; several books had accumulated still in their wrappers, and his own library catalogue was incomplete, but he found a growing restlessness overwhelming him. He decided he was hungry, and since the woman who came in to clean and cook hadn't been able to come over the icy roads, he'd have to do something about it himself. A feeling of relief accompanied the thought of being busy. He went through the hall to the kitchen and opened the door. . . .

. . . The riverbank was gentle in descent; nevertheless it was treacherous with its generous coating of ice. He edged along cautiously, sliding his feet several inches at a time rather than lifting them to walk. He heard laughter ahead of him and looked up in surprise. They were skating today. He watched in pleasure as the figures glided and darted effortlessly in a blur of flying scarves and stocking caps.

There were twelve children. He counted them and there were exactly twelve, laughing and shouting as they played. They were all very proficient, more so than the mediocre assortment the ice usually attracted, rather as if they were practicing for an ice carnival. He edged closer.

"There he is!" one of the little ones shouted excitedly. In a second they were all skating rapidly toward him. In consternation he glanced behind him to see if they might have sighted someone else he had missed, but it seemed obvious that he was their target. They converged on him and skates were thrust out toward him.

"I'm afraid you're mistaken," he started, but they appeared not to hear.

"Put them on! Put them on!" they chorused clapping their hands.

"I can't skate," Harrison protested trying to back away.

"How do you know that?" another voice asked interestedly.

He whirled about and stood face to face with a blond, bare-headed girl. She had two red spots on her cheeks from the cold, and her eyes sparkled blue lights. "How do you know?" she repeated.

"I never did it," Harrison said simply.

"See. You don't really know, do you?" she answered logically. "Put them on."

Hands reached out eagerly to help with the skates and then he was skating hand in hand with the girl. They skated out to the center of the ice where the children made a circle around them. The children wore tight, vivid pants and high-necked sweaters in the brightest colors he had ever seen: reds and yellows and blues so dazzling that they hurt his eyes almost. The girl was similarly dressed, her pants a screaming orange, her sweater forget-me-not blue that wasn't as clear as her eyes. He was aware of himself fleetingly, of his baggy old slacks that were no longer presentable enough for school, of his gray, shrunken sweater that had one elbow out. But as he looked into the deep, shining eyes of the girl he forgot; he knew only that he was warm and vital.

"Who are you?"

"Gabrielle. Come, we must lead them."

"Why?"

"They expect it of us. This way."

She led him and they were streaking across the ice faster and faster, and behind them, as if attached with invisible cords, the children followed in a serpentine line. Gabrielle turned on one skate and was facing him, both of her hands in his. "You're quite good," she said.

"Where did you and these children come from? I've never seen you about before."

She laughed and her hair whipped about her head, hiding her face for a moment. She said, "We're leaving them too far behind. Let's go back."

"No!"

She laughed again and was off and away from him before he could turn around. The children were brilliant specks on the white glare of the ice far in the distance. He pumped harder and harder to catch up with Gabrielle. "Wait for me! We'll go to my house and have hot chocolate. It's just over there!"

She smiled over her shoulder and nodded. The children were doll-sized now and he could begin to make out their features once more. He waved to them and they all waved back, their voices, faint with distance, seemed to be joined in a song.

Harrison sang too, feeling a surge of power flow through his legs as he sped over the ice. He felt free and clean and strong and he marveled at his ability to skate so well. Ahead Gabrielle had joined the youngsters and all together they were coming to meet him. Their blades flashed in unison and he looked down to see his own blades cutting through the ice. His heart froze within him. There was a crack, and even as he watched, it grew wider and he could see the swift, black water below. He turned to his left away from it and watched it appear silently, magically, as a thin, black line separating the two halves of the river.

"Gabrielle! Get off! Get off!" he called frantically, but the children sang and waved and he knew they didn't hear. He pointed down at the growing, widening crack, and they laughed. Now they were close enough to see the half-dollar-sized red spots on their cheeks, to see the color of their eyes and the whiteness of their teeth.

"Get off! Off!" he screamed over and over as he clambered for the bank, his feet slipping from under him again and again. The crack now appeared to be frozen lightning, streaking out in many directions, sending erratic patterns up and down the length of the river.

Gabrielle and the children skated on, and beyond them a cake of ice up-ended and disappeared into the torrent. Then another and another was swallowed silently and still they skated toward him. In horror he watched as the cracks appeared on their ice and one by one they were isolated from each other. He was falling again and desperately he lunged out to grab a stump on the river's edge. When he turned again he saw Gabrielle standing still on the other side. Her eyes followed the progress of the cracks and then turned to meet his. She seemed to be waiting. The children, for the first time, appeared to realize what was happening and they turned panic-stricken faces toward Harrison. He could but stare back, the words dead in his throat.

Gabrielle was out of her skates and barefooted, running swiftly across the gaping breaches, gathering them before her. Together they leaped across the last of the cracks and stood on the opposite bank. They didn't look back.

Harrison cried out, "Gabrielle!" She walked hand in hand with the youngsters, diminishing rapidly until he could see them no longer. He ran. He ran along the bank, his skates dropped, forgotten. He had to get across. His feet rang hollowly on the frozen bank and he ran and stumbled and ran again until his breath didn't come, until his lungs heaved uselessly and he finally fell and lay still, gasping. Time didn't exist and it might have been seconds or hours later when he pulled himself to his knees and looked about wildly. There was a light and he crawled to it, slipping and sliding, clawing at the ice, clutching at the air.

His groping fingers found a handle and he fell inside the door almost unconscious. . . .

He stumbled into his kitchen and collapsed into a white enameled chair with a red-checked cushion. Behind him the door swung back and forth whispering past the frame and finally came softly to rest. He looked about him maniacally, hanging onto the tabletop, his breath coming in convulsive gulps and he felt as if his heart might explode. He still felt the cold ridges along one cheek, on both legs and arms and all up his body where he had lain on the ice.

"What's happening to me? My God, what's happening to me?" he whispered. "What's happening?" he repeated under his breath and clutched at his face with both hands as if to blot out the memory.

He had another fruitless session with Dr. Glaston the day before school resumed. Then the finals were in for grading; goodbys had been exchanged with a class of personless students; faculty meetings were posted to plan for the coming semester. Now he attended every meeting there was; he welcomed Miss Frazer's standing offer for a ride home and even accepted her invitation to dinner in her apartment.

He was surprised at himself at being there, and, being there, at enjoying himself. The meal had been delicious and Miss Frazer was amusing. She was nearing forty, a rather square figure that couldn't be glamorized by her expensive clothes. Her hair was graying, but curled about her ears like a girl's. She was new at the university, had traveled a good deal and could tell about it charmingly. Harrison was glad he had come. Miss Frazer was exactly what Dr. Glaston meant when he said he needed amiable companionship, to be alone less. When the clock chimed the half hour after nine, he looked at it in disbelief.

Miss Frazer must have sensed that he was readying himself to leave and very briskly she rose to her feet and said, "You've enjoyed yourself, haven't you? You'll have to come back after the new semester starts. We can play chess."

So Harrison began "seeing" Miss Frazer. Late in February they had dinner and played chess until nearly midnight. When she said, "See you next week?" at her door, it seemed natural to agree. He didn't bring it about; it just happened that way, and it was pleasant to have somewhere to go, someone to talk to. He decided Dr. Glaston had been entirely right, and he found that he was sleeping better, without the haunting dreams that had threatened for a while to make sleep a form of torture.

It was Thursday, dishes were stacked in the sink and the chessboard was set up with a partially completed game. It was her move. She leaned back in her chair studying the board intently, one hand reaching for her cigarette lighter. She flicked it several times and put it back down. "Get a match, will you, please. Second shelf, right side."

He smiled to himself. She hadn't even seen it, had made no move to block his coming Knight fork. He pushed the door to the kitchen. . . .

. . . He left the apartment building uneasily, lingering in the doorway, aware of a foreboding sense of danger. The street was empty with only a fitful squeaking through the bare treetops that made a futile canopy overhead. Still he paused, unable to locate the source of his discomfiture. When he began walking down the street, he was cautious without reason, the not right feeling of things persisted; a primordial fear had roused and was worrying at his consciousness. He stepped off the curb to cross an alley, and before he could back up or get fully across he was engulfed and swept up by a mob of yelling men and women.

Hands pushed at him and bodies pressed against him as he tried to resist the force of the mob. He was carried along by it as a leaf is inescapably a part of the stream that floats it. They were cursing, shrilling, incoherent, infuriated mad men and he was one of them. A wild intoxication flowed through him and he clapped his hand on the shoulder of the shoving man at his side. The man turned to look at him, but his eyes were vacant as if he moved in a trance. His mouth dribbled little specks of sputum from the corners and he cried hoarsely, "Kill him! Kill him!"

Harrison recoiled sharply and was jabbed in the side by a little woman carrying a stick. Her eyes were empty above a working, screaming mouth. She was lost in the swirling bodies. Somehow Harrison found himself half-turned, being pressed onward sideways, and always before his horrified eyes were the vacuous expressions, the calm, almost peaceful emptiness of the upper faces and the filth of the gibbering, screeching mouths. He was yelling too, begging them to let him go, helplessly flowing along with them.

Someone would be trampled to death, he thought as he stumbled and frantically caught at an arm to restore his balance. The police would come and break it up. They filled the streets, overflowing into the sidewalks and yards. On and on they weaved, gaining speed and strength by the second, their voices an intolerable din. Harrison felt he couldn't breathe; he hurt from the constant jabbings he received as he kept trying to shove his way to the side of them. He couldn't see the ending of the long, senseless stream of robotic shapes. Now they were virtually running and he had to run also, or die under their feet. They wouldn't stop if he fell, and he hated them and was afraid of them, knowing that no matter how fast he ran, he was part of them and couldn't leave them behind.

They stopped abruptly, as definitely as a single unit with no preliminary slowing down, no shoving. Only Harrison was caught off guard and his momentum carried him several yards ahead of the rest. The mob had become ominously silent, unbelievably silent. He whirled to his right and saw the inviting blackness of an unpaved alley. He looked again at the mass of stilled bodies as immobile and expressionless as manikins, as if someone had turned them all off. It was as if they waited for further instructions. Nowhere did he see comprehension or even awareness, and slowly he began to edge to the side toward the waiting alley of escape. Their eyes didn't see, but their heads turned almost imperceptibly to follow his progress. A colder terror seized Harrison, gripping his bowels, jerking his stomach spasmodically. He backed away from them almost fainting with fear, and suddenly his nerves could stand it no longer and he screamed shrilly and raced madly down the blackness of the alley. He could hear them as they were released from their trance-like stance, and now he knew it was him they wanted. He ran until his legs buckled under him and he fell headlong through a door. . . .

He fell to his knees gasping and panting for breath. Dimly he became aware of Miss Frazer's hands on him loosening his collar, undoing his belt. He had got away! In relief he opened his eyes.

"Keep breathing deeply," Miss Frazer said firmly. She was tugging at him, apparently trying to back him against the wall, and still dazed, he helped until he was propped up by it. "I'll get you a drink," she said.

The unaccustomed whiskey burned harshly, but the terror melted away, leaving confusion and a sense of embarrassment over making a fool of himself. He avoided Miss Frazer's appraisal ashamedly and started to rise, but her competent hands held him down with his back against the wall.

"Stay right there for a few minutes," she ordered, stared at him for a moment and turned to get the bottle and a glass from the counter. "I think I need this more than you do."

"I'm sorry I frightened you," he muttered, "but I am all right. I stumbled."

"Yes, you stumbled," she agreed dryly. "And your heart decided to run a race all by itself, and you couldn't breathe. Do you know what happened to you?"

"I stumbled," he repeated stubbornly. "And right now I feel like a fool," he added through tight lips. It happened again! he cried to himself despairingly. Why?

Miss Frazer took several steps backward, and when he did get up alone, she seemed surprised. "Harrison, have you done that before?"

He nodded. "But it isn't my heart. I had Dr. Glaston give me a complete check. My heart is perfect." He shuddered violently and looked directly at her in desperation. "Do I look like I'm losing my mind? Am I going crazy?"

"Don't be ridiculous! There could be a lot of things to cause you to fall. Blood pressure. Disease of the inner ear . . ."

"The doctor checked everything," he cut in rudely. "Organically I am in excellent condition. I live through it, but it doesn't take any time," he cried wretchedly. "I go through the door to somewhere else, and then I come back, but it doesn't take any time!"

Miss Frazer frowned down at the tabletop a moment, raised her eyes to meet his and finally said slowly, "I don't know what you're talking about, Harrison. But believe me, I do not think for a moment that you are any more insane than most of us. Now you sit still while I make coffee and we'll talk."

Haltingly at first, with much hesitation over words, he began with the first time it had happened to him. Then more surely when she didn't laugh or interrupt, he continued with words flowing effortlessly until he concluded, "I remember how miserable I felt with freezing rain soaking to my skin. I remember the feeling of the tightness of the left skate. It was almost tight enough to rub a blister. And later I was cold where I had been against the ice. Those things are real! They happened!"

"Walter Mitty's other life was real to him," she suggested.

"But he dreamed of things he wanted to do," Harrison cried. "He was his own hero. God, I hated that man I was! I'm ashamed of him. He—I could have done something about the children. I could have helped that old man. I could have tried to reason with the mob. Do you think I'd daydream about a coward?"

"Harrison. Harrison. You are talking nonsense. No one can control his dreams. You have to believe me, this is a dream of a sort. So you ran. That's one of the classic dream patterns."

Wearily Harrison rose from the chair, and he felt old and tired. Quietly he said, "In my real dreams I never run."

"Don't go yet, Harrison. Are you sure you're all right?"

"I'm sure," he said. "I'm sorry about all this. I didn't mean to . . ." He stared at his hand outstretched for the door and he felt that he couldn't move. Fascinated, he reached out for the knob and again a paralyzing dread mastered him and he was unable to open the door. Suddenly he turned and crossed the room unsteadily to stand at the counter, gripping the edge of it tightly. "I can't seem to open the door," he muttered, despising himself.

"Harrison, I'm going to open the couch and fix you a bed. It makes a very comfortable bed, and I'll give you a sedative so you'll get a good night's sleep. And in the morning I'm going to take you to Dr. Blakesley."

Harrison stood there not answering and she left the kitchen. He closed his eyes tightly a moment and again turned to face the door. He still couldn't force himself to touch it. Panic was rising within him unbearably as he tried, and uncontrollable, atavistic fear made him cower back away from it. He knew he would have lost consciousness, or started screaming, if he hadn't left it.

He lay in the unfamiliar room and drifted aimlessly midway between sleep and wakefulness as the two pink pills she had ordered him to swallow dulled the razor edge of his thoughts. The mob wouldn't have listened to him. It had been a trick of his twisted mind that led him to think they awaited his orders. Running wasn't the real crime. Other people seemed always to know what to do, like Miss Frazer, and his wife years before, and his mother long before either of them. He thought pleasant thoughts about his mother and somehow she grew more like Gabrielle, merging with the girl until only the golden-haired girl remained. She had known what to do, but there had been a difference. Why? He tried to rouse himself from the lethargic nonawareness of his wandering mind and hold onto the question. Why had Gabrielle been different? It was important. He couldn't remember, and trying, he fell asleep.

"Oh, no, you don't!" Miss Frazer said as she poured their breakfast coffee. "You promised me you'd see Dr. Blakesley this morning and you are going to do it."

"You really think I need a psychiatrist then? Just because I fell down and was frightened for a time?"

"Have you opened a door yet?"

Harrison looked behind him at the kitchen door standing open and shook his head. It had been opened by her.

Miss Frazer chatted amiably through breakfast, and in the car on their way to the university where Dr. Blakesley lectured two mornings a week. Harrison wasn't listening to her, and she seemed to realize it, and made no effort to draw him into her soliloquy. There had been something, he was thinking, something he had almost grasped, and missed.

Miss Frazer parked the car and led the way into the Natural Science Building, holding the door for him. Sheepishly he followed her. She hadn't given him a chance at a door all morning. Gabrielle would have, he thought with assurance. Unlike the others, she had given him the opportunity to act first and he had failed. But she hadn't assumed he would. He was acutely conscious of Miss Frazer's startled grunt as he pushed past her and opened Dr. Blakesley's door. . . .

. . . There were eleven other men in the room, many of them drinking coffee. The air was thick with stale smoke and the press of bodies too long in one place. Harrison looked straight ahead stoically, pretending he wasn't listening to the nasal voice inches away from his ear.

"Y'know he done it, Harrison. All that evidence against him. What more do you need?"

He sat without moving, making no sign. The foreman leaned across the table to point an accusing finger at him. "If he gets off, he'll keep doing it. You know that!"

"He might not be guilty," Harrison said stiffly.

"Everybody knows he's guilty!"

"He never denied it!"

"He wouldn't be here if he wasn't guilty!"

Harrison felt a numbness creeping along his body, and incongruously all he wanted to do was sleep. He put his head down on his arms, pretending to be thinking about it. The voices continued persuasively.

"The judge will be lenient, Harrison. It's not like you were sentencing him to die or anything like that."

"But he'll die," he mumbled.

"We'll all die," the other one answered impatiently.

"If he didn't do it, he wanted to. That's just as bad."

"That's as bad as doing it," someone else echoed solemnly, and it was taken up and reiterated over and over.

"We don't know that he did. We don't know," Harrison protested desperately.

"Harrison, we're all agreed that he's guilty. Are you with us?"

"I can't decide."

"Have you ever decided anything in your life?" asked a new voice.

Harrison looked up at the speaker and it was Dr. Glaston.

"I'm sorry, Harrison," he said. "I had to tell you the truth. There wasn't a thing wrong with your heart. I'm sorry."

"I know," Harrison said. Why did he say that? What a curious thing for a doctor to say.

"You really do have to make up your mind, you know. They'll be calling us back soon," Dr. Glaston said gently and returned to his seat.

Harrison licked his lips and met the gaze of the foreman. Mutely he nodded and the Greek chorus rumbled approval. They filed back into the courtroom awkwardly, embarrassed by the stares of avid curiosity their re-entrance aroused. Harrison stood before his seat until they were all present and as one they sat down.

The accused sat turned away from them as if he alone in the room had failed to notice that they returned. The judge cleared his throat.

The prisoner stood and faced them, but Harrison kept his eyes on the straggly hairs on the red neck before him. He couldn't bring himself to look at the tormented face of the guilty man. The verdict was read and a great shout broke out among the spectators. Above and through it rang out the judge's gavel demanding order. Slowly the noise subsided. The man on Harrison's left whistled softly under his breath.

"Betcha he wants us polled," he said knowingly.

"Polled?"

"Yeah. Wants us to stand up one at a time and say it."

Harrison felt the lump return to his stomach where it swelled. The man at his side grinned as if he knew.

"Won't take long," he said wisely. "Then you can head for the john."

They were both silent as the first man, the foreman, repeated, "Guilty," firmly, and then the next, and the next. The prisoner remained turned away from them, only beginning to move toward the light as the man next to Harrison heaved himself to his feet. "Guilty," he said quickly and sat down again. Harrison felt frozen to his chair, only stirring when the judge frowned disagreeably at him. On both sides the men were pushing at him and somewhere to the side he heard, "You better not renege now."

He rose swaying and stared into the eyes of the other man, into the face he knew so well. The face was empty, emotionless, unlived-in-looking. It was *his* face.

He yelled and leaped from the jury box racing from the courtroom, out the double doors in the rear before anyone seemed to realize what was happening. He ran as if pursued by all the devils of hell, but through a void of silence. No one chased. The streets were deserted; not even a dog barked at his flight. He ran to the corner and across the street and nothing moved along its length except him. It wasn't fair, he sobbed. It wasn't fair to make him be the one to decide. The system was wrong! He wasn't a bad man. He wasn't guilty, but was he innocent? No man could decide it. It wasn't fair. Why didn't someone come and stop him? They could stop him if they tried. He pushed himself away from a building and staggered on, wheeling back to crash into it dizzily. He had to keep going.

The sidewalk ended and he plummeted into a wall ahead of him, stumbling down to his knees. He forced himself back to his feet, but stood half crouched over, hunched as if in great pain. His fingers groped blindly for something to hold, finally finding a handle. He gripped it hard and stood stiff and still waiting for his breath to return.

It was a door handle. He turned it and the door began to swing open. He could go through it, let Miss Frazer and the doctor take care of him—the circle completed. He thought about the man back there who looked like him, but was empty and so very, very guilty. He at last recognized the enormity of the guilt. Not of being; that was accidental. But, having being, of the failure to be more than the insubstantial shadow that hovers awhile and then passes, leaving nothing of itself to mark its passage. Not on one single individual in need, not on a woman and their unborn children, not on humanity as an entity. He had failed them all. And now this, the final test, the ultimate decision, the opportunity most men recognize somewhere along the way, but that he had never before faced knowingly.

Deliberately he placed his foot back again and withdrew from the doorway. They would not come. To be forced to choose was not to choose at all. They knew. He looked down the empty streets. It would take much longer to walk back the path he had run before, but he started, and in starting, he felt peace, and he walked straight and tall through the empty streets. . . .

Inside his office the doctor rose as the hall door was pushed open. He didn't recognize the man who paused in the act of crowding in past Miss Frazer, but assuming it was Harrison, he was prepared to see him display the neurosis the opening of doors triggered. He was not prepared to see him slump to the floor—the unmistakable stamp of death already composing his features.

A woman complained that her husband had been cured of alcoholism by the A.A. "When he was drunk," she said, "he was so cheerful and generous." "He's still miserable, but after that prefrontal lobotomy, he doesn't care." If solipsism as a world system is correct, I must be someone's pawn because if I were managing the show, things sure would be different. Ugly as sin, wicked as sin, the wages of sin—I am certain fragments like these are filed in the brain under many labels for reference. Why they are pulled out and joined to each other in those dark recesses to form a story remains a mystery. If only a writer could know his own filing system, could go browsing through the accumulated data there. I am so much smarter, know so much more about everything when I am writing than when I am not. I wonder what other fragments and snatches are at this moment being shuffled, what new stories are cohering.

The Most Beautiful Woman in the World

THE most beautiful woman in the world awakened smiling a soft, secretive smile. Before opening her eyes she touched the pillow where he had been. He was gone, had been as discreet as he had promised; she stretched and smiled, luxuriating in her memories of him.

"I didn't believe them," he had whispered, "but it's true. You are the most beautiful woman in the world."

His hands, his kisses . . . "Ahh," she heard herself sigh, and sat up. She was alone, however; no one had heard. Suddenly she felt that she had to be up, had to see the day, and let the day see her. She touched her cheeks and knew they would be rosy, aglow, knew if she looked in her mirror her eyes would reveal depths: laughing, happy eyes with deepening pools of understanding where a man could forget as if in Lethe's waters. He had said that last night. She had no need for the mirror, no need to check his words; she felt as beautiful throughout her being as he had found her to be.

She got up then and danced to the window, picking up a gold chiffon peignoir on the way. "Hello, day," she said softly, feeling the caress of the cloudlike material as it ruffled and ballooned in the morning breeze.

Before her the trees bowed and she accepted their obeisance, a spark of delight firing her eyes. "Hello, trees! Hello, birds! Hello, world!" she called, still softly, wanting to reach out and enfold the shivering trees, wanting to embrace the world in its entirety. She laughed at herself, hugged her arms about her breasts and pirouetted across the room, alighting sprawled on the pale gold of the bed.

After a moment she raised her head and regarded the bed. Was it an acre wide? She had promised herself that one day she would own a bed an acre wide. Of course, it wasn't. But how much was an acre?

She touched a silver bell and the door opened soundlessly, admitting Felicia; sometimes the door opened even before the bell responded to her touch. She suspected that Felicia had developed extra senses, possibly even telepathy to compensate for her lack of a voice. Felicia was dumb. She wondered if Felicia could hear the bell before it sounded, could hear her thinking of touching it. She smiled at the mulatto and chatted. Felicia touched her arm and she looked at the bruise there. She made no attempt to cover it. She was reminded of a story she had read, or heard, about a duke, or a knight, or perhaps a king whose lady had bitten his neck, scarring him. How proud of the scars he had been! She wished her bruise would not fade, wished she could fence it somehow and preserve it. . . .

Felicia fussed about her, combing her hair, arranging her clothes, making the bed, silently urging her to have her breakfast, and she found that her appetite was marvelously hearty. Someone had found strawberries already, so early in the season, or were they imported from the south? She poured herself a second cup of coffee, adding thick cream, forgetful for a moment of Felicia. The colored girl touched her arm again, gently, reminding her of the Directors' meeting that morning; she had to get dressed.

She shook her head at the long-sleeved dress. Something young and gay, and sleeveless—to show off the two bruises on her arm. She examined them carefully, smiling deep inside as she did. Felicia returned with the yellow swirl-skirted silk that she loved and she let herself be dressed, cooperating now. A touch of lipstick and she would be ready for the Directors. She glanced at the mirror then, but a cloud passed over the sun and the room was shadowed. She forgot to check her appearance and ran instead to the window. She hoped it wouldn't rain until that night, and that it would rain very hard then, hitting the roof with force, with a gusty wind brushing the branches across her windows. Primitive weather, she told herself. That was what she wanted for that night. There had been a golden moon the night before, and the air had been quiet; for this night she wanted weather. The sun reappeared and she nodded, satisfied. It would wait to rain.

Then it was late and the meeting would have started. She walked lightly at Felicia's side, chattering away at the poor girl who could only nod, and smile, and sometimes touch her arm, opening her mouth as if to speak. She never did, though. Felicia left her at the door and she entered the crowded room after pausing to take a deep breath. Directors' meetings always were a strain on her.

They turned to stare at her in her frivolous dress and she smiled radiantly, extending both hands. They didn't fool her. She knew they wished she would go away, take a trip, or busy herself with society nothings, or get married and have children. They didn't want her to take the chair at the head of the long table; they knew they had to smile at her and kiss her hand, and pretend they were delighted with her for being present. One of them saw the bruises and there was an excited clacking among them. A doctor was summoned. She held her head high as he touched her arm with cool fingers that were swift. He rubbed something on the three bruises with a bit of cotton, and it was cooler than his fingers had been. She kept her head high, turned disdainfully, saying not a word about the marks. Then she was seated and the meeting was started.

It bored her and she allowed her mind to wander away from the drone of voices. Sunlight on dust motes caught her fancy and she watched the vortex, counting how long it took for a single mote to be whirled out of sight. At the count of nine it was gone. The voices were continuing, speaking of business affairs that she couldn't even pretend an interest in that day; she leaned back in her chair relaxing, letting her eyes close as if in thought. Now and then one of them addressed her directly and she heard herself answering, calmly, intelligently, but she wasn't there. They were discussing a new process that her company was developing. It would revolutionize industry. Preliminary work had been disappointing, but they were hopeful. She had heard it so many times before, she thought. Sooner or later it worked, and they all made money and had their pictures in the papers and magazines, and then they got excited about a new process, and the older one was forgotten. Yesterday's successes, today's forgotten toys. The notion pleased her and she laughed inside, telling herself to remember it to repeat to him that night.

Her approval was asked for and she gave it in a bored manner, not even bothering to open her eyes through the period of questioning that followed. Someone said they were to make pictures then, and she yawned. Again. She almost wished that she wasn't the world's most beautiful woman. She didn't remember when she had come to accept the title, only that one day she didn't laugh it off when it was suggested, and she knew then that it was true, probably had been true from the start, and knew that it really didn't matter as much as any of them seemed to think. Her real beauty, she had discovered to her surprise, lay deep within her where they couldn't see it, couldn't photograph it, where it didn't matter to anyone else as long as she knew about it.

They went to the photographer's studio, where he, a virtuoso, as bored with it all as she was, directed her to assume this pose, and that, while he manipulated his cameras and lights. She posed for the pictures, wearing the foolish hat they wanted her to, answering the foolish questions the reporters kept asking her. Some of the questions were impertinent, but she kept her good humor, and her boredom, and got past them all in good form. There was admiration on their faces when she glanced at them and she knew she had won the round. These sessions were always like the continuation of the same fight, separated into rounds that were started when she posed, as if trying to catch her off guard when her mind was on the photographer and not on the questions themselves. So far she had come through them swimmingly. The hairdresser brushed her hair back into place and the session was over. The camera was taken away; the many lights were dimmed; the reporters left; the Directors left, murmuring together in quiet tones. She felt very tired and longed for a nap.

Felicia appeared, solicitous and soothing, her open Irish face comforting, and she let herself be babied back to her room, where she lay down to rest for a while. Business was exhausting, she admitted to the girl tidying up the room. Felicia said quieting things and she dozed. When she awakened, the room was darker and she wondered if it were night already. Her lassitude remained with her, and her white garment felt scratchy and rough when she turned restlessly to try to sleep again. She felt very thirsty, reached across the narrow bed, but found no water on the stand. With a sigh she got up and crossed to the dresser where her pitcher was. She raised her eyes to the shadowy mirror along with the glass of water, and with a choking cry she flung the glass into the mirror as hard as she could. She stumbled back to the bed and fell down on it, swirling off to sleep before she could even pull the sheet over her shivering body.

When she woke up again she had vague memories of having been overtired. Felicia hovered about her and she said, "I even dreamed you were talking to me, dear. I'm sorry," she added, immediately contrite for her cruelty. Felicia opened her mouth and she had to turn away, hurt by the girl's attempts to speak. Felicia had awakened her, almost forcing her to get up and dressed for another of the infernal meetings. Why did they have to have this crisis right now when she was caught up in her own emotional crisis? He hadn't come to her last night, and, finally, when dawn had streaked the sky and hope had died, she had fallen asleep with tears on her cheeks. She felt a gnawing anxiety that he had been hurt, that he might then be lying injured somewhere, with no one knowing, no one helping him. Quietly she let Felicia help her dress, not caring if her dress that day had long sleeves or short. His bruises were fading away, but her wrists were sore. She rubbed them abstractedly, unable to remember what she could have done to chaff them. Bracelets too tight? She felt confusion about the past few days, as if she had been asleep a good deal, waking up only to semiawareness from time to time. It puzzled her. From across the room she thought of the dream, when she had broken the mirror, and she turned to glance at it. It was whole: a large, ornate baroque mirror done in a gold frame that was centuries old, reflecting back the golden bed that was wider than many bedrooms, the stirring silk curtains at the French windows, the ivory carpet as soft as clouds. She moved a step and for an instant caught her own reflection, but the room was too dark to see herself clearly, and she didn't really care that morning. She knew her beauty would be unaffected. Her hurt was inside only. She bypassed the breakfast tray, noting that even the strawberries were absent that morning, wondering if he had arranged for them to be there yesterday. Yesterday?

She wasn't certain. Perhaps it had been longer than that. She seemed to remember being ill, of having a doctor a time or two. She pulled up her sleeve and examined the bruises, three of them, faded, almost gone; she wondered, gazing at them, if they could have faded so much overnight. Or was she remembering wrong? Had they always been on her wrists?

Felicia was drawing her to the door and she shrugged it away. It didn't matter very much. At the door she turned one more time and examined her room, looking for something . . . She didn't know what it was she searched for. The room was as always: rich, tasteful, strewn with her expensive garments, scented with her exquisite perfumes . . . She turned bewildered eyes to Felicia, and in turning she thought she caught a glimpse of something else: hard and mean, bare, a cubicle of white with a cot-bed . . . She shivered and hurried after the neat little Italian . . . or was she Irish? She didn't know.

The meeting was more tiring than the last one had been; there were more photographs to be made, more reporters to be answered. She balked momentarily at more pictures, but they insisted and led her to the studio. She was brusque with the questioners this time, and her head started to ache fiercely from the funny little hat that fitted too tight and the awkward pose that became more and more uncomfortable. Her discomfort forced her to keep her eyes closed, grateful for the bandage someone provided for her eyes and forehead. They looked at the fading bruises again, and treated them. This time when the doctor asked her how she had received them, she told him, listening to the plaintive note in her own voice, and, to her surprise, finding herself sobbing suddenly at the absence of her lover. The Directors had withdrawn, though, and it was all right. Doctors had to respect confidences. He promised he would, and she stopped weeping.

Through most of the photography session, far in the background where they thought she couldn't hear them, the Directors continued to discuss the new process being developed by the company. She caught snatches of their conversation:

". . . radically different. Improved almost immediately, and continued improvement for six days before the present relapse."

"With stepped-up treatments the improvement should be constant. We can expand operations, increase the number of treatments per week. . . ."

". . . first really hopeful treatment . . . suggests actual cure, not simply palliative . . ."

She became bored with it and turned her attention away from them. The headache was worse and she heard a moan escape her lips. The doctor was there instantly, holding her hand, his cool, firm fingers on her wrist. The reporters stopped their questioning; with a start she realized that she had been answering them all along, even though she could remember none of the questions, nor the answers she had given to them. The doctor said that would be enough for then, and he gave her something for her headache.

There followed a period of illness, of medications that caused her to sleep for longer and longer periods, of half-awareness, of treatments, of hands on her, of voices . . . but mostly the noth-ingness of drugged sleep.

Margaret Lester awakened to the sound of the heavy-handed attendant entering her room noisily. She stiffened on the narrow bed, fearing the rough hands of the thick woman. "I'm awake," she said tightly. "I'll get up by myself."

"Suit yourself, Miss Lester," the woman said, slurring her speech. "Doctor wants you in his office in half an hour. You gonna make it?"

"Yes," Margaret said, not taking her eyes off the woman.

The attendant shrugged and left; Margaret heard the key in the lock and shuddered. Like an animal, she thought. She got up swiftly, afraid the attendant would return—to "help" her. She didn't look in the small mirror over the dresser, but pulled the brush through her hair, gazing out the window at the cold Feb-ruary scenery beyond the steel mesh. She thought it must be the longest winter she had ever known, an eternity of winter. She tried not to think of when she had first come awake in this little room. Trying to recall brought back the headaches. Trying to recall the autumn, or last summer . . . She stood at the window and shook her head violently. She would not think of all the things she didn't know. Later, after she was away from this place, away from that awful woman who hated her so, away from the things they did to her, she would try to remember. Now she didn't know, and it didn't matter.

She did know that she should not look in the mirror over the dresser. She finished with her hair and pulled on a simple, blue tailored dress. Her body was sore and aching, and she looked with dismay at the many bruises that covered her arms, feeling them also on her back, on her legs. She felt old and tired, unut-terably tired, unspeakably old. When she was ready she stood by the door so the big woman with hard, heavy hands wouldn't come into the room for her. Sometimes, if she was fast enough, alert enough, the woman hardly touched her.

"You ready?" the attendant asked, opening the door.

"Yes."

"Come on, then." She took Margaret's arm and when she tried to pull away the rough fingers clamped down on the flesh, biting deep and hard, leaving marks that were sore, that were turning blue almost before she released the cruel grasp. Margaret moved quickly, keeping in step with her.

Outside the doctor's door they paused and Margaret took a deep breath, hoping to steady herself; it was always an ordeal, trying to understand what he wanted her to say, knowing she was answering wrong, but not knowing what was right. The attendant squeezed her arm again and she moved, entering the office.

"Good morning, Margaret," Dr. Spaulding said warmly. His cool hand held hers for a moment and he led her to the soft, reclining chair at the side of his desk. "How are you this morning?"

"Fine," she said, her mouth dry, her hands knots in her lap. She wanted to complain about the attendant, about her sore, aching arms, but he might think she had been difficult that morning. If one became difficult, there was the room where the—thing was. Her mind was blank; no images or words went with the flood of terror that drenched her.

"You certainly are looking fine," Dr. Spaulding said. He swiveled his chair around so that he was looking out his window. "Want to finish telling me the incident you started last week? When you were seven . . ."

This was the part she detested. She strained to remember the story, and found nothing. But there had to be! You told him things and he told you what they meant and pretty soon you were sent home. Her mouth felt stuffed full of cotton and she wondered if he knew she was making them up. "I was in the second grade," she said hesitantly. "I hated school. . . ." She stopped in confusion; he had turned and was looking at her kindly.

"Don't you remember it?" he asked.

She shook her head.

"All right. Something else then. Did you dream last night?" She shook her head again, and he nodded. Desperately she opened her mouth to make up a dream for him, but he said, "Never mind, Margaret. I want to give you a present. I bought a purse for you. It's blue, and there is a comb in it, and a lipstick, and a compact. Why don't you put on lipstick for me?"

She touched the purse and liked the softness of the blue leather. It shone dully in the light from the window. She didn't pick it up.

"Go ahead," he said. "It's yours."

She still didn't pick it up. Her fingers traced a crease in the soft leather. She said, "It is very pretty." He nodded, pleased with her. Looking at the purse she said, "I'll be going home soon, won't I?"

Again he nodded. "We have decided that you are almost ready to leave here. You've made excellent progress these past two months. You will be coming back to see us once a week for a while." She started, and he said kindly, "To talk, as we've been doing these past weeks. You don't mind that, do you?"

She could feel him watching her, and her hand slid back from the purse and found her other hand still clenched in her lap. "I don't mind," she said.

"Let me get the lipstick out for you," Dr. Spaulding said. He fumbled in the purse, withdrawing the lipstick and a dull-gold compact. She felt something curling up tight in her middle, and there seemed to be a vacuum just beyond her ears, a distant soundlessness that might come closer and closer. She watched him place the lipstick on his desk, and by it he put the compact, opened now, with the globe of light from the ceiling fixture reflecting back a full moon in the round little mirror. The mirror tilted back, its weight tipping the compact over backwards, the moon descending in an arc, setting. He righted it and nudged it towards her. The mirror caught and held a shelf of red bound books. It was another test, she realized. Or, perhaps, the only real test.

"Margaret, do you remember the day we talked about beauty, and the importance of feeling lovely inside yourself?"

She nodded mutely. The soundlessness touched her and retreated.

I'm alone, she thought clearly, *and no one cares in this whole world. I am ugly and no one wants to look at me. I am getting old and I am tired and I don't like this world where it is a sin to get old and tired and be ugly. . . .* The soundlessness came like waves driven before a storm, each crest higher and broader than the preceding one. In the troughs his voice still reached her, but the troughs were fewer and fewer, and his words were disjointed and senseless: ". . . your job well . . . amazing progress . . . outpatient status . . . lipstick . . ."

Her gaze didn't leave the compact, but she saw him pick up the lipstick, saw her fingers accept it. She watched her ugly fingers play over the smooth tube, open it, unscrew the lipstick up a half inch. *Think of it as another test. Pick up the compact and put on the lipstick. Be a good, sensible girl and they'll let you go home, away from this place, from that woman with her hurtful hands, and that—room. Don't look at the fingers! It doesn't matter what they look like. After you go home you won't have to look again. . . . After I go home . . . It's just a test! A silly test!*

There was the lipstick in her hand, but she couldn't feel it with her fingers. She thought: *All my life with everyone turning aside when I try to get near. Whispers . . . hidden smiles, or grimaces. Ugliness, sinful ugliness. Why a sin? And now they'll say, ugly and crazy! They might even be afraid of me. Ugly is wicked . . . witches are ugly, and devils. Insane is wicked . . . It doesn't matter. I can stay away from them, in my own apartment, safe, no one there to hurt me. First the test, and then I can go home.*

She held the lipstick and reached for the compact with its round little mirror. A wave of soundlessness receded and she heard, ". . . tomorrow a hair set, and new clothes . . ." The wave crashed in higher and it was a longer time before the next trough. There was a note of . . . anxiety? in his voice when she heard, ". . . and rest for now. You don't have to put on the lipstick now . . . a nap . . ." But she did have to! She had to pass this test so she could go home.

The fingers she could no longer feel held the compact. The bookshelves flashed in the mirror, the deep, rich brownness of the door; the mirror tilted and an expanse of the ceiling was caught, then the globe-moon, shaking, wobbling against a white sky. Faster then: the door again, shelves, from somewhere a clock appeared, the moon, the door, shelves, moon . . . faster and faster . . . shaking, wobbling images flashing . . . his hand reaching . . . a face. She threw the compact as hard as she could and everything stopped. She didn't hear it hit or shatter.

It was not a wave coming in then, but the tide, higher and higher, and in the vacuum there was nothing.

The most beautiful woman in the world awakened smiling a soft, secretive smile. She touched the gold satin pillow lightly where he had been after so long an absence, and her smile deepened. She had known he would return to her, knew he could never leave her again. She ran her hands over her body and knew the beauty went deep, that it went all the way through her, and that he had found all of it. There were marks on her from their laughing scuffles, and their passion. She reveled in the marks, touching first one and then another, each bringing back memories. Her excitement surged anew and she caught her breath, eyes closed, for a few moments until her joy became manageable again. She knew it showed in her eyes, making them shine; she felt her happiness curling up the corners of her mouth; there was a low exultant laugh quivering in her throat to bubble up to the surface from time to time. She knew she could no more conceal her joy than a fountain could conceal its gurgling water. She sang, throwing back the covers, dancing to the wide windows to see the day and to let the day see her. "I am pretty, oh, so pretty. . . ."

I've returned again and again to this introduction and finally came to realize that I have nothing to say about the story or how I came to write it. Once thought of, it had to be written, so I wrote it.

The Planners

Rae stopped before the one-way glass, stooped over, and peered at the gibbon infant within the cage. Darin watched her bitterly. She straightened after a moment, hands in smock pockets, face innocent of any expression what-so-god-damned-ever, and continued to saunter toward him through the aisle between cages.

"You still think it is cruel and worthless?"

"Do you, Dr. Darin?"

"Why do you always do that? Answer my question with one of your own?"

"Does it infuriate you?"

He shrugged and turned from her. His lab coat was on the chair where he had tossed it. He pulled it on over his sky-blue sport shirt.

"How is the Driscoll boy?" Rae asked.

He stiffened, then relaxed again. Not facing her, he said, "Same as last week, last year. Same as he'll be until he dies."

The hall door opened and a very large, very homely face appeared. Stu Evers looked past Darin, down the aisle, a question on his face. "You alone? Thought I heard voices."

"Talking to myself," Darin said. "The committee ready yet?"

"Just about. Dr. Jacobsen is stalling with his nose-throat-spray routine, as usual." He hesitated a moment, glancing again down the row of cages, again at Darin. He didn't ask what ever it was bothering him, said instead, "Wouldn't you think a guy allergic to monkeys would find some other line of research."

Darin looked also, but Rae was gone. Sometimes she didn't come back for months and months; sometimes her visit was a daily occurrence, or even several times daily. What was it this time? The Driscoll boy, the general trend of the project itself? He wondered if she had a life of her own when she was away. "I'll be out at the compound," he said. He passed Stu in the doorway and headed toward the vivid greenery of Florida forests.

The cacophony of jungle noises hit him at the door. There were four hundred sixty-nine monkeys on the thirty-six acres of wooded ground the research department was using. Each monkey was screeching, howling, singing, cursing, or otherwise making its presence known. Darin grunted and headed toward the compound. "The Happiest Monkeys in the World," a newspaper article had called them. "Singing Monkeys," a subhead announced. "Monkeys Given Smartness Pills," the most enterprising had proclaimed. "Cruelty Charged," added another in subdued, sorrowful tones.

The compound was three acres of fenced-in, carefully planned and maintained wilderness, completely enclosed with thirty-foot-high, smooth plastic walls. A transparent dome covered the area. There were one-way windows at intervals along the fence. A small group of people stood before one of the windows. The committee.

Darin stopped and gazed over the interior of the compound through one of the windows. He saw Heloise and Skitter contentedly picking nonexistent fleas from one another; Adam was munching on a banana; Homer was lying on his back idly touching his feet to his nose. A couple of the chimps were at the water fountain, not drinking, merely pressing the pedal and watching the fountain, now and then immersing a head or hand in the bowl of cold water. Dr. Jacobsen appeared and Darin joined the group.

"Good morning, Mrs. Bellbottom," Darin said politely. "Did you know your skirt has fallen off?" He turned from her to Major Dormouse. "Ah, Major, and how many of the enemy have you swatted to death today with your pretty little yellow rag?" He smiled pleasantly at a pimply young man with a camera.

"Major, you've brought a professional peeping tom. More stories in the paper, with pictures this time?" The pimply young man shifted his position, fidgeted with the camera. The major was fiery; Mrs. Bellbottom was on her knees peering under a bush, looking for her skirt. Darin blinked. None of them had on any clothing. He turned toward the window. The chimps were drawing up a table, laden with tea things, silver, china, tiny finger sandwiches. The chimps were all wearing flowered shirts and dresses. Hortense had on a ridiculous flop-brimmed sun hat of pale-green straw. Darin leaned against the fence to control his laughter.

"Soluble ribonucleic acid," Dr. Jacobsen was saying when Darin recovered, "sRNA, for short. So from the gross beginnings when entire worms were trained and fed to other worms that seemed to benefit from the original training, we have come to these more refined methods. We now extract the sRNA molecules from the trained animals and feed it, the sRNA molecules in solution, to untrained specimens and observe the results."

The young man was snapping pictures as Jacobsen talked. Mrs. Whoosis was making notes, her mouth a thin, lipless line, the sun hat tingeing her skin with green. The sun on her patterned red-and-yellow dress made it appear to jiggle, giving her fleshy hips a constant rippling motion. Darin watched, fascinated. She was about sixty.

". . . my colleague, who proposed this line of experimentation, Dr. Darin," Jacobsen said finally, and Darin bowed slightly. He wondered what Jacobsen had said about him, decided to wait for any questions before he said anything.

"Dr. Darin, is it true that you also extract this substance from people?"

"Every time you scratch yourself, you lose this substance," Darin said. "Every time you lose a drop of blood, you lose it. It is in every cell of your body. Sometimes we take a sample of human blood for study, yes."

"And inject it into those animals?"

"Sometimes we do that," Darin said. He waited for the next, the inevitable question, wondering as he waited how he would answer it. Jacobsen had briefed them on what to answer, but he couldn't remember what Jacobsen had said. The question didn't come. Mrs. Whoosis stepped forward, staring at the window.

Darin turned his attention to her; she averted her eyes, and almost as quickly fixed her stare again on the chimps in the compound. "Yes, Mrs. uh . . . Ma'am?" Darin prompted her. She didn't look at him.

"Why? What is the purpose of all this?" she asked. Her voice sounded strangled. The pimpled young man was inching toward the next window.

"Well," Darin said, "our theory is simple. We believe that learning ability can be improved drastically in nearly every species. The learning curve is the normal, expected bell-shaped curve, with a few at one end who have the ability to learn quite rapidly, with the majority in the center who learn at an average rate, and a few at the other end who learn quite slowly. With our experiments we are able to increase the ability of those in the broad middle, as well as those on the deficient end of the curve so that their learning abilities match those of the fastest learners of any given group. . . ."

No one was listening to him. It didn't matter. They would be given the press release he had prepared for them, written in simple language, no polysyllabic words, no sentences containing more than one clause. They were all watching the chimps through the various windows. He said, "So we gabbled the gazooka three times wretchedly until the spirit of camping fired the girls." One of the committee members glanced at him. "Whether intravenously or orally, seems to be as effective one way as the other," Darin said, and the perspiring man turned again to the window. "Injections every morning . . . rejections, planned diet, planned parenthood, planned plans planning plans." Jacobsen eyed him suspiciously. Darin stopped talking altogether and lighted a cigarette. The woman with the unquiet hips turned from the window, her face very red. "I've seen enough," she said. "This sun is too hot out here. May we see the inside laboratories now?"

Darin turned them over to Stu Evers on the inside of the

building. He walked back slowly to the compound. There was a slight grin on his lips when he spotted Adam on the far side, swaggering triumphantly, paying no attention to Hortense, who was rocking back and forth on her haunches, looking very dazed. Darin saluted Adam, then, whistling, returned to his office. Mrs. Driscoll was due with Sonny at 1 P.M.

Sonny Driscoll was fourteen. He was five feet nine inches, weighed one hundred sixty pounds. His male nurse was six feet two inches and weighed two hundred twenty-seven pounds. Sonny had broken his mother's arm when he was twelve; he had broken his father's arm and leg when he was thirteen. So far the male nurse was intact. Every morning Mrs. Driscoll lovingly washed and dressed her baby, fed him, walked him in the yard, spoke happily to him of plans for the coming months, or just sang nursery songs to him. He never seemed to see her. The male nurse, Johnny, was never farther than three feet from his charge when he was on duty.

Mrs. Driscoll refused to think of the day when she would have to turn her child over to an institution. Instead she placed her faith and hope in Darin.

They arrived at two-fifteen, earlier than he had expected them, later than they had promised to be there.

"The kid kept taking his clothes off," Johnny said morosely. The kid was taking them off again in the office. Johnny started toward him, but Darin shook his head. It didn't matter. Darin got his blood sample from one of the muscular arms, shot the injection into the other one. Sonny didn't seem to notice what he was doing. He never seemed to notice. Sonny refused to be tested that day. They got him to the chair and table, but he sat staring at nothing, ignoring the blocks, the bright balls, the crayons, the candy. Nothing Darin did or said had a discernible influence on the boy. Finally the time was up. Mrs. Driscoll and Johnny got him dressed once more and left. Mrs. Driscoll thanked Darin for helping her boy.

Stu and Darin held class from four to five daily. Kelly O'Grady had the monkeys tagged and ready for them when they showed up at the schoolroom. Kelly was very tall, very slender and red-haired. Stu shivered if she accidentally brushed him in passing; Darin hoped that one day Stu would pull an Adam on her. She sat primly on her high stool with her notebook on her knee, unaware of the change that came over Stu during school hours, or, if aware, uncaring. Darin wondered if she were really a Barbie doll fully machined to perform laboratory duties, and nothing else.

He thought of the Finishing School for Barbies where long-legged, high-breasted, stomachless girls went to get shaved clean, get their toenails painted pink, their nipples removed, and all body openings sewed closed, except for their mouths, which curved in perpetual smiles and led nowhere.

The class consisted of six black spider monkeys who had not been fed yet. They had to do in order six tasks: 1) pull a rope; 2) cross the cage and get a stick that was released by the rope; 3) pull the rope again; 4) get the second stick, which would fit into the first; 5) join the sticks together; 6) using the lengthened stick, pull a bunch of bananas close enough to the bars of the cage to reach them and take them inside where they could eat them. Each monkey had an identical cage, screened from each other's view. At five the monkeys were returned to Kelly, who wheeled them away one by one, back to the stockroom. None of them had performed the tasks, although two had gone through part of them before the time ran out.

Waiting for the last of the monkeys to be taken back to its quarters, Stu asked, "What did you do to that bunch of idiots this morning. By the time I got them, they were all acting like they'd been goosed."

Darin told him about Adam's performance and they were both laughing when Kelly returned. Stu's laugh turned to what sounded almost like a sob. Darin wanted to tell him about the school Kelly must have attended, thought better of it, and walked away instead.

His drive home was through the darkening forests of interior Florida for sixteen miles on a narrow, straight road.

"Of course, I don't mind living here," Lea had said once, nine years ago when the Florida position had come through. And she didn't mind. The house was air conditioned; the family car, Lea's car, was air conditioned; the back yard had a swimming pool big enough to float the *Queen Mary*. A frightened, large-eyed Florida girl did the housework, and Lea gained weight and painted sporadically, wrote sporadically—Poetry—and entertained faculty wives regularly. Darin suspected that sometimes she entertained faculty husbands also.

"Oh, Professor Dimples, one hour this evening? That will be fifteen dollars, you know." He jotted down the appointment and turned to Lea. "Just two more today and you will have your car payment. How about that!" She twined slinky arms about his neck, pressing tight high breasts hard against him. She had to tilt her head slightly for his kiss. "Then your turn, darling. For free." He tried to kiss her; his tongue was stopped, and he realized that the smile was on the outside only, that the opening didn't really exist at all.

He parked next to an MG, not Lea's, and went inside the house, where the martinis were always snapping cold.

"Darling, you remember Greta, don't you? She is going to give me lessons twice a week. Isn't that exciting."

"But you already graduated," Darin murmured. Greta was not tall and not long-legged. She was a little bit of a thing. He thought probably he did remember her from somewhere or other, vaguely. Her hand was cool in his.

"Greta has moved in; she is going to lecture on modern art for the spring semester. I asked her for private lessons and she said yes."

"Greta Farrel," Darin said, still holding her small hand. They moved away from Lea and wandered through the open windows to the patio where the scent of orange blossoms was heavy in the air.

"Greta thinks it must be heavenly to be married to a psychologist." Lea's voice followed them. "Where are you two?"

"What makes you say a thing like that?" Darin asked.

"Oh, when I think of how you must understand a woman, know her moods and the reasons for them. You must know just what to do and when, and when to do something else . . . yes, just like that."

His hands on her body were hot, her skin cool. Lea's petulant voice drew closer. He held Greta in his arms and stepped into the pool, where they sank to the bottom, still together. She hadn't gone to the Barbie school. His hands learned her body; then his body learned hers. After they made love Greta drew back from him regretfully.

"I do have to go now. You are a lucky man, Dr. Darin. No doubts about yourself, complete understanding of what makes you tick."

He lay back on the leather couch staring at the ceiling. "It's always that way, Doctor. Fantasies, dreams, illusions. I know it is because this investigation is hanging over us right now, but even when things are going relatively well, I still go off on a tangent like that for no real reason." He stopped talking.

In his chair Darin stirred slightly, his fingers drumming softly on the arm, his gaze on the clock, whose hands were stuck. He said, "Before this recent pressure, did you have such intense fantasies?"

"I don't think so," Darin said thoughtfully, trying to remember.

The other didn't give him time. He asked, "And can you break out of them now when you have to, or want to?"

"Oh, sure," Darin said.

Laughing, he got out of his car, patted the MG, and walked into his house. He could hear voices from the living room and he remembered that on Thursdays Lea really did have her painting lesson. After the lesson there was always the single cocktail with Dr. Lacey, who then meticulously shook hands with Darin and walked stiffly from the house, an elderly, white-haired leonine figure until he got to the MG where suddenly he simply looked foolish. Darin was grinning when he entered the living room.

Lacey left five minutes after Darin arrived. Lacey said vague things about Lea's great promise and untapped talent, and Darin nodded sober agreement. If she had talent, it certainly was untapped so far. He didn't say this.

Lea was wearing a hostess suit, flowing sheer panels of pale-blue net over a skintight leotard that was midnight-blue. Darin wondered if she realized that she had gained weight in the past few years. He thought not.

"Oh, that man is getting impossible," she said when the MG blasted away from their house. "Two years now, and he still doesn't want to put my things on show."

Looking at her, Darin wondered how much more her things could be on show.

"Don't dawdle too long with your martini," she said, leaving the living room. "We're due at the Ritters at seven for clams."

The telephone rang for him while he was showering. It was Stu Evers. Darin stood dripping water while he listened. "Have you seen the evening paper yet? That broad made the statement that conditions are extreme at the station, that our animals are made to suffer unnecessarily."

Darin groaned softly. Stu went on, "She is bringing her entire women's group out tomorrow to show proof of her claims. She's a bigwig on the S.P.C.A., or something."

Darin began to laugh then. Mrs. Whoosis had her face pressed against one of the windows; other fat women in flowered dresses had their faces against the rest. None of them breathed or moved. Inside the compound Adam laid Hortense, then moved on to Esmeralda, to Hilda . . .

"God damn it, Darin, it isn't funny!" Stu said.

"But it is. It is."

Clams at the Ritters were delicious. Clams, hammers, buckets of butter. With them was a mountainous salad and beer, and, finally, coffee liberally laced with brandy. Darin felt cheerful and contented when the evening was over. Ritter was in Med. Eng. Lit. but he didn't talk about it, which was merciful. He was sympathetic about the stink with the S.P.C.A. He thought scientists had no imagination. Darin agreed with him, and soon he and Lea were on their way home.

"I am so glad that you didn't decide to stay late," Lea said, passing over the yellow line with a blast of the horn. She always liked to drive. He let her. It wasn't worth fighting about. Very little that came up was worth fighting about. "There is a movie on tonight that I am dying to see."

She talked, but he didn't listen, training of twelve years drawing out an occasional grunt at what must have been appropriate times, enough so that she didn't question that she had his attention.

"Ritter is such a bore," she said later. They were nearly home. "As if you had anything to do with that incredible statement in tonight's paper."

"What statement?"

"Didn't you even read the article? For heaven's sake, why not? Everyone will be talking about it . . ." She sighed, exaggerating it. "Someone quoted a reliable source who said that within the foreseeable future, simply by developing the leads you now have, you will be able to produce monkeys that are as smart as normal human beings." She laughed, a brittle, hard sound that was without meaning.

"I'll read the article when we get home," he said. She didn't ask about the statement, didn't care if it was true or false, if he had made it originally or not. He read the article while she settled down before the television. Then he went for a swim. She hadn't quoted it exactly right, but the gist was there. The water was warm, the breeze cool on his skin. Mosquitoes found him as soon as he got out of the pool, so he sat behind the screening of the verandah. The bluish light from the living room went off after a time and there was only the dark night. Lea didn't call him when she went to bed. He knew she went very softly, closing the door with care so that the click of the latch wouldn't disturb him if he were dozing on the verandah. He didn't care.

He knew why he didn't break it off. Pity. The most corrosive emotion endogenous to man. She was the product of the doll school that taught that the trip down the aisle was the end, the fulfillment of a maiden's dreams; shocked and horrified to learn that it was instead another beginning, some of them never recovered. Lea never did. Never would. At sixty she would purse her mouth at the sexual display of uncivilized animals, whether human or not, and she would be disgusted and help formulate laws to ban such activities. Long ago he had hoped a child would be the answer, but the school did something to them on the inside too. They didn't conceive, or if conception took place they didn't carry the fruit, and if they carried it the birth was of a stillborn thing. The ones that did live were the ones, usually, to be pitied more than those who fought and were defeated *in utero*.

A bat swooped low over the quiet pool and was gone again against the black of the azaleas. Soon the moon would appear, and the chimps would stir restlessly for a while, then return to deep troubleless slumber. The chimps slept close to one another companionably, with no thought of sex then. Only the nocturnal creatures, and the human creatures, performed coitus in the dark. He wondered if Adam knew of his human captors. The colony within the compound had started almost twenty years ago, and since then none of the chimps had seen a human being. When it was necessary to enter the grounds, the chimps were fed narcotics in the evening to insure against their waking. Props were then changed, new obstacles added to the old conquered ones. Now and then a chimp was removed for study, usually ending up in dissection. But not Adam. He was father of the world. Darin grinned in the darkness.

Adam took his bride aside from the other beasts and knew that she was lovely. She was his own true bride, created for him, intelligence to match his own burning intelligence. Together they scaled the smooth walls and glimpsed the great world that lay beyond their garden. Together they found the opening that led to the world that was to be theirs, and they left behind them the lesser beings. And the god searched for them and, finding them not, cursed them and sealed the opening so that none of the others could follow. So it was that Adam and his bride became the first man and woman and from them flowed the progeny that was to inhabit the entire world. And one day Adam said, "For shame, woman, seest thou that thou art naked?" And the woman answered, "So are you, big boy, so are you." So they covered their nakedness with leaves from the trees, and thereafter they performed their sexual act in the dark of night so that man could not look on his woman, nor she on him. And they were thus cleansed of shame. Forever and ever. Amen. Hallelujah.

Darin shivered. He had fallen asleep, after all, and the night wind had grown chill. He went to bed. Lea drew away from him in her sleep. She felt hot to his touch. He turned to his left side, his back to her, and he slept.

"There is potential x," Darin said to Lea the next morning at breakfast. "We don't know where x is actually. It represents the highest intellectual achievement possible for the monkeys, for example. We test each new batch of monkeys that we get and sort them—x-1, x-2, x-3, suppose, and then we breed for more x-1s. Also we feed the other two groups the sRNA that we extract from the original x-1s. Eventually we get a monkey that is higher than our original x-1, and we reclassify right down the line and start over using his sRNA to bring the others up to his level. We make constant checks to be sure that our standards aren't slipping in order to allow inferior strains to mingle with our highest achievers, and we keep control groups that are given the same training, the same food, the same sorting process, but no sRNA. We test them against each other."

Lea was watching his face with some interest as he talked. He thought he had got through, until she said, "Did you realize that your hair is almost solid white at the temples? All at once it is turning white."

Carefully he put his cup back on the saucer. He smiled at her and got up. "See you tonight," he said.

They also had two widely separated compounds of chimps that had started out identically. Neither had received any training whatever through the years; they had been kept isolated from each other and from man. Adam's group had been fed sRNA daily from the highest level of intelligent animals they had discovered. The control group had been fed none. The control-group chimps still had to master the intricacies of the water fountain with its ice-cold water; they used the small stream that flowed through each compound. The control group had yet to learn that fruit on the high, fragile branches could be had if one used the telescoping sticks provided to bat them down. The control group huddled in the open, or under the scant cover of palm trees when it rained and the dome was opened. Adam long ago had led his group in the construction of a rude but functional hut, where they gathered when it rained.

Darin saw the women's committee filing past the compound when he parked his car. He went straight to the console in his office, flicked on a switch and manipulated buttons and dials, leading the group through the paths, opening one, closing another to them, until he led them to the newest of the compounds, where he opened the gate and let them inside. Quickly he closed the gate again and watched their frantic efforts to get out once more. Later he turned the chimps loose on them, and his grin grew broader as he watched the new men ravage the old women. Some of the offspring of the miscegenation were black and hairy, others pink and hairless, some a mixture of the two. They grew rapidly, lined up with arms extended to receive their daily doses, stood before a machine that tested them instantaneously, and were sorted. Some of them passed through a disintegration room, others out into the world.

A car horn blasted in his ears. He switched off his ignition and got out as Stu Evers parked next to his car. "I see the old bats got here," Stu said. He walked toward the lab with Darin. "How's the Driscoll kid coming along?"

"Negative," Darin said. Stu knew they had tried using human RNA on the boy and failed consistently. It was too big a step for his body to cope with. "So far he has shown total intolerance to A-127. Throws it off almost instantly."

Stuart was sympathetic and noncommittal. No one else had any faith whatever in Darin's own experiment. A-127 might be too great a step upward, Darin thought. Ateles spider monkey from Brazil was too bright.

He called Kelly from his office and asked about the new arrivals, the spider monkeys, they had tested the day before. Blood had been processed; a sample was available. He looked over his notes and chose one that had shown interest in the tasks without finishing any of them. Kelly promised him the prepared syringe by 1 P.M.

What no one connected with the project could any longer doubt was that those simians, and the men, that had been injected with RNA from the Driscoll boy had actually had their learning capacities inhibited, some of them apparently permanently.

Darin didn't want to think about Mrs. Driscoll's reaction if ever she learned to what extent they had been using her boy. Rae sat at the corner of his desk and drawled insolently, "I might tell her myself, Dr. Darin. I'll say, 'Sorry, ma'am, you'll have to keep your idiot out of here; you're damaging the brains of our monkeys with his polluted blood.' Okay, Darin?"

"My God, what are you doing back again?"

"Testing," she said. "That's all, just testing."

Stu called him to observe the latest test of Adam's group, to take place in forty minutes. Darin had forgotten that he was to be present. During the night a tree had been felled in each compound, its trunk crossing the small stream, in effect damming the water, pooling it. At eleven the water fountains were to be turned off for the rest of the day. The tree had been downed at the far end of the compound, close to the fence where the stream entered, so that the trickle of water that flowed past the hut was cut off. Already the group not taking RNA was showing signs of thirst. Adam's group was unaware of the stopped flow.

Darin met Stu and they walked together to the far side, where they would have a good view of the entire compound. The women had left by then. "It was too quiet for them this morning," Stu said. "Adam was busy making his rounds; he squatted on the downed tree for nearly an hour before he left it and went back to the others."

They could see the spreading pool of water. It was muddy, uninviting-looking. The tree chosen for this experiment had been carefully placed, so that the pool created by its damming of the stream was in a spot where the dirt was loose, where the water was certain to be a suspension of dirt. At eleven-ten it was generally known within the compound that the water supply had failed. Some of the older chimps tried the fountain; Adam tried it several times. He hit it with a stick and tried it again. Then he sat on his haunches and stared at it. One of the young chimps whimpered pitiably. He wasn't thirsty yet, merely puzzled and perhaps frightened. Adam scowled at him. The chimp cowered behind Hortense, who bared fangs at Adam. He waved menacingly at her, and she began picking fleas from her offspring. When he whimpered again she cuffed him. The young chimp looked from her to Adam, stuck his forefinger in his mouth and ambled away. Adam continued to stare at the useless fountain. An hour passed. Darin had a cup of coffee and a sandwich pressed on him by one of the lab boys. He munched without tasting it. At last Adam rose and wandered nonchalantly toward the drying stream. Here and there a shrinking pool of muddy water steamed in the sun. The other chimps followed Adam. He followed the stream through the compound toward the fence that was its source. When he came to the pool he squatted again. One of the young chimps circled the pool cautiously, reached down and touched the dirty water, drew back, reached for it again, and then drank. Several of the others drank also. Adam continued to squat. At twelve-forty Adam moved again. Grunting and gesturing to several younger males, he approached the tree trunk. With much noise and many meaningless gestures they shifted the trunk. They strained at it again, shifted it again. The water was released and poured over the heaving chimps. Two of them dropped the trunk and ran. Adam and the others held. The two returned.

They were still working with it when Darin had to leave, to keep his appointment with Mrs. Driscoll and Sonny. They arrived at one-ten. Kelly had left the syringe with the new formula in Darin's small refrigerator. He injected Sonny, took his sample, and started the tests. Sometimes Sonny cooperated to the extent of lifting one of the articles from the table and throwing it. Today he cleaned the table within ten minutes. Darin put a piece of candy in his hand; Sonny threw it from him. Patiently Darin put another piece in the boy's hand. He managed to keep the eighth piece in the clenched hand long enough to guide the hand to Sonny's mouth. When it was gone, Sonny opened his mouth for more. His hands lay idly on the table. He didn't seem to connect the hands with the candy with the pleasant taste. Darin tried to guide a second piece to his gaping mouth, but Sonny refused to hold a piece a second time.

When the hour was over and Sonny was showing definite signs of fatigue, Mrs. Driscoll clutched Darin's hand in hers. Tears stood out in her eyes. "You actually got him to feed himself a little bit," she said brokenly. "God bless you, Dr. Darin. God bless you!" She kissed his hand and turned away as the tears started to spill and flow down her cheeks.

Kelly was waiting for him when the group left. She collected the new sample of blood to be processed. "Did you hear about the excitement down at the compound? Adam's building a dam of his own."

Darin stared at her for a long moment and then nodded. The breakthrough? He ran back to the compound. The near side this time was where the windows were being used. It seemed that the entire staff was there watching silently. He saw Stu and edged in by him. The stream twisted and curved through the compound, less than ten inches deep, not over two feet anywhere. At one spot stones lay under it; elsewhere the bottom was of hard-packed sand. Adam and his crew were piling up stones at the one suitable place for their dam, very near their hut. Now and then a young chimp would stumble into the water too close to them, and Adam would growl at it or throw water at it. One of the chimps threw a stone at a youngster, and Adam cuffed the offender, sending him sprawling face down in the water. Adam stood his ground until the chastised one resumed work. The dam they built was two feet wide and only a foot above the water level. A planned safety measure, or accident? The dam was less than five feet from the fence, fifteen feet from where Darin and Stu shared the window. When the dam was completed Adam looked along the fence. Darin thought his eyes paused momentarily on his own before they continued the sweeping look. Later he heard that nearly every other person watching that scene felt the same momentary pause as those black, intelligent eyes sought out and held other intelligence.

". . . next thunderstorm. Adam and the flood . . ."

". . . eventually seeds instead of food . . ."

". . . his brain. Convolutions as complex as any man's."

Darin walked away from them, snatches of future plans in his ears. It was getting dark already. Or, he looked at his watch in surprise, not so early after all. There was a memo on his desk. Jacobsen was turning over the S.P.C.A. investigatory committee to him. He was to meet with the university representatives, the local S.P.C.A. group, and the legal representatives of all concerned on Monday next at 10 A.M. He wrote out his daily report on Sonny Driscoll. Sonny had been on too good behavior for too long. Would this last injection give him just the spark of determination he needed to go on a rampage? Darin had alerted Johnny, the bodyguard, whoops, male nurse, for just such a possibility, but he knew Johnny didn't think there was any danger from the kid. He hoped Sonny wouldn't kill Johnny, then turn on his mother and father. He'd probably rape his mother, if that much goal-directedness ever flowed through him. And the three men who had volunteered for the injections from Sonny's blood? He didn't want to think of them at all, therefore couldn't get them out of his mind as he sat at his desk staring at nothing. Three convicts. That's all, just convicts hoping to get a parole for helping science along. He laughed abruptly. They weren't planning anything now. Not that trio. Not planning for a thing. Sitting, waiting for something to happen, not thinking about what it might be, or when, or how they would be affected. Not thinking. Period.

"But you can always console yourself that your motives were pure, that it was all for Science, can't you, Dr. Darin?" Rae asked mockingly.

He looked at her. "Go to hell," he said.

It was late when he turned off his light. Kelly met him in the corridor that led to the main entrance. "Hard day, Dr. Darin?"

He nodded. Her hand lingered momentarily on his arm.

"Good night," she said, turning in to her own office. He stared at the door for a long time before he let himself out and started toward his car. Lea would be furious with him for not calling. Probably she wouldn't speak at all until nearly bedtime, when she would explode into tears and accusations. He could see the time when her tears and accusations would strike home, when Kelly's body would still be a concrete memory, her words lingering in his ears. And he would lie to Lea, not because he would care actually if she knew, but because it would be expected. She wouldn't know how to handle the truth. It would entangle her to the point where she would have to try an abortive suicide, a screaming-for-attention attempt that would ultimately tie him in tear-soaked knots that would never be loosened. No, he would lie, and she would know he was lying, and they would get by. He started the car, aimed down the long sixteen miles that lay before him. He wondered where Kelly lived. What it would do to Stu when he realized. What it would do to his job if Kelly should get nasty, eventually. He shrugged. Barbie dolls never got nasty. It wasn't built in.

Lea met him at the door, dressed only in a sheer, loose gown, her hair loose and unsprayed. Her body flowed into his, so that he didn't need Kelly at all. And he was best man when Stu and Kelly were married. He called to Rae, "Would that satisfy you?" but she didn't answer. Maybe she was gone for good this time. He parked the car outside his darkened house and leaned his head on the steering wheel for a moment before getting out. If not gone for good, at least for a long time. He hoped she would stay away for a long time.

There is a charming children's story in which a small boy is given butter to carry home to his mother. He carries it through the jungle on his head, and it melts and runs down his face. His grandmother scolds him and gives him a second cake of butter. This time he carries it in his pocket and it melts and runs down his legs. And so on. Finally the grandmother shows him how to fashion a container of cool, wet leaves, and this time he gets the butter home whole and sweet. The moral is that that which is contained must shape the container. Who would capture the wind must not use a sieve. And the windsong? How does one capture the windsong?

Windsong

W<small>E ARE THREE.</small> We drive along the coast slowly until Paula says, "This one." Then we get out of the car and walk around the house nonchalantly, wade through the dunes to the ocean and swim there alone, away from the crowds that form a solid crust like soiled snow up and down the public beaches. How Paula knows this house is empty, but not that one, we don't know. She is never wrong. Subliminal signs that only she can perceive? A shade drawn wrong, a chair outside that should have been moved from the sun, a garment, long since dried, sun-bleached even, still flapping in the wind? We never know, and she can't tell us.

Paula is the windsong, quick, nimble, restless, long hair salt-dulled most of the time, too thin, sharp elbows, knees, cheekbones, collarbones. No makeup; she is in too much of a hurry. A nail breaks and she bites it even again. Her gaze flicks here and there, noting everything, lingering on nothing, and she says, "We have to go back. A storm is coming." How does she know?

Gregory says she noticed the gray in the water far out near the horizon. That and the feel of the wind on her skin, and the way the clouds scudded now, all were clues for her. But he can't tell when a storm is coming. Gregory is her twin brother. Both are fifteen this summer. Gregory is the rock around which the wind sings and flutters, departing to pry into this and that, but always whirling back again. Gregory can give reasons for most of her conclusions, but he can't reach the conclusions intuitively as she can.

Dan Thornton stirred in his seat and opened his eyes slowly. There was no sound that had roused him, nothing out of the ordinary. He listened for a moment to the familiar soft humming of the computer at his right side, and before his gaze turned to it he knew the play of lights would be normal. The instrument panel before him showed nothing abnormal either, no flashing amber light, or worse, the steady throbbing of the red light. Systems okay. He yawned and stretched. Time to make the routine checks. He opened and closed relays, turned the television camera on and studied the passengers, all piled up in boxes like rows of frozen goods on a supermarket shelf; he turned the camera off again. Readings on his instruments all normal. He got out the food capsules carefully, and put them on a sectioned dish and slid it into the recon unit. He waited until the light went on, killing two more minutes, then slowly drew out the dish of scrambled eggs and bacon, toast and honey. He dropped another capsule into a cup and slid it in, and sat down with his breakfast. Presently he had coffee and his first cigarette. Then he looked over the book titles on spools. He dropped the spool he selected and some of the thread-tape unwound as it rolled across the cabin. He kicked it hard and abruptly sat down. The computer was calling him.

The alarm clock hummed, and Thornton woke up groggily, feeling the ache of unrested muscles. He turned off the clock before it could start its second phase: a raucous buzz that sounded like fifty men with fifty saws clearing a swath through a forest. His hand left the clock and groped for his notebook and he wrote down the dream details before they began to flit away. He paused and tried to remember something: a dream within the dream? Nothing came of it, and he wrote about the cabin he had seen, and the books on spools like thread. The reconstituter for food struck him as a particularly good idea, one he had never encountered before. He finished the dream sequence and only then stretched and felt each muscle protest again.

He padded in bare feet across the room to the bathroom and stood under a hot shower for ten minutes. The icy follow-up failed to revive him and he knew that his efficiency would be at about 60 percent of normal unless he took his zoom-wowie pills. He looked at the small bottle disdainfully, but swallowed two capsules and only then looked at his face.

"This is the way we start most of our days, old man," he said to the face. "Aches, try to shock the system into awareness, then the pep pills and a gallon of coffee. It's no good, old man. You know it's no good."

The old man in the mirror didn't answer, and he was almost sorry. The day the image did answer he'd quit, just walk out and never come back, and that would be nice. Shaving, he repeated to himself, emphasizing each syllable of it, "That would be nice!"

At the office he was met by his secretary, who handed a memo to him. Meeting for nine sharp. The Secretary would be present. End. He crumpled it and nodded to Jeanne. It was 8:45.

"Coffee?" he asked.

The girl nodded as he started through the doorway to his inner office, a cubicle ten-by-ten. "I poured a cup, and there's more in the pot," Jeanne said. "Shall I start on the mail?"

"Sure, honey. And, Jeanne, try to winnow it way down, huh?"

She smiled sympathetically and he started on the coffee. He tried not to look at his desk, which Jeanne had cleaned up as much as possible, but which still was a jumble of plans, memos, doodles, slide rules, schematics. The coffee was blistering hot, strong, black. The day began to seem less infernal. When he left for the conference in ten minutes he was carrying his third coffee with him. He grinned at Jeanne, and his stride was purposeful and his back straight.

There were fifteen men at the conference that morning, and

all of them looked as bad as Thornton, or worse. They had all been driving on twelve-to-eighteen-hour days for seven months now, and the end was not in sight. Thornton could almost envy the union-protected maintenance men. He nodded to others and there were low greetings and hurried conversations in the short-hand that passed for talk. He thought, one bomb right here, right now, and poof, there goes the Special Institute for Applied Research.

He saw that the Secretary was already in the room, cloistered by several bodies near the window, speaking in his low mono-tone to Halvern, the Director of the Institute. The clock chimed softly and Halvern moved toward the long table, the Secretary following, still talking, like a priest mumbling incomprehensible prayers.

Introductions were unnecessary, since the Secretary had been there before. Thornton thought of his bomb and enlarged it a bit in his mind, still not The Bomb, of course, but slightly bigger than the one he had contemplated earlier. Would the war stop then? He knew it would not, but there would be those on the outside who would sanctify him. He grinned at the thought, and for a moment he was afraid the grin had reached the outside of his face, but there were no looks askance, and deliberately he turned his thoughts from that line and became attentive to what the Secretary was saying:

". . . imperative that we solve this final problem before nego-tiations are finalized. When the talks begin, our activities in the field will be curtailed . . ."

Thornton added: *and we have stalled the Secretary-General about as long as possible.*

"Naturally we are trying to bring about peace talks as rapidly as we can, *on the surface anyway where we can point to our ef-forts,* but it is difficult to negotiate with an enemy that is so xeno-phobic. *You mean he hates our guts, with reason, and he doesn't believe a word we say.* I repeat, the President has informed me that it is imperative that we complete our plans for the Phalanx and try it out under battle conditions so that we will better be able to assess its potentials in the event we are faced with a major land war. . . ."

Thornton turned him off, letting his gaze slide from the Secretary's hand-tooled-leather face to the window that framed a vista of Tennessee hills touched with early spring. Dogwoods and redbuds were in bloom, and a strong wind whipped them unmercifully. Kite wind. Sailing wind. Sailing . . . He smiled inside and wished he could go sailing along the coast on the curious flat-bottomed skiff Gregory had picked up somewhere in the distant, almost forgotten past. Twenty-five years ago, by God! For a moment the thought of his boyhood friend stirred something, and his hand toying with a pencil tightened its grip painfully.

He wrenched his attention back to the Secretary, who had left the familiar rah, rah, team talk, and was on something new finally. "I am scheduling the first simulated battle test for one month from today, and the first actual battle test for sixty days subsequent to that date." There was more of it, but Thornton perversely blocked it out. So they would all work for twenty hours a day instead of eighteen. He shrugged inwardly and decided that he didn't care. With wow-zooie pills and coffee they would all stay on their feet until they collapsed, and it didn't matter what shape they would be in when the year was over. One year in the Institute, one year off resting, then back to the university to pick up the threads of class work, lectures on Advanced Programming Theory, and his own small quiet lab. And back to his family, of course.

Thornton returned to his office after the meeting and was confronted with the meaningless garble from other departments that he had to translate into a program. Very deliberately he didn't try to understand most of the problems that he worked with. He didn't want to know what the Phalanx would be able to do and what it would not.

He divided his day into thirds: the first third, from 8:45 until 1:00, he worked on the advanced programming that was his to do: after lunch, 1:30 until 5:30, he went over the papers prepared by others, sometimes accepting them, often sending them back; from 7:30 until exhaustion stopped him he worked with the computer searching for errors. Then dream-laden sleep until 7:30 the next morning. At 5:30, three days a week, he spent half an hour with his analyst, and it was to him that he reported any interesting ideas that had come to him during his dreams, awake or asleep. His analyst, Dr. Feldman, believed implicitly in the creative ability of the unconscious to serve up workable ideas, which generally were brushed aside because they were far afield of the patient's area of interest. Now that he was aware of the sort of things that Feldman was looking for, Thornton also searched his dreams and his reveries for those ideas, and was surprised to find how many of them there were. Surprised and excited. This was something that he planned to take with him from the Institute when he left. Most of it he planned, swore he would leave behind him forever.

He told Feldman the dream without consulting his notes: "I was in the cabin of a spaceship, carrying cryopassengers to a distant star system. I was responsible for them. Everything was functioning smoothly." He told in detail how he had prepared his breakfast, and then went on to the book incident. "It was a variation of the microfilm process, I suppose, simplified somewhat. I read the title the way you would read the label on a spool of thread; it even had the feel and texture of a spool of thread. I dropped it, though, and woke up then. My clock went off."

Feldman didn't interrupt him, simply nodded when Thornton came to the end of it. When Thornton pulled out his notebook and read from his notes, he was chagrined to find that he had omitted parts of the dream.

Feldman said, "The dream that you remember, what kind of a dream was it?"

"Kind? Oh, I see. I think it was black and white. I don't remember any color. I didn't feel it particularly, I don't think."

"Yes. Could you come out of it at any time? Did you realize that you were dreaming?"

"I don't think so. I have done that, and noted it afterward, but not this time."

Feldman worked on the dream within a dream, but Thornton couldn't remember if there had been one or not. Short of hypnosis, Feldman decided, it would stay repressed for the time being. Thornton and Feldman had discussed dreams in the past, and he knew that Feldman believed there were three major types of dreams: the hypnagogic dreams that float in and out of awareness on falling to sleep, and on awakening, the kind that fade in and out of a short nap when you know you are dreaming and can even take a hand in directing the dream sometimes. Then there was the next stage where the dreamer had no control, but was really more an observer than a participant, although he could be both at the same time, watching himself from a distance. The third kind was the sort that Thornton rarely had, or if he had, seldom remembered: the dream that is a reality in itself, the dream that can result in a heart attack if it is a nightmare, or in orgasm if it is sexual, the dream that exists, that can change the dreamer just as a living experience can.

Feldman was smiling happily when Thornton looked at him at the end of the questioning, and Thornton knew that finally he was proving interesting to the psychiatrist. After seven months of unshakable normalcy, he had done something interesting. He felt a stab of fear and wished he hadn't talked so much, had let it go at the remembered dream, but even as he thought it, he knew that it would have been impossible. Feldman would have known, and resistance would have delighted him even more than mere repression. For a moment he hated the smiling man, but it passed, and he grinned back briefly.

"You think I'm going to earn my keep, after all?"

"When you have something come up after this length of time, I must assume that there is the possibility that it can be connected with the work here, yes. We shall see. I am scheduling you for an hour tomorrow, starting at five. Is that convenient?"

The question was rhetorical.

"You should give thought to the spool of thread that you tried to rid yourself of," Feldman said. "As you fall asleep, think to yourself, spool of thread, spool of thread. Who knows, perhaps it will come to you." He held open the door and Thornton left.

Thornton knew that early in their dealings Feldman had had him in deep hypnosis, that he had few secrets from the man, that probably Feldman had left him with some posthypnotic cues, and he wondered if it had been a suggestion, or an order, that he should think of a spool of thread, and even as he wondered about it, he knew that, coming from Feldman, a suggestion could have the force of an order given at gunpoint. His smile was without mirth as he remembered what Feldman had said once when asked why he didn't merely hypnotize all his patients and have them recite their dreams and fears to him.

"Ah, but the associations, the meanings would be lost then, perhaps. Why do you repress this and not that? This is what is interesting, not what you repress particularly, although it *can* be. No. I might nudge you from time to time, but I want you to bring them out with the proper associations, the associations that only you can make."

Spool of thread, spool of thread . . .

He remembered, dreamed, of losing his first tooth, and the thread his mother had tied around it, her gentle insistence that he pull it himself, and her promise, after a look of surprise and amusement, yes, they would send it to his father. He drifted out of the dream-reverie and was wide awake thinking about his father, who had been a good man, kind and wise, a colonel in the army. He got out of bed and paced his tiny room smoking furiously, but the image of his father naked and bruised, shaved clean, dragging one foot, being pulled hobbling down a street crowded with Oriental faces that were grimaces of hate, the image remained, just as he had watched it on television. A good man, he repeated soberly. But he might have done the things they accused him of doing. He might have.

He swallowed a pill and returned to bed and found himself repeating: spool of thread, spool of thread. He wanted to get up again, but the pill was quick and he felt lethargy stealing over him. He would be achy in the morning, always was achy when he resorted to sleeping pills. Spool of thread . . .

He dreamed discordant, meaningless dreams, fantasies without basis in reality. And slept deeper, and was less restless on the single bed.

We walk through the museum arm in arm and it is Paula who is leading us, although she is in the middle. Her steps are light and quick, and she talks incessantly. She pauses before the paintings of the new artist, Stein, and she squints and cocks her head this way and that, then she pulls us on to the next one. She is changed now, her hair still long and straight, but shining clean, smelling of sun and fresh air, and she has done something to her face, something so subtle that I can't decide what it is. I find myself staring at her again and again, and she smiles at me, and for an instant I find the wild girl who lived for the ocean only five years ago. Then it is gone and she is saying, "It's such a joke! He's wonderful! Don't you see it?" There are fifty paintings, arranged in aisles that meet and interconnect so that it is hard not to repeat an aisle. There is no arrow pointing this way, no numbers on the paintings, but Paula has led us through them to the end, and she is laughing with delight. The artist is there, regarding Paula with deep and penetrating interest. She runs to him and kisses him on his bearded cheek and says, "Thank you. I won't tell." And she doesn't tell. Gregory goes back to the beginning and works his way slowly to us once more, and when he comes back, his eyes share her mirth, but he won't tell either. I know that he can explain it though she can't, but he needed her to tell him there was something to explain. I return later and study the paintings alone for a long time, and I don't know what they found. I am lost there. The paintings are grotesque, hideous, and mean nothing, and the arrangement is meant to befuddle even more, not enlighten.

Paula loves the city as she loved the beaches. She runs and dances through the streets joyously, tasting what no one else tastes, smelling what no one else smells, seeing what is not there for my eyes to see. She sings in the city like a fresh breeze from the ocean.

Paula plans to leave school in the spring. She wants . . . she doesn't know what she wants, but it is not in school. She will travel, perhaps marry. I feel tightness in my throat and I ask if she will marry me and she stops, frozen, and finally after a long time she says no. I am angry with her and stalk away. Gregory says that she is like a bird; she must fly here and there before she stops, and love would stop her. I hate them both, their closeness, their awareness of each other. I want to kill them both. Especially Paula. My hands are fists when she comes near me, and the smothering waves of love-hate immobilize me at a place where the pain is unendurable.

She knows. Paula is like a spring wind then, gentle and soothing, and I am filled with her presence. For two weeks we are together and she is in every cell of me, deep in me where she can never escape now. Then she is gone. Gregory knows where, but he doesn't tell me. He plods with his books, getting every detail of every subject letter-perfect, but he never originates anything, never offers anything new, and he is like a shadow without the wind. I know his loss is greater than my own, but I don't care about that. I return to California, where I am still in school, and the jet is my scream of anguish that I cannot utter for myself. I want her out of my life. I want never to see her again. I want her dead so that no one else can have her.

Dan Thornton strode across his mammoth office and began pushing buttons on a four-by-eight-foot console on one side of his desk. Three doors flew open from other rooms, and shaking men entered; he waved them to seats and waited for the Secretary.

"I have your answer," he said to the Secretary on his arrival. "It is simply this:" He was dying, his throat tightening and choking him, his heart pounding harder and harder . . .

He sat up shivering. He reached for the notebook and the light, and wrote quickly and lay down again. He thought he had been wakeful off and on most of the night, and now the sky was lightening, a pale gray touched with peach tones. He squeezed his eyes tighter, desperately wanting sleep to return, deep, untroubled sleep, and he knew that it would not.

Feldman said slowly, "You are aware of what the Phalanx is, yet you consistently deny any real knowledge of it to yourself. Why is that?"

Thornton shrugged. He thought of his wife and three children and talked of them for a few minutes until Feldman stopped him.

"I know about them. Tell me about the spool of thread."

He free-associated for a while; he had learned to do it quite well, but privately he thought it was nonsense. He paid little attention to his own voice when he free-associated. It wasn't as if he were being analyzed for a medical purpose, he had told himself early in the business. Feldman was paid to keep tabs, that was all. He had nothing to hide, nothing of interest to learn about himself, so he cooperated, but he didn't pay much attention.

Feldman said, "Maze," and he answered, "Art Museum." He sat straight up on the couch. He was shivering. Feldman nodded to him when he swung around to look. "So that is that," Feldman said. "What it is actually I don't know, but you do now, don't you?"

Thornton shook his head violently, shivering hard. He remembered the feeling of being lost at an art exhibit years ago. "It was so meaningless," he said. "This exhibit was arranged like a maze, and the artist came over to me while I was standing there feeling stupid, and he told me that it meant nothing. I had worked hard trying to puzzle it out, and he said it had no meaning. It was arranged like a maze.

Feldman looked disappointed. His silence invited Thornton to keep talking, but there was nothing more to say about it. Thornton said, "The Phalanx is the final solution of the problem of modern warfare. It is an armored computer designed to control at least twenty-five subunits at this time, and it will have the capacity to control n subunits when it is completed. The subunits to this point have been built to scout jungle trails, and go through undergrowth where there are no trails searching out the enemy. They come equipped with flame throwers, grenade launchers, rocket launchers, communications units, infrared sensors, mass sensors, mine-laying and mine-detection devices, chemical-analysis labs, still and movie cameras, audio sensors and transmitters . . ."

He became aware of Feldman's bright, unblinking gaze and he paused and grinned at the analyst. Softly he added, "But the main problem with the Phalanx is that it doesn't know what a smile is on a friendly face. It can't distinguish between friend and enemy. It can't tell if the metal it senses is a gun or a hoe. It has no way of knowing if the mass-burdened heat source is a man with a howitzer or an ass with a load of firewood on a metal frame. And no matter how many changes the psychocybernetics lab sends to me, I can't program those things into it." He stood up and stretched. His gaze followed a low long shaft of sunlight coming through the venetian blind where a slat was crooked. "I'm going for a walk," he said. He sensed that Feldman made a motion toward him, but there was no effort to stop him or force him to complete his hour.

"Tomorrow at five," Feldman said, and that was all.

His thighs burned as he climbed. He had wanted to climb the hill ever since the first tracery of white blossoms had appeared high on its side, but no time, no time. And now his thighs burned. He should write to Ethel tonight. Hadn't even opened her last letter yet. He had put it down somewhere and had forgotten it. On the dresser in his room? On his desk? He groaned to himself at the thought of his desk, and he slipped on a moss-covered rock and banged his knee. Sitting on the damp, pungent ground, he rocked back and forth nursing the knee for a few minutes, catching his breath. He had come farther than he had realized. Below him almost hidden, he could see the Institute building. It had started as a simple two-story building, but had been extended in three directions, like dominoes, and at the end of one of the newer additions there was construction going on. He had a vision of it worming its way over the hills, growing like a snake through the mountains, creeping through valleys, over crests, following watercourses. . . . He closed his eyes and composed part of the letter to Ethel. It would be dull, he decided, faltering after the initial hope-you-are-well bit. Ethel was a good woman, but dull. God, she was dull. He remembered the shock he had felt the day he understood that Ethel had settled in on herself, that she would change no more, only become more what she was, more dogmatic, less malleable, more picture-pretty and smug. Ethel was forty. She had been forty on her twenty-fifth birthday, would be forty on her eightieth. But she was good, kind, considerate, a good mother, a faithful and helpful wife, good social animal. . . .

They could say that about him. A good man. Plodding maybe, but a good man. Wouldn't hurt a fly. Good to his kids, a real father.

He leaned back against a tree trunk and watched the sunset without thinking.

A good man.

The breeze on his cheek was warm and fragrant with spring. Gradually he forgot about the cold, damp ground beneath him. He thought about the three kids. Bang, bang, bang, three years, three kids. That was the way they had wanted it. Have them all together, raise them together and be done with that part of it. By the time we're both forty, they'll be almost grown, and we'll still be young. Well, he was forty-four, and they were grown. But he wasn't young. Ethel wasn't young. Both of them were good, good, good, but they were not young. He dreamed of romping with the kids and the romp was wrong. They were glad when he tired of it and left them. He dreamed of his daughter's soft cheek against his as she whispered secrets to him, and his yawn that had driven her away. Yet, he did love her with an intensity that sometimes had startled and frightened him. Perhaps that was why he had driven her away. He remembered her flying past him on her bicycle, hair streaming behind her, thin legs pumping harder and harder . . .

We go down the coast in the skiff with the wind driving us hard. Feeling of fear, exhilaration, alertness, watching for the sudden wave that could topple us. Paula's hair streaming out in the wind, hitting my face, stirring something in me, making me look at her through different eyes for a moment. And the intolerable ache that is Paula. The searing, burning, unbearable pain that means Paula, and the release that was just as sudden and even more intense.

He jerked from the tree and was on his feet. He shuddered once and started down the hill. He had been dreaming of his wife and the kids. Of his daughter . . . A flush of deep shame swept over him and he stumbled blindly back to the Institute.

"Dr. Thornton, there has to be a way to program these abstracts, as you call them." Melvin Jorgenson paced. He was a restless man. Even pacing failed to satisfy his need to move, and in his hands he carried and played with a pen whose point he extended and retracted over and over, each time making an audible click. Thornton noticed that he was pacing in time to the click, or was he clicking in time to his tread? He said nothing and waited. Maybe they were going to fire him.

The Director was there also, and it was to him Jorgenson was addressing himself, although he prefaced his remarks with Thornton's name. The Director looked unhappy.

"You know that we have been experimenting with various techniques," Jorgenson said, glancing at Thornton, but still talking to the Director. "We have a simple psychomodular unit in operation now, much like the one you described in your book of several years ago. That gave us the necessary line to follow, but as I say, this is a simple unit."

He continued to talk and pace, and by listening to him very carefully and ignoring the clicks as much as possible, Thornton finally understood that there was to be a major revision on the Phalanx, and he was to program the revised version with all the data that already had gone into the obsolete model. He started to laugh and continued to laugh until someone, the Director himself, brought him water. He said that he had strangled on a smothered cough, that he had caught cold when he had fallen asleep out in the woods a few nights ago. He allowed Jorgenson to lead him to the new unit ready to be connected to the Phalanx, and he asked the right questions, intelligent questions, and he made intelligent notes and finally said, sure, why not?

"The Phalanx," he wrote in his diary (because writing it, even though he would have to destroy what he had written afterward, set it in his mind: once written, never forgotten, he had learned early in his school career, and so had gone through school laboriously copying passages, notes, sometimes almost whole textbooks; he had remembered all of it, still remembered all of it), "is apparently a small building, and only on close approach can you see that there are treads under it, hidden by sides that come almost to the ground. There are pseudo windows, a pseudo exterior that can be made to conform to any local style of building. Inside . . ." He put the pen down and walked to the window. It was raining hard. He was slightly feverish; he really had caught a cold, and he had taken the afternoon off on the instructions of the infirmary doctor. He was supposed to be sleeping now, but the sound of the rain was unsettling instead of soothing, and he wanted to be out in it, walking bareheaded under the driving, stinging sheets of water. He thought yearningly of the pneumonia that would almost certainly follow, and the discharge from present duties, and the long rest afterward. Rest, travel, sunbathing, reading, being conducted through the computer laboratories of major countries throughout the world. His name would be magic after a year on the Project, even if they hadn't brought it off yet. Eventually they would, and then everyone connected with it would be known, not to the public but to their peers, where it mattered. He pulled the blind over the window and returned to the diary.

"Inside the 'house' are the computer, its weapons, and sensors, with a monitor board in the center. Here it is that we are forced to maintain human surveillance. A man has to oversee the data that are brought in, has to be able to jump over intervening bits of data to connect those things that have no apparent reason for being linked together. For instance, if a fire is to be started to clean out an area, the man has to note the weather—a fire during a thunderstorm is a futile gesture. He has to note the wind, the placement of other units, the relative value of migratory birds in the area, for example. Or the possibility of livestock that will be killed by smoke downwind from the area. All of these we can program in, if we can formulate them in clear, unambiguous language. We don't dare let the Phalanx get confused."

He dropped his pen again and went to the bathroom and took his temperature. It was up, 102.6. He lay down. He was thinking of the statements that could confuse the Phalanx unless all parts were satisfied: A.B, A+B, A/B, A→B, A≡B . . . They couldn't do it. How describe a smile in clear and unambiguous language? The Phalanx couldn't be unmanned. Nor could it be manned in the usual sense. The Phalanx and its offspring were to be the call boxes, like the police telephones that were spaced all over cities. Imagine, he told himself, what it would be like if the call box on the corner not only alerted the precinct station, but watched suspicious characters, measured and weighed them, analyzed them, noted what weapons they carried, made countless other observations about them, came to a decision that they were okay, or not okay, and if not, then apprehended them, or killed them. Imagine that. What if it made a mistake and burned down a city block in error? *Sorry 'bout that.*

But if they could make it work, wouldn't it be good? Wouldn't it be better than armies over the face of the earth? Good, good, good . . .

Dan Thorton couldn't lift his arm because they had pinned gold braid on it. Real gold. They got the other arm and he wanted to beg off, but they insisted, refusing to hear his pleas. With the fastening of the braid on his other arm all he could do was stand, trying not to sway, knowing the weight would topple him if he swayed. He was paralyzed from goodness, he thought.

They had this old brain hanging around, see. The guy died on the operating table, abdominal surgery, and his head was intact, going to waste. So they put the brain in this jar of nice warm nutrients and fed it now and then and it went on ticking away, thinking its own thoughts. Then they put electrodes in it, this is the sight center, this the kinesthetic . . . And they put return wires and hooked them to an EEG and they watched the pens go up and down, up and down, and they kept getting cuter with it until they could get that little old brain to tell them what was on its mind. Not much, as it turned out. You see, that little old brain had gone crazy as a bedbug from the various things they had done to it, but still those pens went up and down, up and down, and it couldn't stop, couldn't refuse to cooperate, couldn't do anything but soak up the nutrients and sit there ticking away.

"Doesn't he look natural, like he might get up and talk to us any minute."

But don't look behind that eyeball, ma'am. Empty behind it. That one too, and that.

Most of them go mad, if not immediately, then as soon as they are hooked to the computer that is sending messages at the rate of a million bits a second. They had time, and psychomodular units to work with. They found a unit that did not go mad when they linked it to a computer. It was a simple computer, however.

If chips are black and white, and this object is green, then this object is not a chip. If tiles are red and blue, and this object is green, then this object is not a tile. And so on, and on, and on, at the rate of one million bits a second. The brain ticked away and did not go mad. They made it more complex. The object was green and round. Then more complex: green, round, and weighs n grams . . . The brain did not go mad. Yet. They hooked it to the Phalanx, and the brain went mad.

Dan Thornton stood with his arms dangling, paralyzed by his own goodness and the heavy gold braid that testified to the goodness and watched the brain go mad. How they could tell it was going mad was by the way it made the pens go up and down, up and down. It was drawing paper dolls, all joined at feet and hands.

We stare at each other across a roomful of people and somehow we come together without either of us moving. I hold her tight against me and murmur into her hair that smells of sea winds and sunshine, and my murmur has no words, but says that I love her. "It's been a long time, Dan," she says. Her eyes are shining and I feel that she is happy to see me. Again she is different. The wild girl is deeper, harder to find now, but still there. She says, "Let's go somewhere else." We walk the streets, her hand in mine, our steps matched, even though she has to take long strides to keep up. We walk for hours, see the night out, watch silently when the last star is lost in a lightening sky.

I am defending my father. She stops me with cool fingers pressed against my lips. "You are shocked that you can love someone who is capable of evil," she says, as if surprised at me. "We are all capable. It's just that most of us never get the chance to do more than small evil things." I argue that he wasn't evil, that he never hurt anyone in his life. She is skipping at my side, not listening, and I know she thinks I am foolish. I am angry with her, almost as angry as when she said she would not marry me. I ask her again and she shakes her head. I ask her what she is doing, how she is living, and she is amused that I don't know of her. She puts a slim book into my hand, says I should not open it until she is gone again, and that won't be until Monday.

The weekend is an agony of pleasure, and on Monday she is gone. The book is poetry that I cannot understand. They say she is brilliant, a genius, that she is the eyes and ears of the world. And I can't understand her poetry.

Two weeks later I marry Ethel and we plan to have three children right away.

"Dr. Thornton, if you'll just raise your hips a bit. That's right."

He was being taken somewhere on a stretcher on wheels. It was too hard to try to understand, so he let himself be carried and cared for, and sometime later he knew that he had the pneumonia that was to release him and send him home. After the serious part of it passed and he was told to take it easy and soak up sun on the wind-protected sun porch, he thought about the Project, and he knew he wouldn't ask to be relieved from it. The Institute brought in Carl Brundage, an old friend of his, to substitute for him until he was well enough to resume a full schedule. Carl stopped in to talk when he had time, and that helped the slow days along.

"The major mistake is in the lack of selectivity in the psycho-modular units they are forced to use. Most of them belong to enlisted men, untrained minds that probably never used a tenth of their potential. You have to think of that one unit as pre-programmed, you see. It can accept no new training, can't learn anything, can't develop any of its potential; it is the coordinator, that's all. The mistake lies in thinking that it is more than that. But that's all it needs to be," he added, deep thought furrows aging his face for a moment. Something . . . ? Whatever the thought had been, it had not come to consciousness, however, and he shrugged. It would. He knew the workings of his own brain, knew that he might feel twinges of this sort off and on for a while, then a new idea would hit him and the twinges would go away until another new idea was being born.

"Are you going to be allowed to watch the first test on Monday?" Carl asked.

"Sure. But it will be a failure." Moodily he repeated that to himself after Carl had left to do the work that he, Thornton, was supposed to be doing.

He rested over the weekend, sleeping deeply and heavily under massive sedation. Monday was clear and warm with high cirrus clouds forming milky streaks in a perfect sky. The wind velocity was five to ten miles an hour, air temperature a mild 71. Thornton rode in a jeep to the demonstration site, twelve miles from the Institute building, in a narrow gouged-out valley, where spring was arriving later than on the more exposed hill-sides. Pale-green spears of unfolded leaves tipped the trees here, and the dogwoods still bore tiers of snowy flat blossoms.

The Phalanx sat in the center of the small valley, looking like a miner's cabin. At the signal given by the Director, the sides of the Phalanx rose slightly, enough for ten small, rounded sub-units to roll out from the interior. The units were called the bugs. They were painted randomly in browns and greens, and when they moved away from the Phalanx, they merged with the earth and the undergrowth. The test was to be in two parts; the first was without the psychomodular unit hooked in, the second would use it.

Scattered in the valley and on three sides of the surrounding hills were Institute men, taking the part of the enemy. Thornton had expected to be one of them, and he was grateful for the pneumonia that had turned him into a spectator. The ten bugs were only a part of the force the Phalanx could control. Two of them carried sprays that threw out an arc of a water-dye solution; in battle that would be fire. Two others recorded on film and soundtrack everything in a radius of up to ten miles, terrain permitting. Another moved along with a radar antenna spinning, homing in on a helicopter that thundered overhead, while its companion followed a flight of birds, then picked up a jet making a pencil-thin contrail.

Each bug seemed to function as planned. Thornton waited. The sun heated his thighs and he remembered how they had burned on the climb up the hill the day he had caught the cold. His driver, one of the junior programmers, shifted excitedly and pointed to one of the bugs that was leaving the ground, skimming over the tops of bushes, over a runoff stream. The Phalanx had everything under control. It didn't fall apart until three rabbits were flushed from the bushes and ran straight at the mine-detecting bug. The dye thrower swung around and sprayed the rabbits, and with them the mine detector that was immediately frozen in its tracks. The Phalanx had been programmed to put out of commission any of the units that were scored on. Following the rabbits the dye thrower rolled over a "mine," and it also was immobilized.

One by one the subunits proved vulnerable to the unexpected, and within half an hour the Phalanx sat alone, unprotected, and the men moved in and "captured" it.

Thornton watched the slumping figure of the Secretary and the unbowed figure of the Director, who was gesturing expansively. The second session would take place after lunch, after the psychomodular unit was hooked in and the men resumed their positions.

With the psychomodular unit in place, the test was more impressive. Some of the men on the hill were killed by the dye throwers, others were "gassed," but none were taken prisoner. The Phalanx was not equipped to take prisoners. This time the Phalanx refused to be fooled by rabbits deliberately introduced by the men, and it sent a unit after the men themselves. It shot down three crows and two jets and a hawk. When it went mad, in less than an hour, it had the units destroy each other, and turn on the Phalanx itself.

While technically a failure, the second session of the test gave great satisfaction. There was a rally that night, conducted by the Secretary himself.

Thornton's son was of draft age, or would be in a month. He could understand the tenor of the country that clamored for an end to the draft, an end to the endless wars, an end to the frustrations that dulled the young men and made them restless in school, made them marry too young, drive too hard and fast, experiment with drugs and danger wherever it was presented to them. He didn't need or want the Secretary to outline this for him, but the Secretary did. His voice was sad and rousing by turns. Thornton used his illness as an excuse and left early.

The work continued. The psychomodular units continued to go mad. Thornton convalesced without incident and discontinued the heavy sedation, and went back to a shortened workday. He also went back to his sessions with Dr. Feldman.

There was an air of excitement at the Institute now. Success was in the smell of the spring air turning into summer, and the scientists and technicians were lightheaded. Thornton too. Carl was almost embarrassingly grateful to him for having become ill so that he had been called in. He worked like a man possessed, trying to spare Thornton all he could. Thornton knew that other departments were working even harder than his own. The psychocyberneticist and the perception psychologist must not sleep at all, he thought one night when he met them both in the hall. He had returned for his notebook, after napping for three hours. He would return to sleep, but they seemed prepared for an all-night stint.

How does man know what he sees? How does the brain communicate with itself? with the hormonal system? with the autonomic nervous system? He didn't envy them their work. When they found another answer, he got it in the language of formulae and symbols that he then translated to binary digital language and put in the Phalanx. This was tested, and if it was wrong he took it out again, and they went back to the original problem.

Thornton dreamed often of the Phalanx and its bugs now. "Are the others reporting dreams about it?" he asked Feldman.

"They dream of everything," the analyst said.

Thornton wondered if Feldman was curious about why his dreams seemed never to concern sex. "When I was young," he said, "I was as horny as anyone, I guess. But now . . . After I got married and settled down, it seemed less important. I guess I'm one of those fortunate people who isn't driven by sex so much. I've hardly missed Ethel at all," he added. It surprised him to say it and know that it was true. Of course, when he had been ill, he had missed her. She would have been good to have around then. She had a way with sick people, soothing, gentle, comforting. But normally his work was enough, and the momentary pangs of longing seemed almost directionless, certainly not aimed specifically for her. Or anyone else.

"Were you ever in love?" Feldman asked when the silence lengthened.

"Sure. A couple of times. High-school stuff; then, of course there was Ethel."

"What about the high-school stuff? Any particular girl who stands out now?"

He couldn't remember the name of any one girl he had admired in high school.

That night he had three programs to check. Carl had admitted mistakes in them. "Garbage in, garbage out," Carl had said, flinging the papers down on Thornton's desk. "And I can't find the garbage." He had been disgusted with himself for letting the error slip past in the first place, and even more so for not finding the error after it was known to be there.

The three programs comprised a whole; the error could be in

the first of them, throwing off the next two; or it could be in the last step of the third program. There were over fifteen hundred steps involved.

Thornton worked on it until 1 A.M., knocked off half an hour to stretch and have a sandwich, then went back to it again. At 3 A.M. he realized that Feldman was pushing him for some reason that he couldn't fathom. For months his relationship with Feldman had been casual, in the line of duty, but now it was different. The difference in Feldman was like the change that came over a cat that had been playing with a ball and was presented with a mouse. The same gestures, but with a new intensity, a new concentration. He wandered out into the night to smoke and let his room clear of the smoke there. He was coughing badly with each cigarette, the after-effect of pneumonia, he guessed.

He had talked to the psychocyberneticist about the selection of the psychomodular unit, and Jorgenson had been bitter and in agreement with his theory that they could expect no great stride forward until they were allowed to select for themselves. He knew the Director had brought it up with the Secretary, but no word had filtered down as yet about the outcome. Meanwhile the units continued to go mad and the Phalanx tried to commit suicide periodically.

He didn't like the phrase "tried to commit suicide," but it was how they all talked about it. He remembered his mother and her suicide that followed the execution of his father. He remembered the pictures of the mangled children that had arrived in the mail, and the letters, and phone calls, and his mother's anguish and final surrender. He would not have got through that period without Paula and Gregory. His hand froze in the process of lifting his cigarette to his lips.

Paula! He hadn't thought about Paula for twenty years. Not since he had gone to hear her speak and read her poetry. Ethel had been so bored by it. They hadn't stayed for all the program, but later he had gone back and met Paula at the reception that followed. She never appeared surprised to find him, he had thought then when her face lighted with pleasure at his approach. Never surprise, only pleasure to see him again. He almost asked her if she loved him then, but he didn't. Again she seemed different, wiser, but not only that. In touch with something that he couldn't grasp, perhaps. Tuned in, the students said of her, adoring her and what she wrote for them.

He inhaled deeply and held onto a tree until he had his breath back. Coughing made him dizzy, made his head swell and throb. He thought fleetingly of himself dying, dead, and Paula coming to the funeral, weeping over his lifeless body, pleading for another chance with him. A bitter smile twisted his face and he pulled hard on the cigarette, finishing it, not caring if he coughed or not. Another paroxysm and he knew that he did care. He waited for it to pass and returned to his room and the programs that had to be corrected.

Toward dawn he threw himself down on his bed and fell asleep instantly.

We pull ourselves up the steep rocks of the cliff, and when we get to the top we have no breath left for talking. Paula is sweating, and she rubs the back of her hand over her face carelessly, leaving a smudge of dirt there from her forehead to her chin. I lie back with my eyes closed, trying not to cry yet. Hoping never to cry over my mother. Paula says, "Mom and Dad say you can live with us until you go to school in the fall. Okay?"

It isn't really a question. I can go with them, or I can go with my aunt and uncle who came from Ohio for the funeral. The state won't let me stay alone yet because I am only seventeen. My aunt told me that much. She is angry because my mother, her sister, killed herself. It was irreligious of her. It was selfish of her. I despise my aunt.

I feel Paula's toe digging my side and I squirm, wanting not to cry. She giggles and the bare toe prods again, digs and wiggles against my side. I look at her and I know that I won't cry now. I jump up and grab her, meaning to shake her, but I just hold her, and she stops giggling. We don't move for a long time until Gregory interrupts us. He hasn't noticed anything, so maybe it wasn't so long, but that moment goes on and on.

When we go back to my house my aunt is furious with me. She says that I am selfish too for leaving now when people have been coming by to pay respects. She is going to lecture me, but Paula goes to her and puts her dirty hand on my aunt's smooth, clean sleeve, and Paula says something I can't hear. Then she says, "It's going to be all right. We'll take care of him." My aunt bursts into tears and falls down in a chair crying like that, shaking, ugly with crying, and Paula, Gregory and I leave her there.

Thornton woke up, remembering the dream in detail. He made notes of it for Feldman's benefit. He rolled over and went back to sleep.

The work went slowly and badly. They had plateaued and apparently could go no further. But all of them could see the next step so clearly, and all of them knew that without the next step the Project was a failure. The Secretary returned and huddled with the Director and several other top men, and following this meeting there was something not so open, something uglier about the Project. No leaks came from the meeting, and there was a dearth of rumors for once. A new brain was installed, and hope rose as it continued to function after twenty-four hours, then thirty-six hours. A field test was scheduled, but before it could be held the brain went mad.

Gloom settled heavier over the men, and mistakes were made that would have been unthinkable four months in the past. They analyzed the results of the last psychomodular unit and its stresses and the final breaking point, and it was then that Thornton learned that this brain had been selected. He knew vaguely who Lester Ferris had been, but he didn't know how he had died, or when, or how his brain had come into the possession of the Institute. Ferris had been a child prodigy, a brilliant mathematical physicist who had shaken up the world of physics at the age of fifteen. Crippled in body, with a mind that sang, he had drawn the attention of the entire world with theories that might be proven in some distant future, or might never be proven, but were unmistakably original and brilliant. He had settled down at the Institute for Advanced Study at the age of twenty-five, and as far as Thornton knew no more had been heard from him.

Thornton began reading the daily papers that were brought to the Institute, and every time they had a brain that was more successful than previous ones he searched the obituaries, but he didn't ask anyone any questions. No one was asking questions.

He and Feldman went over the incident of his mother's suicide several times, and slowly he found that he was remembering things about Paula that he had forgotten completely. Feldman knew her work and was impressed that he, Thornton, had been her lover. Thornton found that he could talk of it freely as if it had happened to someone else.

Sometimes Thornton went for walks in the woods, now dark green and summery, harboring snakes behind rocks and logs, alive with rabbits, birds, insects that sang and whirred and buzzed. He didn't do it as often as he would have liked because there was no time. His year was running out. The second test was due within weeks, and although the idea of a battle test had been abandoned, the field test was still on the schedule. They were learning what kinds of brains were best suited for the symbiotic relationship with the computer that was called Phalanx, but they were unable to find just the right one. The brains continued to go mad.

They had a Delphi session, with each man answering questions about the sort of mind, the kind of mentality that would work with the Phalanx. Thornton bit his pencil and slowly filled in the answers to the printed questions. Afterward they read them aloud and talked about them. The papers were gathered by the Director.

"What do you think now of Paula Whitfield?" Feldman asked.

"Oh, she's a promiscuous bitch. Exciting, probably very beautiful still. She was, you know, but in a wild, unpremeditated way. Not the cover-girl look of studied loveliness."

Feldman nodded. "Your wife is very lovely," he said after a moment. He was making idle talk now that the hour was almost over and Thornton had been wrung out.

"Ethel is beautiful," Thornton said. It surprised him. She really was. He had a letter from her in his pocket then. She would meet him and they would drive to Florida and go from there to Nassau. She was excited about the trip. She was lonesome for him.

"Is Paula Whitfield really promiscuous?" Feldman asked curiously. "There's no hint of that in her work."

"She sleeps around," Thornton said, hearing the contempt in his voice. "She's got a couple of illegitimate kids, you know." He shrugged and got up. "I guess that's unfair. I don't really know what she's like now. It's been twenty years since I saw her. A genius with the morals of an alley cat. That's what she was then."

He opened the door. Feldman said, "Tomorrow, five, one hour? Okay?" Thornton looked back and nodded, and Feldman added, "Why did you put her down as the one mind that could exist with the Phalanx?"

He ate little dinner, and walked afterward. He hadn't. He knew he hadn't. He visualized the sheet of questions and his answers, and he knew that his memory would reproduce it faithfully for him. He hadn't put her name down. The questions had all led to that one, of course: Can you name anyone who you think would qualify as a psychomodular unit?

He had left it blank.

He saw it again in his mind, and it was blank.

He felt a stab of fear. What was Feldman after with him?

He wouldn't recommend Paula, even if the thought had occurred to him. When Gregory died, she had written that crazy poem about the boy who chose death rather than killing. Gregory had died under enemy fire. He had mailed her the firing pin of his rifle, then had walked upright until he was felled. A stupid, banal act of insanity. It had made all the papers, his death, and the bitter poetry that had flowed from Paula afterward. She was practically a traitor, as Gregory certainly had been. Again he wondered what Feldman was trying to do. He returned to his desk and worked until midnight.

He dreamed that night of the psychomodular unit fixed in the island inside the house that was the Phalanx. It was a sealed tank that looked very much like an incubator, with rubber gloves built into it so that the operators could push their hands into them and handle the thing inside. There were six pairs of the gloves. To one side of the tank a screen had been placed to show electroencephalograph tracings. Thick clusters of wires led to desks close by, and on them were screens that showed chemical actions, enzymic changes, temperature of the nutrient solution and any fluctuations in its composition. Going into the brain were wires with electrodes, the input and output wires, and they too were tapped so that the men at the desks could know exactly what was going in and out. Thornton's hands tightened and he thrust them deep in his pockets.

He wanted to plunge his hands into the gloves and handle the thing inside the tank.

The Phalanx had been in operation for seven days and nights. The lights twinkled steadily, and in the back the EEG tracings were regular. The technicians had replaced the walls about the computer so that it stood a house within a room, a tank within the house, a brain within the tank. There was still work to be done, still many programs to plan and translate and feed to the Phalanx, but any good programmer could do them now. They were talking about increasing the number of bugs to an even four dozen, and no one doubted that the computer could keep them all under control.

Thornton stood in the doorway looking at it for the last time. His work was done, his year over. Others would be interviewed now, or already had been, and they would feel the excitement coursing through them at the chance to work at the Institute for a year. He turned and left, picking up his bag at the main door. A car was outside to take him to the gate, where Ethel would meet him. Feldman was on the steps waiting. He thrust a book into Thornton's hand.

"A goodby present," he said. Thornton wondered if he had seen tears in the analyst's eyes, and decided no. It had been the wind. The wind was blowing hard. He rode to the main gate, and when he left the car and walked through, he dropped the book. He got in his own car and drew Ethel to him.

"I was so afraid you'd be different," she said after a moment. "I didn't know what to expect after your year among geniuses. I thought you might not want to come out at all." She laughed and squeezed his hand. "I am so proud of you! And you haven't changed, not at all."

He laughed with her. "You too," he said. He wondered if there had always been that emptiness behind her eyes. She pressed on the accelerator and they sped down the road away from the Institute.

Behind them the wind riffled through the book until the guard noticed it lying in the dust and picked it up and tossed it in a trash can.